After spending most of his time at Oxford University drinking in pubs and singing folk songs, Ian Morson reluctantly had to find work as a librarian in the London area, dealing in other writers' novels. He finally decided he had to prove he could do better, and William Falconer grew out of that decision. The medieval detective has appeared in eight novels to date, and several short stories in anthologies written by the Medieval Murderers, a group of historical crime writers. Ian also writes novels and short stories featuring Nick Zuliani, a Venetian at the court of Kubilai Khan, and Joe Malinferno and Doll Pocket, a pair living off their wits in Georgian England. Ian lives with his wife, Lynda, and after sampling the joys of life in Cyprus, they now reside in Hastings.

Master William Falconer Mysteries

Falconer's Crusade*
Falconer's Judgement*
Falconer and the Face of God*
A Psalm for Falconer*
Falconer and the Great Beast*
Falconer and the Ritual of Death
Falconer's Trial
Falconer and the Death of Kings

*available in Ostara Publishing editions

FALCONER
AND THE
RAIN OF BLOOD

A William Falconer novel
By

IAN MORSON

Ostara Publishing

First published by Ostara Publishing 2013

Copyright © Ian Morson 2013

Hardback   ISBN 9781906288 969
Paperback ISBN 9781906288 976

A CIP reference is available from the British Library

Printed and Bound in the United Kingdom

Ostara Publishing
13 King Coel Road
Colchester
CO3 9AG
www.ostarapublishing.co.uk

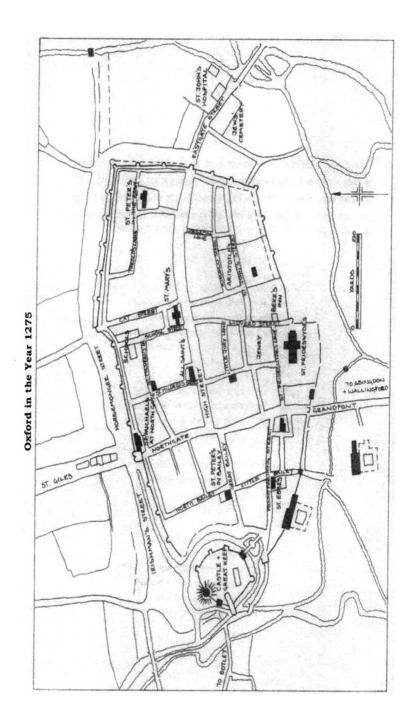

Oxford in the Year 1275

Prologue

Later, it was difficult to pin down exactly when it all began.

It could be said that the primary cause was the arrival of Sir Hugo de Wolfson, crusader knight, in Oxford on the Feast of St John Chrysostom in September, 1275. By the time he rode through Eastgate, he was hot and feverish, but then he had been travelling for days and might expect to feel a little out of sorts. What he didn't know about was the fate of one of his companions with whom he had shared a cabin when crossing the English Channel, and who had complained of a sore mouth. The man had, since they had bade each other farewell, sickened and died close to Canterbury. Sir Hugo had ridden hard for ten days and, still to travel further north, had decided to break his journey in Oxford. His decision had fatal consequences for several people in the town.

It may also be said that it began a lot earlier, when knights of Western Europe pledged themselves to retrieving the Holy Lands from the Islamic invaders. Many knights returned to England with booty and tales of noble deeds. Some carried unexpected and unwanted stowaways with them in the form of disease. The ill-fated attempt led by Louis of France in 1270 resulted in Prince Edward of England rushing to Louis's support with a band of fellow knights including Sir Hugo de Wolfson. Edward and Sir Hugo made it to the Holy Lands, but Louis did not. The saintly French king died that August of a pestilence, and was reduced to muttering 'Jerusalem, Jerusalem' on his death-bed in Carthage. Edward and his knights actually saw little combat as a peace was negotiated with the Muslim ruler, Baibars, in 1272. Though Sir Hugo de Wolfson remained, some of the English knights accompanying Edward returned to their homeland through the port of Damietta on the coast of Egypt. Red plague was rife in the town, and the knights hurried on. The crusaders fled across the sea to Venice, but one knight unwittingly took with him an unwelcome companion. And so began the plague's insidious crawl through mainland Europe.

A trader called Peter Hawkmoor was the last link in the chain to Sir Hugo, who thought he had escaped the plague in the Middle East. Unfortunately, it had lain in wait for him in France. The trader he shared a cabin with on the cog Cockerel as it crossed from Honfleur to Portsmouth had made an error of judgement. Hawkmoor had tarried in a small French town to the east of the port, where he knew a widow intimately. She had felt unwell, but had put on a pretence of jollity for her generous visitor. Unknown to Hawkmoor, she was now desperately ill, and he was unaware his dalliance had ensured his

7

own death. Unwittingly, he also passed sentence on his cabin companion and on those Sir Hugo himself encountered later.

However, some say it only really began when the town constable of Oxford took the terrible decision to close all the gates in and out of the town. It was a decision Peter Bullock came to regret, but at the time he thought it was the correct one. He locked the whole town into close confinement with the red plague to prevent its spread elsewhere. He was not comforted by the thought that other communities in the past had done so, and that down into the future would doubtless carry out similar selfless acts. Not after what came about in the febrile atmosphere of the plague town in that month of September, 1275.

Some even say now that what swept through Oxford would have happened anyway. That it was a result of too much learning infecting brains with a murderous plague that ran as rampantly through the town as did the red plague of small pox. That mankind was not meant to know so much. That books, and a reaching for an understanding of the world that was rightly the perquisite of God alone was bound to drive a person mad and cause a rash of deaths.

Others merely said what happened came about because the prophet Merlin had predicted it would.

Chapter One

The Feast of St Frithestan of Winchester, 10ᵗʰ September, 1275

'*Woe to the red dragon, for his banishment hasteneth on. His lurking holes shall be seized by the white dragon, which signifies the Saxons whom you invited over; but the red denotes the British nation, which shall be oppressed by the white. Therefore shall its mountains be levelled as the valleys, and the rivers of the valleys shall run with blood.*'

The old man closed the book reverentially, and his rheumy eyes looked up at his guest, who was pacing the small upper room that formed the library of Oseney Abbey. The tall man was fifty if he was a day, and his greying, curly locks were thinning. But he still gave out an air of authority and vigour that the old man found reassuring. The man was a teacher of the clerks at the university close by the abbey, and needed to seem authoritative. The young men required firm guidance, and it was hard to know who provided that these days. Ever since old King Henry had died, and his son Edward had come to the throne, the world seemed to have changed beyond measure. And not for the better, either. Aldwyn was Welsh, and he had heard that the new king was proposing to invade his homeland. The old monk, his mind wandering as it was wont to do recently, suddenly realised that his guest had asked him a question.

'I'm sorry, what did you say?'

The man, who was indeed a regent master in Oxford, smiled, and his piercing blue eyes wrinkled at the edges.

'I was asking you if you believed all that Geoffrey wrote in his History.'

Brother Aldwyn looked scandalised at the master's deprecating remark. He patted the book on the table at his right hand reassuringly.

'It is as true a retelling of the history of Britain as has ever been recorded. From the days of Brutus's landing on the island of Albion at Totnes. How King Lud founded London, and my homeland got its name of Cambria from Brutus's son Camber. And Geoffrey's recording of Merlin's prophecies is as I myself remember them told to me by my father.'

Aldwyn closed his eyes recalling the prophecies his father had recited to him when he had been a stripling no older than most of those youths who thronged the streets of Oxford today. The passage he had just read out to his visitor was the opening of Merlin's portents, and concerned the feuding between the true Britons of Wales, and the Saxon invaders who laid claim to the country next. Of course since those times there had been the Norman invasion too, which he

9

felt sure was in the prophecies somewhere if only he could decipher the text. Aldwyn felt that he had almost lived through all those times, immersed as he was in the chronicles of Oseney Abbey. And proud as he was of Merlin's red dragon, it was a humiliation to record how the Anglo-Saxon white dragon held supremacy. Worse still, the Prince of Wales, Llewellyn ap Gruffyd, had bribed the old King Henry to recognise his title with an amount of money he – or Wales – could ill afford. The sum of 3,000 marks had now to be found annually, and Llewellyn was not popular with his subjects for the burden imposed on them. His own brother, David, had rebelled against him, and losing the battle with his sibling, had sought refuge in England. That was another sore on the back of the Welsh pony.

The regent master coughed gently, to remind the misty-eyed Aldwyn of his presence. He had come to the abbey ostensibly to pay his quarterly rent for the hall he used in Oxford to accommodate a handful of students. His payment for being a regent master was small, and the fees the students paid supplemented that income, even after the rent to his landlord – the abbey – was paid. Oseney Abbey owned many plots of land in the university town, including Aristotle's Hall in St John's Street, where William Falconer had lived for almost fifteen years. The rent paid, he had called on the abbey's librarian, Aldwyn, because he sought some information about the past. It was something to do with the year 1225, around the time when the Friars Minor first came to England led by Agnellus of Pisa. The year, if he guessed right, when Master William Falconer thought he had been born.

Aldwyn dragged himself back to the present, and smiled at Falconer ruefully.

'Still and all, you do not want to know prophecies of what is to come, but what happened in the past. Am I right?'

William Falconer nodded in agreement. Old Aldwyn was the latest in a long line of chroniclers at the abbey, and if he was to learn anything about his own origins, he needed the old monk's memory to be functioning well. So he nudged Aldwyn's recollections into action.

'Two Englishmen, who came with Agnellus, were responsible for founding the Franciscan friary, I understand.'

The old monk nodded, almost seeming to be dozing off. But then he roused himself enough to reply.

'Yes, two friars with the same name – Richard – arrived in Oxford in November of the eighth year of Henry's reign.'

That year – 1224 – was the year before Falconer's presumed birth date. Though he knew little about his childhood, he had always been told he was born in the ninth year of Henry's reign. But that was all he did know, and it was the reason he was here at Oseney making enquiries about the Franciscan friary that had eventually grown like an excrescence on the town wall on the south side of Oxford.

'Yes, and I am told that one of them helped at the hospital of St Bartholomew's.'

Aldwyn smiled as nostalgia washed over him.

'Ah, yes, Bartlemas leper hospital.' He gave the familiar name for the building rather than its formal title. 'Thirteen prebends were paid for originally, and Augustine brothers here at Oseney were involved in its running, which is why I assume you have started your quest here. Then in that year, a Grey Friar joined us. I recall that Richard Ingworth was the Franciscan in question. I also remember that the hospital possessed many relics, including St. Edmund's comb, which was a sure cure for headaches.'

Falconer frowned, an anxious look forming on his weather-beaten face.

'But, a leper hospital, you say?'

Aldwyn waved a hand by way of reassurance.

'Not at the beginning. It was set up to care for the poor infirm of Oxford. Though it later became a place of sanctuary for lepers, and that was what attracted Richard Ingworth to it. The Grey Friars were ever dedicated to those poor outcasts of our world.' He scrutinised William Falconer more closely all of a sudden. 'But what brings you to ask about Bartlemas?'

Falconer's brilliant blue eyes darkened, and he cast his glance down to the floor.

'I am curious about someone who was taken in there. But it was some time ago. Are there any records kept, would you know?'

Aldwyn shrugged his shoulders.

'I believe there are records of those who passed through the hospital's doors, but how accurate they are I cannot say. Let me make enquiries, and when you next come to pay your rent, I may have some news.'

Falconer would have liked a faster response to his enquiries, but knew Brother Aldwyn of old. Living in a monastic world governed by regular and timeless routine, he would not be hurried along at the pace of the secular realm. And in truth, Falconer wasn't sure his quest was all that urgent. Finding out about his own birth and ancestry had been a subject he had ignored for many years. Such long-ago events had seemed irrelevant to him. Until he had met Saphira Le Veske.

*

Saphira was a Jew, and placed great store by her birthright. Her surname was one she had adopted in the Christian style when she married her now long-deceased husband. But two weeks ago, lying beside Falconer in the bed in her rented house in Fish Street, she told him of her true family name. And tried to explain the intricacies of the Jewish naming of names.

'It is only living with Christians that we Jews have adopted surnames like Le Veske. Before then, everyone simply took their father's first name to describe their ancestry. And besides, Le Veske is just a version of the French word for bishop or priest — *l'évêcque*. It means that some ancestor of my late husband's was a rabbi.'

Falconer eased on to his elbow and faced his lover, tearing his eyes from her rounded breasts with difficulty.

'Then tell me what your name really is, strange woman in my bed.'

Saphira prodded his belly, which she had noticed was growing more soft and rounded lately.

11

'We are occupying *my* bed, regent master William Falconer. And you are supposed to be a celibate cleric, who I should by rights throw bare-arsed out into the street. As if you needed reminding of that fact.'

Saphira pulled the covers over her bare chest. Falconer grinned, and held up a placatory palm.

'*Pace*, Saphira ... But then if you are not Le Veske, what do I call you?'

'I was born Saphira, daughter of Habib of Nimes. Now, there's a name to conjure with.'

'Habib is Arabic!'

'And yet my father was a Jew. So he must have come to France by way of Outremer or North Africa. We Jews are good at fitting in wherever we live, and fashioning our names to suit. So you can see how our very name speaks of our origins.'

She settled back on the feather pillow, tucking her hands behind her head, and exposing her nipples again in the process. Her shock of flame-red hair spread across the white linen.

'Now, tell me of your family.'

Falconer had nothing to say, because he knew nothing, having been brought up an orphan by Augustine monks in far-off Bardsey Abbey. No-one there had told him of his parents, other than to hint that his mother had died in a hospital near Oxford at his birth. His surname had been given him by a prior to whom the boy's blue eyes had suggested the piercing stare of a bird of prey. Sadly, even that attribute had proved incorrect, and though his eyes had been good enough to carry him through a career as a mercenary, he now needed eye-glasses to see anything clearly.

Still, if he looked closely, he could see well enough, and he saw that Saphira's bare nipples were hardening in the cold air of her bedroom. He had then slipped his hand underneath the covers, and for a while his childhood was forgotten. But later he began to think about who he was, and he spent the following two weeks making enquiries. Largely frustrated, and guessing the hospital near Oxford was St Bartholomew's he had finally spoken to Brother Aldwyn on the occasion of his quarterly payment of rent for Aristotle's Hall.

*

The Feast of St Eanswida, 12ᵗʰ September

After waiting a day or so for Aldwyn's news, Falconer became impatient for information. He decided he would go to the leper hospital himself and see what he could find out. It was late afternoon, and his teaching duties were over for the day. He had a rendezvous with Saphira later, but felt some fresh air and a brisk walk would be beneficial. Bartlemas hospital was beyond East Gate on the Cowley Road that led south-east towards London. He could be there and back before dark. Though he knew the centre of town and its market stalls would be quiet at this time of day, he chose to cut through the narrow lanes that wound through from South Gate, past St Frideswide's Church, and along Schitebarne Lane. He loved the dark, winding alleys and vennels that made up the real Oxford for him. Here stood the low, half-timbered houses of the working population of the town. You didn't find the rarified atmosphere of intellectual speculation on the numbers of angels on a pin-head here. This was the *sordidissimi vici* of stews, cheek by jowl with stinking tanners' homes, and those of book binders who used the leather made by their smelly neighbours. To Falconer it had the odour of honest toil and sweated labour, and he returned to wallow in it when he was tired of the other world of his fellow regent masters and their petty concerns.

Emerging hard by East Gate, he had to step back sharply into the mouth of the lane as a horseman rode hard in through the entrance to the town. The rider saw Falconer only at the last minute and pulled his horse up abruptly with a warning cry.

'Have a care, man. You were nearly under my horse's feet.'

Falconer was inclined to suggest the rider in his turn might care to exercise some care, but looking up, he saw the man was as shocked as he had been. The stocky figure of a crusader knight sat firmly on his massive charger, which was lathered in sweat and covered in the dust of the road it had travelled. The rider himself was no better off, covered as he was in dust, cut through on his face by runnels of sweat. He looked dead beat, his bearded face drawn and lined with utter weariness. Falconer bowed mockingly, and waved the rider past with a wave of his arm. The knight grunted, and pricked his horse forwards with a jab of his heels. Falconer watched as the horse and rider plodded on at a more sedate pace into the town.

Falconer turned and acknowledged the watchman at the gate, who had stood open-mouthed at the near collision.

'Take care, Tom, or you may catch a fly in that.'

Old Tom Inge clapped his mouth closed involuntarily, and then waved a finger at Falconer.

'Have a care yourself, Master William, or I may close the gate before you can get back in.'

Falconer smiled.

'Then I shall have to pay the penalty, and supply you with a jug of ale as usual.'

Blushing, the old man grunted, knowing that Falconer's jest had the ring of truth. Inge was known to accept a drink by way of allowing people back through the wicket gate after curfew. He turned back into his little box that protected him from the worst of the weather and the cold at night, and Falconer passed through the gate and on towards the leper hospital.

*

While Falconer delved into his past at Bartlemas, another man was also thinking about matters in Oxford. Edward was a handsome man despite the strange droop to his right eye that he had inherited from his father, King Henry. At the age of thirty-six, he still had a thick mane of black hair. And he was a tall man, standing head and shoulders above the common crowd. His long arms and legs gave him an advantage in swordplay and mastering a stallion. They also gave

13

him his nickname of Longshanks, though no-one used that soubriquet any longer. Last year he had been crowned Edward, King of England, and was now travelling with his court around his kingdom. They had just descended on Woodstock with his retinue of cooks, carters, clerks, grooms, doctors, tailors, huntsmen and knights. Sometimes his court could swell to six hundred, though today he was travelling with a third of that number, even taking into account the merchants, players, beggars and prostitutes who also tagged along. He was actually travelling light – for a king – as his trip was one with a particular purpose. Now, pacing the great chamber that was his audience room in Woodstock Palace, a day's journey north of Oxford, he suddenly felt diminished. He turned on the patient, soberly-clad man who attended him.

'Damn it, Robert. Am I to be circumscribed by lawyers and pen-pushers?'

It seemed to the king that the times were an age of lawyers and quibblers, and not of warriors and monarchs any more. He waved his hands above his head as though he were trying to swat away so many buzzing flies. Robert Burnell, Chancellor of England, shrugged his shoulders, not caring to inflame Edward's anger any further. He could have pointed out that it had been the king's idea to set up the Commission into local government, but that would only make matters worse. Burnell knew Edward had an orderly mind, and was seeking to consolidate the laws of England in much the same way as he saw his fellow rulers doing across Europe. But his chief purpose in so doing was to define royal rights and possessions, not to cede rights to those beneath him. Edward had a well-developed sense of his own importance and power. Now he was angry.

Burnell rode out the storm of Edward's anger, knowing the real cause of the explosion. It was nothing to do with the fifty-one laws set out in the First Statute of Westminster, and now approved by bishops, abbots, barons, earls and knights of the realm. The new laws covered an astonishing numbers of subjects dear to Edward's heart – extortion by royal officers, lawyers and bailiffs; writs and methods of procedure in civil and criminal cases; the custom of wrecks; freedom of elections and so on. This had all pleased Edward, and when the Parliament also forbade usury to the Jews, he felt he had achieved a great deal in a short time. No, Burnell knew that, despite his anger, the king secretly loved all this casuistry.

What had actually peeved Edward was Llewellyn ap Gruffyd's refusal to attend his coronation. Ostensibly, it was all over the fact that Llewellyn's own renegade brother, Daffyd, had sought refuge in England and whether Edward should or not have give him succour. But Edward was sure it was more to do with the Prince of Wales – so called – chancing his arm in a battle of wills with him. Though Llewellyn had bent the knee to Henry, Edward's father, and was seen as a petty vassal to the King of England, the prince thought he could improve his own esteem at home by avoiding bowing before the new king. Besides he owed thousands of marks to Edward, which he did not have. So it had all come down to a quibble over the treaty Llewellyn had signed with Henry, and that was why Edward was railing at lawyers.

14

As Burnell waited patiently, a light flickered in Edward's eyes. Like his father, the king had a droopy right eyelid, and for a moment it seemed he was winking at his Chancellor. Burnell knew better, however, and kept his own eyes to the ground. Edward had come to a decision, and began to explain it.

'We thought to be magnanimous, by taking the court to Chester. There, the Prince of Wales could have made his due obedience, but he didn't. Time has now run out for him.'

Robert Burnell inclined his head, and nodded his approval of Edward's clever ruse. The trip to Chester, from where the king's retinue was returning, had actually been a trap for Llewellyn. The options before him had been either to meet with Edward and bow the knee, or to appear rebellious and refuse to meet him. Llewellyn had decided that to agree to meet Edward was impossible for him now. But by refusing to meet Edward so close to his own domain, he had fallen into the king's trap The Welsh prince had incautiously chosen the worse option, just as Edward and Burnell had thought he would.

Robert Burnell was a man from modest origins, who maintained an air of quiet, self-effacing charm. He had made himself indispensable to Edward even before he became king, and at one time had been spoken of as a future Archbishop of Canterbury. His attraction to women, however, and the production of at least five bastard children had eventually ruled him out of that race. But now, he was in a far more powerful position as Chancellor. He was often able to place an idea in Edward's head that might come to fruition as the king's own idea. The Chester ruse had actually been his. He now chanced his arm on a matter he knew also bothered the king.

'Perhaps, as we are close by Oxford, we can find a way to resolve the other little matter that I know vexes you, your Majesty. I have good cause to go to Oxford on your behalf to press de Bosco on the Welsh students. I could be your emissary there.'

There was a good reason the Burnell should visit Oxford in Edward's place. There was a long-standing belief that any king who entered the university town would soon thereafter lose his throne. Edward was not superstitious, but it was prudent not to tempt fate. The business in Oxford could well be dealt with by Burnell, and the king knew it. Without saying a word, Edward turned his gaze from the window out of which he had been looking, and faced Burnell. This time, the little, sombrely-clad man was sure it was a wink of approval that the king gave him.

15

Chapter Two

Feast of St John of Chrysostom, 13th September

He knelt before the altar, the stone seeping cold into his knees. He raised his arms in adoration of the crucifix suspended high in front of him. Then he fell forwards on to the chilly slabs, his face turned aside so his left cheek struck the stone floor jarringly. He made the shape of the cross with his outstretched arms and body, hugging the coldness to him in a sort of religious ecstasy. He tried to calm his boiling brain, but he couldn't. The theft of the first book had been so simple.

The chest in which it had lurked, the darkness of the interior suited to the book's murky and disgusting content, was in a communal area in the hall. The purpose of the chest's location was so that a student lodging at the hall could borrow a text for study. But the room was often left unattended, and anyone could walk in from the street and claim a book for their own. Of course there was a ledger on a stand next to the chest, where a borrower was required to make their mark. For a while, book in hand, he had contemplated the half-filled page, the space a tempting invitation to make a statement of his purpose. But he had resisted the temptation, satisfying himself with the theft alone. He had walked out with the book in the sleeve of his grey robe.

The book now resided under the simple pallet in his starkly bare cell along with others he had taken since. Their presence was still a rankling sore, for he had not thought beyond the act of stealing. Now, he tossed around his brain the possibilities open to him. He could expose the books' heresies in public, but that would only serve to disseminate its contagion. No, he had known the minute he had stolen the latest book that he would have to destroy them all. The idea at first filled him with horror – the destruction of any book was an action barely to be contemplated when each precious text took a scribe so long to copy. But the contents of the books were an abomination, so they deserved no better fate than to be burned in the fires of Hell. A fire that should be shared with their authors. This thought gave relief to his concerns about what had happened yesterday, when he had had to resort to a violent act. In his mind this was now justified.

He sighed in pleasure at the resolution of his quandary, and his breath blew out in a chilly draught across the floor of the chapel. As his cheek grew numb from the cold slab under it, so his brain cooled from its former fervour, and he began to talk with God.

*

16

Sir Hugo de Wolfson awoke that morning in his bed in Dagville's Inn with his throat feeling raw. He ran his fingers through his thick, but greying hair and sat up. For a moment he felt dizzy, but shook his head, and forced his weary bones from the bed. After dressing, it was all he could do to swallow some watered ale and bread. And even then he had to soak the dry bread in the ale to make it palatable. It had been his intention to travel onwards to his destination in the north that day, but he felt weak from a feverish cold. He resolved to recover by spending another day in Oxford, and told the inn-keeper, Thomas Dagville, so. He also made enquiry for a physick, and Dagville gave him direction to an apothecary in Kepeharm Lane off Fish Street.

'You cannot miss it for the lane is almost opposite the House of Converts.'

Dagville was making reference to a sturdy stone house in the middle of Great Jewry. The people of Oxford knew little of its occupants, but as its rents were paid to the main Domus Conversorum set up by the old king in London, they assumed it served the same purpose. To accommodate those Jews who sought conversion from their faith. Dagville laughed cruelly at the situation of the Jews.

'There have been some who lodged inside, but they are so stubborn it is said that few have come to the true faith. You see how foolish they are. The Jews do not have the wit even to understand the wrongness of their ways.'

Dagville failed to mention that amidst the 'errant' Jews who lived in Oxford was a physick who was far superior in his knowledge and skills to the local Christian apothecary he had directed the crusader knight to. Old Samson was a wise and skilful Jewish healer, who Thomas Dagville's own wife had resorted to for help with her last, difficult birth when Spicer the apothecary had failed her. Dagville thought it better not to send this stiff crusader to a Jew though. So he recommended Will Spicer of Kepeharm Lane instead. De Wolfson pushed himself out of his chair, his bones aching.

'I thank you, Dagville. It is nothing but a small fever. But I have still to travel far, and do not wish to be delayed any longer than need be. I am sure Spicer will fix me up.'

De Wolfson tugged his cloak around him, though the day was already warm, and stepped out of the inn into the mayhem that was a normal market day in Oxford.

Oxford was well situated to benefit from trade moving from north to south and east to west. Inside the walls, the town was cut into four by roads running in those directions, so that the very layout of the town was in the form of a Christian cross laying on its side. Northgate Street ran down across Carfax into Fish Street, through Great Jewry to South Gate. Great Bailey in the west ran from the castle where the constable, Peter Bullock resided, through Carfax in the opposite direction, and along High Street to East Gate. These crossed roads teemed with traders, ranging from the straw-sellers in East Gate, past the pig market, wood-merchants, purveyors of earthenware, to glove-makers and bakers of good white bread. From South Gate the stalls were home to fishmongers, tanners and sellers

17

of faggots, through to the corn-merchants at North Gate. The houses
behind the stalls were only two stories high but stretched back a
long way behind their narrow frontages. They were huddled in nature,
cheek-by-jowl, and close to the ground from which they rose, as if
rendered from the mud of the streets. It made the thirteen parish
churches of Oxford all the more striking with their tall spires reaching
up to heaven.

The ailing crusader knight at first fought against the flow of people.
A group of young clerks filled the roadway, some clad in sober clothes,
some in parti-coloured tunics. One of the more sober, grey-robed youths
was reading a book and he bumped into de Wolfson. On hearing a
curse, he might have argued. But thought better of it when he looked
up to see a sturdy knight staring him in the face. He stepped aside, a
scowl on his face, and walked on, his mind back deep in his tome.
De Wolfson would have pressed on in his haste to find the apothecary,
but he soon tired of the effort of pushing through the crowd, and let
his pace conform to the slow passage of shoppers. Soon, he was
moving with the flow of the crowd rather than against it. Making this
more leisurely way towards Carfax, he lingered over a stall displaying
well stitched leather gloves, wiping his runny nose with his fingers
before picking up one of the samples to test its quality.

'It is the best of cut and stitching, sir knight, and well able to stand
the vicissitudes of battle, even in the heat of Outremer.'

John Burewald, the sharp-eyed glove-seller, had expertly assessed
his potential customer. The stocky figure of de Wolfson was clad in
a loose nondescript tunic under his cloak, which now hung open,
but it was easy to spot the broad shoulders of a fighter. And his face
still bore the effect of the unbearable Holy Land sun. De Wolfson
merely grunted, as he was not seeking to buy gloves. He had a pair
of stained but still serviceable gloves in his saddlebags back at the
inn. He shoved the glove he had picked up back at the man, and
moved on before the glover became a nuisance. At Carfax, he turned
south, as instructed by Dagville, and followed the crowds down
Fish Street.

He stopped to admire a display of fresh fish, the glittering eyes
staring back at him blankly. Alice Lane was standing beside him
buying pickled herring which she hoped would stretch to feed her
large family back home. He was caught with a fit of coughing, and
hawked and spat in the foul gutter that ran the length of the street.
Alice shrank back in disgust, and de Wolfson grunted an apology,
almost knocking over a Franciscan friar as he stepped away. Drifting
on past other fish stalls at the pace of the general mob, he realised
when he came to the South Gate that he had missed his way. He
turned back and retraced his steps, trying to recall from Dagville's
instructions if Kepharm Lane was to the right or left. He was
momentarily distracted by the sight of a pretty woman emerging from
a house on the opposite side of the street. Her shapely figure fitted
her flowing green dress well, and her unruly red hair escaped the
confines of her linen snood, suggesting a woman of lively temperament.
She crossed the street ahead of him, and disappeared down a narrow
lane bounded on one side by a sturdy stone building with a square

tower. De Wolfson recalled the landlord's mention of the House of Converts.

'This must be the building,' he muttered to himself. 'I was to turn here, was I not? But which way?'

His head ached, and he cursed his fever-addled brains. But, mindful of the pretty red-head and the fact he had not slaked his lust in a month or more, he followed the vision of pulchritude down the narrow lane. He was soon to realise that he was going in quite the wrong direction, but by then he had lost the red-head, and found himself after a few twists and turns walking down Grope Lane. Not that he knew its name, but the familiar sign of a brothel put any idea of finding a remedy for his fever out of his mind. He scratched at his crotch and stepped through the open doorway.

It was still morning, and the house was quiet, but Sal Dockerell, the brothel-keeper, bustled out of the back room. She recognised a good customer when she saw one, and when the stocky knight laid down a silver coin, she sent him upstairs to spend some time with a raven-haired slut called Peggy Jardine. Just to make sure, Sal put the coin in her mouth and bit it. She could tell it was a good one.

*

William de Bosco was the chancellor of the university, and today was not the first time he had regretted taking the post. Others before him had actively sought the position, and used its power to further their own ends. The previous incumbent, Thomas Bek, had indeed aspired to be Chancellor of England, but his hopes had been dashed when he used the powers of his position to bring to trial a certain regent master for murder. His idea had been that, taking the responsibility away from the King's authorised officers and assuming it himself, would raise his profile once the master was found guilty. The case had seemed straightforward, but friends of the regent master had turned it on its head, and Bek's reputation had been ruined. De Bosco had been chosen to replace him as a safe pair of hands, who had no great ambition for himself. He was a quiet man, grey by nature and in appearance. For well nigh two years he had occupied the Chancellor's seat almost without anyone realising. But now he had a problem that he couldn't ignore.

Books were going missing from halls and private rooms, from chests and from shelves. It had started a few weeks ago, when a master teaching the *trivium* of rhetoric, grammar and logic at Moyses Hall, found that a few classical texts had gone missing. He had thought it trivial at first, as Boethius, Cicero and Priscian could be replaced, albeit at some cost. But when he spoke to a colleague from neighbouring Durham Hall, he discovered that books from a chest there had disappeared too. Soon it became apparent that many more were lost, and the tally grew. Seneca, Donatus, Statius, Juvenal, Lucan, Horace, Ovid, Perseus, Sedulius, Cato, and Macrobius were all added to the growing losses. Then came the greatest blow. Only yesterday, Regent Master Roger Stephens had come to de Bosco pale-faced and in shock, a gash on his forehead seeping blood.

He had arrived earlier than usual at the school he used in the lane beside St Mary's Church so he could prepare for a lecture on civil law. He wished to consult a reference in the rare twelfth century *Commentary* of Vacarius on Justinian. It was said that Vacarius had lectured on Roman Law at Oxford about 1149, but was forced by King Stephen to desist. Most of his works had been gathered up and destroyed, so the volume carefully locked away in the Law Schools chest was a rarity. Stephens knew something was amiss when he reached the school's door to find it ajar. Peering at the lock, he saw that the wooden door frame had been smashed. Heart racing, he pushed the door open, and stepped into the darkened room, calling out as he did so.

'Hello, who's there?'

The room was eerily silent, though the regent master sensed a presence.

'Is there anyone there?'

He wished he had brought a lantern, for now he had to grope his way across the room to the wall cupboard where the cheap tallow candles were kept. As he took a tentative step towards the centre of the room, a grey shadow detached itself from the prevailing gloom. He flinched, and soon found it was not some insubstantial shadow, but someone very solid with a square object held under his arm. The intruder barged into him, knocking him to the floor, and causing him to hit his head on a bench as he fell. For a few moments he was stunned, and when he pushed himself to his knees, he saw the chest of books had been broken open too. Heart pounding, he crawled on his hands and knees to the repository of law books. Peering inside, he instantly knew what had been in the intruder's arms. The irreplaceable tome by Vacarius was gone.

Chancellor de Bosco had sighed deeply as he listened to Roger Stephens's report, and had sent the man off to have his wound attended to. Today, his mind was turning the problem over and over. He had to admit that the minor, albeit costly, inconvenience of the loss of copies of Priscian's *Grammar* and the like had taken a serious turn. He now knew he would have to do something about it, and thought immediately of the regent master who had caused the downfall of his predecessor, Thomas Bek. De Bosco knew he liked to interfere in cases of murder, and thought that if this book thievery went on, it could well lead to killings. De Bosco needed the man to sort the problem out before it got worse, and someone suffered a worse fate than Roger Stephens. He muttered to himself in a sort of prayer.

'This time I will have you on my side, Regent Master Falconer.'

Having come to his decision, de Bosco turned his mind to the other problem facing him. He had only this morning received warning that no less a personage than the Chancellor of England was arriving in Oxford tomorrow. He had no idea why Robert Burnell was coming, and why the message only preceded him by a day. In a panic, he had called the two proctors, who formed his executive in keeping order in the university. Both were men he had inherited from his predecessor, and they had been re-elected annually since. Roger Plumpton and Henry de Godfree were like chalk and cheese, as

Plumpton, the proctor for the northern nations, was a man who stood by the rules and rarely chanced his arm. De Godfree, on the other hand, had an eye for the main chance, and nearly came a cropper at the same time as Thomas Bek. That he had survived the turmoil spoke volumes about his slippery nature. He was the proctor for the southern nations.

The two nations of the university represented a geographical divide roughly following the course of the River Nene. The northerners, or *boreales*, therefore included the Scots in their numbers, and the southern nation, or *australes*, included Marchers, Irishmen, and Welshmen. They were constantly at each others throats, and the proctors had difficulty keeping the students under control. But this had not been what de Bosco wanted to talk to them about. He wanted their opinion on Burnell's purpose in Oxford. When he had told them who was due to arrive in Oxford, it was surprisingly Plumpton who first spoke up.

'He is paving the way for the king. We know, do we not, that Edward proposes to finally solve the Welsh problem.'

De Bosco looked his proctor in the eye, anxiety written all over his face. He could hear the triumph in Plumpton's voice. The northern proctor was a man who had always taken the king's side, both in the Barons' War and later. Now he found himself firmly in the right, while his colleague, de Godfree, was a supporter of the reviled Welsh. De Bosco wondered how far Plumpton would be prepared to go in his attack on the Welsh. Deliberately, the chancellor tested his resolve.

'Have you heard anything, Roger? Does this mean Burnell thinks the university is not maintaining control of its Welshmen?'

Roger Plumpton's response was suddenly cautious, sensing the chancellor's prevarication.

'Not necessarily that, Chancellor, but the king is on his way back from Chester where he was snubbed once again by Llewellyn. It won't be long before he snuffs out that man's resistance, and the Welsh nation as a whole. Then we might find that the Welsh clerks in Oxford would be uncontrollable.'

De Godfree snorted in derision, eager to pass on any blame to his opponent.

'The Welsh clerks are no problem to Edward, Chancellor. It's Plumpton's Scots he should be concerned about. Why, Bullock the constable had to crack a few Scottish heads with that sword of his only last week.'

And so the argument had raged, leaving de Bosco with still no clear notion as to why Burnell was coming to Oxford. When the day dawned, he could only hope that the Chancellor of England was not coming to oust the Chancellor of the University.

Chapter Three

Holy Cross Day, 14ᵗʰ September

Falconer could hardly concentrate on his teaching duties that morning in the school. He droned on about Aristotle and logic almost without knowing what he was saying. He had covered the ground so many times before with so many shining faces staring at him, he was afraid he had begun to bore the young men in his class as much he had begun to bore himself. His mind was actually on what he had gleaned from the old Franciscan friar at St Bartholomew's hospital the other afternoon. Friar Gualo was even older than Aldwyn, and had a memory for patients who had passed through the hospital's doors years ago, even if he could not recall what he had done the previous day.

'The eighth or ninth year of the old king's reign, you say?'

Falconer nodded, unsure if his trip was going to be worth it. Gualo looked closer to death than some of his wards in the leper hospital. But he insisted on racking his brains for Falconer.

'A woman, you say? I recall the case of a maid who was deaf, dumb, and blind in both eyes. Her parents brought her to the festival of Saint Bartholomew, and she was cured. She skipped away full of joy, perfectly sounding her words. But she was twelve years of age, and so I don't think she is the one you are seeking.'

'No, this woman would have been of full age, and perhaps already with child.'

Gualo frowned disapprovingly.

'She would not have come here merely through being ... *gravidus.*' He took care to use Latin to avoid any common reference to pregnancy passing his clerical lips. 'After all, that is hardly an illness. There was a leper maiden who was here three years before St Godric cured her. Her symptoms were horrible apparently, and her frame wasted.'

The old friar shivered at the thought of someone coupling with a leper.

'But no, she would not do either.'

Falconer sighed, seeing he was getting nowhere. He didn't even believe in miraculous cures, and was prepared to wager that the examples given came about for one of two reasons. Either the sick person was ill through grief or despair, and was cured through a dose of hope, or the person was an astute beggar feigning illness in the first place. He was about to thank the old monk and leave, when Gualo bucked up, apparently recalling a matter long forgotten.

'Could the woman have been carrying out works of mercy here, rather than being a patient? Some women not of gentle birth but still fit for the purpose watched over the sick, and others attended to the household affairs. I do recall a story about a Welsh woman who ...' Suddenly, Gualo's eyes clouded over. 'But then I would be talking out of turn.'

Falconer felt as though he was getting somewhere at last, and encouraged the friar to tell his tale, even if it were unpleasant.

'Friar Gualo, this is important to me. Please tell me what you know, and it will go no further.'

The old man squinted at him, and huffed.

'It was only a tale told in the friary, you understand, between young postulants who should have known better.'

With a sudden shock of surprise, Falconer guessed that one of those postulants was probably Gualo himself. The friar was old enough to have been a postulant fifty years ago. He restrained a smile, imagining the old man as a youth newly entering a celibate life, and revelling in a little salacious chatter. He held his breath, and finally the old man continued.

'It concerned a woman – Welsh, as I said – of uncertain background, and a young Franciscan friar newly arrived in Oxford. He was an Italian, it was said, by the name of Alberoni. It was soon after the Grey Friars had arrived in the town, and before the friary was built. We were lodging in St Ebbe's. The Italian took a fancy to assisting at the hospital. The woman – well, girl really – kept the rooms clean and was entranced by the Italian. One thing ...' He coughed. '... led to another, and she grew in size till she could hide it no more. In fact, I believe the child was ripped out of her like Julius Caesar is said to have been. When the master of the hospital learned of the situation, he had the child sent to his mother's own land. To an island where there was another Augustinian community, and where the boy could be kept an eye on.'

Falconer couldn't believe his ears. Depending on the name of the community, this could be the first morsel of information about his own birth.

'The woman ... she died?'

Just as Friar Gualo was about to reply, a young Franciscan had appeared in the little office where they were sitting together. He was of a severe demeanour with a sour face as if he had been sucking on a sponge soaked in vinegar. His voice was harsh and piping, as if it had not yet properly broken.

'Brother, it is time to return to the friary. Our brothers require your presence for prayer.'

Gualo sighed, obviously used to this fervent young man acting as his keeper.

'Yes, yes, Fulbert. I am coming. I just have to tell Master Falconer ...'

Fulbert's pitiless gaze latched on to Gualo, stopping the words from emerging.

'I am sure the regent master will understand your need to share your prayers with our community.'

The young man switched his gaze to Falconer, plastering a rictus of a smile on his face. Creakily, Gualo rose to his feet, following

Fulbert like some tame dog. Falconer threw a question the old man's way as he passed.

'The island. What was its name?'

'Bardsey. They say that King Arthur is buried there, waiting to be woken. It is also the island of twenty thousand saints.'

Falconer was still turning over in the back of his mind the possibility that he had found the link to his birth, when the time came to move his lesson with his students on to *sophisma*. Needing to concentrate more, he shelved his other thoughts. Some of his pupils loved solving the riddle that was a sophist statement; others found it incomprehensible. Falconer confessed himself as being in the first camp. It was all a matter of liking the riddle for its own sake, and he often likened his predilection for murder cases to sophistry. He gave the students one of his favourite sentences to puzzle over.

'Consider this sophisma.'

He carefully chalked on the slate board, "All men are donkeys or men and donkeys are donkeys." He carefully did not say the words, so as not to give them any particular inflection. Then he eyed his audience, and maliciously latched on to a youth he knew disdained such theoretical arguments.

'Geoffrey Westhalf, give me a proof of the sentence's truth, and also a disproof.'

The pinch-faced boy grimaced, as all his contemporaries' eyes arrowed in on his discomfort. But he was not to be caught so easily, and sneered.

'The sentence is a copulative sentence each part of which is true. "All men are donkeys or men," and "Donkeys are donkeys."'

Falconer smiled, and he heard a stirring from the brighter boys in his flock. He chose Peter Mithian, who was one of his own boarders at Aristotle's Hall.

'What's wrong with that statement, Peter?'

Eager to please his mentor, Mithian grinned widely, his youthful face lighting up.

'Nothing is wrong with what Westhalf said, master, but it is only half the truth.' He looked round for approbation of his pun on the other boy's name. Falconer sternly motioned for him to continue, so he did.

'As well as being conjunctive, the sentence can also be disjunctive, and therefore incorrect.'

Westhalf screwed up his face, making it even more weasel-like.

'How can a sentence be both true and untrue? That is stupid.'

Glad to have trapped his victim, Mithian continued.

'It can also be read as two different, incorrect statements. "All men are donkeys," and "Men and donkey are donkeys."' He paused for effect, and added a rider. 'Though in Westhalf's case, I see a man who *is* a donkey.'

Falconer spent some time calming down the class, and regretted his levity, seeing that he and Peter Mithian had both just made an enemy of Geoffrey Westhalf.

*

24

Robert Burnell's arrival in Oxford was typically discreet. He rode through the North Gate accompanied only by one other person. The Chancellor of England was dressed as usual in modest black robes and hose, and was so unmemorable that the watchman on the gate took more notice of his companion. He was a dark-skinned man with a greasy, black mane of hair, who sat on his horse as though born in the saddle. This companion of Burnell's swivelled his gaze around constantly as if distrusting anyone in the crowd around his master. His eyes, when they alighted on Peter Kepeharm, the watchman at the North Gate, were cold, black pools reflecting no light. Kepeharm blinked, and looked away to deal with a small troupe of players and acrobats who were entering the gate pushing a cart loaded with their possessions. The gatekeeper stopped them, and demanded to know their business, though it was self-evident from the garish masks and brightly painted juggler's clubs on the cart. Their leader, John Peper by name, sighed and, used to being harassed by officialdom, began to explain.

Burnell and his servant rode on oblivious to the scene taking place behind them. He knew where the man he sought resided and jogged steadily down to Carfax. From there, he turned east along the High Street towards St Mary's Church. William de Bosco lodged in a house called Glassen, or Aula Vitrea, because of its extravagant glazed windows. It was located conveniently for the chancellor at the end of Schools Street, where the clerks studied, and behind St Mary's Church, where de Bosco and his predecessors held chancellor's courts to manage the affairs of the university. The passage of the quiet, little man and his swarthy servant drew little attention, and so Burnell was able to surprise William de Bosco in his lair.

*

Brother Aldwyn had searched the records of Bartlemas hospital, but had found no reference to a female inmate who could have been the person William Falconer was looking for. Young girls who had had hysterical fits and miraculous cures of paralysed old women beyond child-bearing age cropped up regularly. But he had found an oblique reference to an incident with a serving girl at the hospital. A terse note in the relevant year told of an operation 'such as Caesar's mother suffered', but with no report as to the outcome. Aldwyn felt vaguely disturbed, as it reminded him of a prediction in Merlin's prophecies. He hurried over to his precious copy of Geoffrey of Monmouth's book to be sure of his recollection. He scanned past the passage he had quoted to Falconer earlier about the red dragon and the white. And there it was.

It shall rain a shower of blood, and a raging famine shall afflict mankind. When these things happen, the red one shall be grieved; but when his fatigue is over, shall grow strong. Then shall mis-fortunes hasten upon the white one, and the buildings of his gardens shall be pulled down. Seven that sway the sceptre shall be killed, one of whom shall become a saint. The wombs of mothers shall be ripped up, and infants born premature.'

It did not please him one bit that these predictions presaged the possible rise of the red dragon, or Llewellyn. There were too many evils accompanying it to excite an old man, even a true born Welshman. But he resolved to advise Falconer of his discovery. And of his fears. He gathered up Geoffrey's tome, tucked it under his arm, and hurried across the open marshland on which the abbey stood, making his way towards Oxford.

*

The door of William de Bosco's solar opened, and Inkpen, his servant, poked his head round. De Bosco looked up from the documents he was examining.

'Is Master Falconer here already?'

He was a little surprised. He had only just asked Inkpen to find the regent master and get him to come to Aula Vitrea. The manservant shook his head.

'No, master, I left a message at Aristotle's Hall but he has not yet arrived. However, there is a man here to see you. I told him you were busy, but he insisted, and said his name was Barnwell, or something similar. He can't be anyone important for he is dressed like a regent master, and I don't know the name. Do you, chancellor?'

De Bosco's face paled, and he found he could not take a breath. Of course he knew the name, even though Inkpen had misheard it, because he was expecting the man. He trembled at the thought that his servant was making the second most powerful man in the kingdom – after King Edward himself – linger in the hallway. He rose from his chair and, regaining his power to breath, hissed at his servant.

'My God, man, show him in at once. It is the king's chancellor, Robert Burnell.'

The blood fled from Inkpen's face also, and he disappeared from view. Only moments later, he was ushering Robert Burnell and his silent companion into the room. His voice cracked as he tried to announce them, failing completely with the second man, whose name he had not discovered in his haste to rectify matters. Burnell seemed quite unperturbed, and as Inkpen's voice died away, introduced the man at his shoulder himself.

'This is Isaac Doukas, my secretary. He is a Greek from the island of Cyprus.'

De Bosco glanced nervously at the other man. He was stocky and dark-skinned with long, greasy black hair tied up at the back, and revealed his calling by the satchel over his shoulder, out of which protruded the feathery ends of several quills. But he was no grovelling, stoop-shouldered clerk, for his eyes were as black as his hair, and gave off no reflection. Indeed, they seemed to suck the very light away from the room in which he stood. Almost as though reacting to de Bosco's imagination, a candle at his shoulder flickered, and the chancellor felt his heart lurch. He started to thrust out a hand to

26

Burnell, but something held him back, and he bowed instead.

'Forgive me for your poor treatment. We were expecting you, but you caught us on the hop. You see, we are having some difficulty with a persistent thief of books, and his behaviour has been getting more worrisome of late. He attacked the last master he stole from.'

He was aghast that he was babbling out such embarrassing facts, but he couldn't stop himself. Burnell waved his hand, not caring to know about a thief, albeit one of such a valuable commodity as books. But de Bosco was so flustered that he continued to babble about his problem, trying to excuse himself but only making matters worse.

'I am in control of the situation, though. I have summoned a most subtle master, who concerns himself with mysteries, and who will be on the trail of the malefactor soon enough. His name is William Falconer.'

Burnell raised an eyebrow, as if he neither knew nor cared about who this master was.

'If, as you say, this thief is resorting to violence, then I think this ... Falconer needs to act quickly. The king would hate to hear of murder within the walls of Oxford.' He stared balefully at de Bosco. 'It would not go well for your tenure.'

De Bosco licked his lips nervously. The post of chancellor was in the hands of the regent masters of the university not in the gift of the monarch. However, most of the masters could be swayed by the king's view on a candidate. Even one who was already occupying the post. He parted his dry lips to speak, but saw that Burnell was of a mind to move on, and held his peace.

'But there is a far more important matter I have come to discuss. I have to tell you that the king is far from pleased by the Welsh at present. He is contemplating a campaign against Llewellyn, and wishes to have no disturbances within his kingdom centred on this rabble. Therefore he has taxed me with the job of ensuring there is not any Welsh rebellion in Oxford.'

De Bosco opened his mouth to protest Oxford's loyalty, but once again Burnell stopped him with a glance.

'You will, therefore abolish the nations here at the university, and so prevent the Welsh and other factions joining together in rioting against the king's authority.'

De Bosco was aghast at such a command, but knew it was pointless objecting to the decision. After all, he had only the day before been talking to his proctors himself about the divisiveness that the Northern and Southern nations created in the town. These nations were a long tradition at the university, but it looked as though their days were numbered. Still, he could not help raising an objection.

'But, but ... I will have to call together the congregation of masters, and speak to my proctors. I dare say they will not be pleased to see their power bases removed.'

Burnell waved a desultory hand, apparently dismissing the proctors and the whole mass of regent masters as though irrelevant.

'I do not know the Southern Proctor, but I have corresponded with Plumpton, and know his views on the matter. I see no problem there.'

De Bosco was shocked he had already been betrayed from inside his own camp. Plumpton, of all people, had gone behind his back. Defeated, he bowed once more to the Chancellor of England. Triumphant, Burnell now placed a friendly arm on his shoulder, and spoke of other matters.

'Now, tell me about this book thief, and the man who will root him out.'

Chapter Four

At sext, in the middle of that particular Saturday, an interesting sight was to be seen in Oxford. Solemn men in black robes appeared from all corners of the town, and began converging on St Mildred's Church in the northern quarter of Oxford. It was to observers as though a dark and gloomy mass of water was flowing down the narrow lanes, pulled by an unseen force towards the church. The Congregation of Regent Masters of Oxford University's Faculty of Arts met periodically to consider matters of relevance to the workings of the university. The Masters of Arts jealously guarded their status and pre-eminence over all other masters, and their numbers specifically excluded the friars and doctors of theology. Perhaps because of their dull garb, or perhaps due to the secretive nature of their gatherings, they were familiarly known as the Black Congregation. In actual fact, the issues coming before the Congregation were often tedious, and not every master who could attended all meetings. However, it was rumoured that today was to be an unusual occurrence. They had all been summoned at short notice by the chancellor for a most serious purpose, and required to attend at midday without fail. Rumours of someone of eminence attending the meeting had ensured that no master stayed away under any pretext. And that had made certain of their promptness too. Soon the church was filled with the black sea of masters, and the doors were closed on the curious outsiders.

Four chairs had been set up just below the altar, two slightly raised above the other two, which flanked them either side. A group of senior masters placed themselves close before the seats to establish their precedence, though they were still not sure what was to take place. Amongst the senior group were the tall, angular figure of Master Gerald Halle, and the coarse features of one of the few foreign Masters, Heinrich Koenig. Others nodded to this pre-eminent group as they moved around seeking a suitable place to sit. After an initial period of subdued conversation, when questions were bandied around from master to master but no answers supplied, the congregation began to arrange itself in the seats either side of the nave. All the masters wore a black tabard, over the top of which was arranged a black sleeveless cope, or a cloak with a hood bordered with fur. All knew how cold the interior of St Mildred's could get, and had ensured they wore something warm. It was likely to be a lengthy business they were summoned to sit through. Headgear saw a mixture of square birettas and simple round pileums. A few had already pulled up their hoods to keep warm, and no doubt in order to doze off beneath them should matters become tedious. Though the wait was protracted by the absence of the chancellor, and speculative whispers broke out, the assembled crowd were not to be kept in uncertainty for long.

As the conversation in the church lulled, William de Bosco finally scurried from the gloom of the side aisle towards the chairs arranged below the altar. He wore a scarlet cope trimmed with black over his robe, and a scarlet biretta on his head, though he looked uncomfortable in such grand robes. The two proctors strode along either side of him, and arranged themselves in the lower chairs flanking the chancellor's chair and the as yet conspicuously empty one. De Godfree's face looked decidedly grim, while in contrast Roger Plumpton's was all smiles. The delay to the arrival of the three men had been caused by the absence of the Northern Proctor, Plumpton who, it turned out, had been in private consultation with Robert Burnell. This clearly explained de Godfree's current grimness, and de Bosco's uncertainty. The three men's entrance, late as it was, had ensured complete silence, and the chancellor finally broke it with a sombre pronouncement.

'You were summoned here for a most serious purpose. The congregation will be addressed by Robert Burnell, Chancellor of England.'

A murmur of shock and surprise wafted through the gathered crowd. Some masters were no doubt excited by the prospect of such a grand figure addressing them. Others, chiefly those whose antecedents were Welsh and who were aware of the king's anger with Prince Llewellyn, were filled with apprehension. All craned their necks to look down the aisle of the church to get a sight of the chancellor. As he walked up to the empty seat next to de Bosco, Burnell's slight and sombrely-clad figure disappointed them somewhat.

*

He had heard the word of God again, and rose from his prostrate position on the cold stone flags before the altar. He was aching and stiff – his limbs frozen by their contact with the floor and the fixed pose he had maintained for so long – but he was exhilarated by God's murmurings in his ears. He flexed his arms and stamped his feet to get the blood flowing around his extremities again. His rational mind might have told him God's words were merely echoes of the gossip he heard from his fellow creatures. But his state of ecstasy convinced him otherwise. God and his angels spoke directly in his head, telling him where next he must strike. He walked stiffly down the nave, and out into the late afternoon sun. Weak though its rays were, they warmed his frozen body, and gave his legs added purpose. The words still buzzed in his brain like bees in a hive, and they had caused his head to ache unmercifully. But it was a small price to pay to be in direct contact with God. The buzzing told him Regent Master John Bukwode of Corner Hall had a collection of magic books that must be taken, and the evil canker destroyed. He shook off a sudden wave of dizziness, and began to make his plans.

30

*

Falconer had received de Bosco's message, and curiosity had finally drawn him to the Chancellor's lodgings. But not before he had skulked in his solar to avoid the Black Congregation. Then, on the way to Glassen, he had been distracted by a chance encounter with someone he knew. Ahead of him in the narrow street that led up to the High Street, he had seen a figure he recognised. The rotund young man, with a rolling gait and a shock of unruly brown hair, could be none other than the boy from the travelling players' troupe. He had to search his brain for the name, and for a while it eluded him. A few years ago, the troupe had been embroiled in a murder that he had solved. At first one of the troupe, the jealous husband of an acrobatic female *saltatore*, had been suspected. His name was John Peper – Falconer could at least remember that. But the boy, who was somewhat slow-witted, was more difficult to place. If the troupe was in Oxford, Falconer wished to know where they intended to perform, so he skipped through the crowd and caught up with the boy. He tapped him on the shoulder, and as the youth turned to face him, he remembered his name.

'Will Plome. What are you doing here?'

It was an innocently worded enquiry, but it seemed to perturb the fat boy more than it should have. His plump face turned red, and his lips formed a perfect O in surprise. Clutching a cloth-wrapped bundle to his chest, he stammered a few incoherent words in reply to the challenge.

'I ... just ... I didn't ...'

The youth fumbled nervously with his parcel, and Falconer regretted his scaring of the slow-witted Plome. He patted him on the shoulder encouragingly and smiled. Plome looked away, as if expecting someone else to leap on him, and ran off clutching the parcel tightly to his bosom. Too late, Falconer realised he had failed to ask where the troupe was to perform, wondering only what had made Will Plome so skittish. When he had last seen him, he had always been cheery and pleasant. But this time his face looked ashen and grimly determined. Falconer wondered what had changed the boy so much. But he was late for his meeting with the chancellor, and hurried on. And by the time he had spoken to de Bosco, Plome and the strolling players were banished from his mind.

His conversation with William de Bosco began awkwardly. He was chastised for having forgotten the calling together of the Black Congregation that very day. In actual fact, he had done no such thing, but no longer relished the meetings of that assembly ever since the time it had tried to judge him for murder. But it was easier to apologise for a poor memory rather than explain his feelings on the matter. He was told by de Bosco, however, that no less a person than Robert Burnell had addressed the gathering concerning the Welsh problem. De Bosco was most vexed by the whole situation.

'The nations are to be abolished, and I shall take the blame. Meanwhile, Burnell has gone back to the king, but has left his clerk behind, who will no doubt spy on me and report back to his master about all my failings. And talking about failings ...'

31

The chancellor finally got to the point of his summoning Falconer. He wanted him to discover who was stealing valuable books from collections belonging to individual masters, and student halls. Falconer, disappointed that his summons was for mere thievery, at first declined to assist. But de Bosco was insistent, a pleading look in his eyes.

'You must help me, Master Falconer. You see, what started as a purely an inconvenience, has become a serious matter. Not only has a master been violently attacked during the last theft ...' He knew he was exaggerating, but it was to a good purpose. '... but now the king himself is showing interest in the university. I dare not let such vandalism progress any further.'

Falconer didn't like the thought of Edward being involved in the university's affairs. And if someone were to die as a result of this spate of thefts, he would probably find himself at the centre of something more clamorous than thievery. Far better then to solve the lesser crime than let it escalate. He nodded a reluctant agreement.

'I will look into it. Tell me who was attacked and I will talk to him.'

'I thank you, Master Falconer. It was Master Roger Stephens of the law schools.'

De Bosco was glad of Falconer's acquiescence. He heaved a sigh of relief, knowing that Burnell's Greek secretary, Isaac Doukas, was in the next room, listening in to the conversation on his master's behalf. The cold, apparently heartless man scared him more than a scribe had any right to, but he needed to show assurance. It would not do to have seemed indecisive at such a time as this. He clapped the regent master on the shoulder in a man-to-man sort of way that he was entirely unused to.

'You will not regret your decision.'

As Falconer walked back to Aristotle's Hall, he wasn't so sure. He turned the man's request over in his mind. William de Bosco was like a willow tree – he swayed with the wind, and so survived the storms around him. But unfortunately that meant he was also in Falconer's opinion a cipher – a symbol of something, but lacking depth. Perhaps that was his purpose – to represent the university without imposing his own opinions on it in the way that Thomas Bek had. Bek had sought a greater power than was his to command, and was fortunate that, once dislodged from Oxford, he had still found a place in Edward's court. A personal friendship with the king counted for a great deal in this world. On the other hand, a king's enmity was not to be recommended, as Falconer knew to his cost. He had performed a service for the king while both men had been in Paris, but it had left Falconer knowing more about the king than Edward cared for in anyone. Knowledge could indeed be a dangerous thing, especially knowledge of the king's private affairs. So since that time, Falconer had hidden away in Oxford, kept his head down, and attended to his teaching duties assiduously. To now be under the scrutiny of Edward's servant, was a worry for him.

Falconer opened the door of Aristotle's, not convinced that de Bosco's final words were correct. He somehow felt he might indeed live to regret getting involved with the thefts. Stepping into the main hall of his rented accommodation, he was surprised to find Aldwyn hovering beside the fire that glowed in the grate. The monk hurried over to him, holding out a well-thumbed tome.

'Master Falconer, I am glad you have returned.'

Falconer could see that the old monk was agitated, and supposed it had something to do with his ancestry. Aldwyn had been examining the hospital records, and he supposed the monk may have found a reference to his possible birthing, and the fate of his mother. He licked his lips, which had suddenly gone dry.

'You have some ... news for me?'

Aldwyn frowned, and patted the book in his hands.

'Grave news, I fear. It is all coming true.'

Falconer shook his head in puzzlement.

'What is coming true? Have you not come to tell me of my birth in the year 1225?'

Aldwyn looked uncomfortable, recalling what had started his researches in Geoffrey's book.

'Ah, yes. The cutting open of the unfortunate maid to save her baby. I suppose that could be what you were looking for.' He nodded his head slowly. 'A birth in the very year you wanted there to be one. But there is no proof it was your birth, nor that the maid was your mother.'

'Even so, did she die?'

'There is no record in the ledger.' He couldn't look Falconer in the eye. 'It was an irregular situation, you understand. But that is not why I came to see you, though it did set me on the right track.'

'The track of what?'

Falconer was becoming irritated by the old man's lack of clarity.

'The truth of the prophecies of Merlin.' Aldwyn waved the book in the air, holding the heavy tome in both hands. 'They are all coming true.'

*

Peter Bullock sat disconsolately in his spartan accommodation in St George's Castle. The old fortification stood on a mound at the western end of the town surrounded by a moat engineered from the stream that ran over the marshy ground outside the town walls. His two rooms, one above the other in the tower, were allocated to him by virtue of his appointment as constable. The aldermen of Oxford had a duty to maintain order in the town – no mean feat when you brought together within its wall rowdy young students, townsfolk jealous of the university's privileges, and neighbouring farmers full of drink on market days. It was Bullock's appointed job to keep the lid on this bubbling stew. A former mercenary, he was used to rough justice, and meted it out quite often with the flat of his old sword, stopping potential riots from occurring with a judicious swipe. But today he was feeling his age. At sixty four, he could no longer wade into the middle of a dispute with the same vigour he had possessed even five years ago. King Henry, who had ruled for as long as Bullock could remember, had died at sixty-five. Who was he – a mere commoner – to expect to outlive the monarch?

He eased his aching back in the fireside chair, and reached for the jug of ale at his feet. A sudden spasm of his spine spoiled his grasp, and the jug tipped over, splashing the ale across the rushes on the flagstone floor. He groaned, and stretched to ease the pain. He heard a clatter of feet on the steps that led up to his private chamber, and reached for his sword, still in its scabbard by his side. The haste with which his visitor was negotiating the spiral stairs suggested this was more than a social call. He eased himself upright, clutching the arm of his chair, just as the caller burst into the dimly lit room. It was Grace from the Dagville Inn, a buxom and round-faced ale-wife, and normally of good cheer. This day, she looked ashen and careworn.

'What's this, Mistress Dagville? You have already brought my dinner today. Have you forgotten?'

Peter Bullock kept bachelor quarters, and relied on the wholesome cooking of Grace Dagville to supply his daily needs. Even as he spoke, he regretted his levity. Looking at the woman's face, he knew he would not be able to lighten what looked as if it was going to be a serious situation. Grace Dagville licked her lips nervously before speaking.

'It's one of our guests at the inn.' She paused, uncertain how to go on. 'You need to see this for yourself.'

Bullock frowned.

'See what, mistress? Can't you tell me what's wrong?'

The robust woman looked around as if fearing someone would overhear what she was too afraid to say. She screwed up the end of her linen apron, which showed signs of what she had been cooking before coming to fetch the constable.

'Constable Bullock, you need to see this for yourself.'

The constable sighed, strapped on his sword, and followed Mistress Dagville back out on to the streets of Oxford. It was evening, and despite it being September, the air was still and humid. In spite of the heat though, Thomas Dagville's wife scurried off, leading the way towards Carfax, the main crossroads in the centre of the town. Her ample buttocks wobbled back and forth under the coarse grey cloth of her skirt, and Bullock pulled at the collar of his jerkin, feeling the sweat run down his back. They were soon at the inn, where an anxious Thomas Dagville stood, looking along the High Street and wringing his hands.

'Constable Bullock, am I glad to see you. You have to tell me what to do.'

Bullock wiped his red face on his sleeve.

'I will be glad to, when I know what this is all about.'

Thomas looked sharply at his wife, who flapped her hands in evident distress.

'I couldn't say anything to the constable in case someone overheard, and then there would be panic. And it would not be good for our business.'

Thomas considered her comments, and nodded in agreement.

'You are right. Though I fear our business is ruined anyway.'

Bullock was getting increasingly annoyed by these incomprehensible statements.

'Dagville, for God's sake show me what this is all about.'

34

The inn-keeper sighed.

'Come on, then.'

He led Bullock upstairs to where he kept his few guests in rooms under the eaves of the inn. He opened one of the low doors, and stood uncertainly in the opening. Bullock brushed past him, and stepped into the darkness. The stench of sweat and vomit immediately hit him. He held his hand over his mouth and nose, and peered into the gloom. At first he could see nothing, but then his attention was drawn to the corner of the room by a rustling sound. At first he thought it was rats, and he raised a foot to kick out at the beasts. But in the gloom the shape of a man lying on a low pallet began to emerge as his old eyes adjusted. He made to go closer, but Dagville held him back by his arm.

'Take care. He is ... feverish.'

Bullock shrugged off the restraining hold of the innkeeper and, covering his face with the sleeve of his shirt, he took a step forwards. He leaned over the man, and saw it was a fit-looking man of middle age with the tanned skin of one who had been in Outremer. Under his tan, however, there was the pallor of a sick man, and as Bullock looked more closely the crusader knight coughed. The constable felt a spray of wet phlegm hit his sleeve, and he lurched back. As an old soldier, he knew enough of sickness and plague to know closeness to a sick man was a danger. He should remove his shirt and wash it when he got back to his quarters.

'Do you see?'

The question came from Grace Dagville, who was now at his elbow. She was pointing at the man's face. But Bullock had already seen what he needed to. The knight's forehead was covered with a hideous rash, and when he had coughed, Bullock could see his tongue had been covered in blisters. The man stirred on his bed, but otherwise seemed oblivious to the people in his room. Bullock backed away, pushing Grace Dagville behind him out of the room. Once Thomas Dagville had closed the door, he ordered the innkeeper to keep everyone else away, and to say nothing about this matter until he had brought a physick to verify what they were facing.

Dagville's face crumpled.

'Isn't it obvious what it is? It's the plague – and in my inn too.'

'Let's not jump to conclusions, Thomas. Plague it may be, but what sort? Until I know for sure, I won't know what action to take.'

He went to touch Dagville's arm by way of reassurance, but recalled the sick man's cough that had sprayed his shirt. The old Jew, Samson, had once told him that plague could be spread that way. He didn't necessarily believe that was true, but he wouldn't take any risks. In fact, he would fetch Samson here immediately, and get some idea of what he was facing. The man was a mine of information about diseases, even if he was a Jew. He wagged a finger at the Dagvilles.

'Keep quiet about this. I don't want a panic. I will be back shortly.'

The inn-keeper and his wife looked pale, but nodded their heads. If this wasn't plague, they didn't want rumours to be spread without good reason. They surely didn't want anyone to be afraid of coming to their inn again. So they were guaranteed to be tight-lipped until the worst was known. Bullock rushed off down the High Street towards the Jewish quarter.

*

Saphira was receiving her next lesson on cures for poisoning and the effects of potions and herbs from Samson. Few outside the Jews who lived in Oxford knew of his secret skills, not only in medicines but also in poisons. If the Christians in whose midst he lived guessed at this knowledge, he might have been singled out for special attention and even worse persecution. So he lived a secret life inside what was a secretive community. He was getting old now, however, and Saphira hated the idea of his knowledge dying with him. For months now she had been mining that fund of information, and today Samson was going to test her on her knowledge of poisons.

His grizzled locks, hanging either side of his old face, gave him the look of the very Devil incarnate to outsiders. But to Saphira his strong visage and sparkling eyes spoke volumes about the humanity of the man. He was both knowledgeable and wise, and adept at using his skills in the best way possible, even though at times he seemed eccentric. Saphira, who knew his odd ways, smiled at her teacher as he snapped his fingers at her. They were in the kitchen at the back of his house, a room with a large open fire dominating one wall. In the centre of the room stood a well-worn table that should have been for preparing vegetables and meats. But this was where the resemblance to Saphira's own kitchen ended. The table was not set up to accommodate Jewish dietary laws, nor any other form of food preparation. Instead, its surface was covered with pots and jars. And strange aromas filled the kitchen, one coming from the pot that now bubbled over the fire. Samson hurried over to it, and carried on stirring it gently.

'Forgive me, child, for being so abrupt, but the concoction needs my full attention.'

Saphira smiled coyly at being called a child, and even found herself blushing a little. This old man indeed made her feel once more like a child learning its alphabet. Except he was teaching her ways of both curing and poisoning people, for sometimes the same brew did both. He pointed to the pot on the fire.

'Albertus Magnus himself wrote down this recipe. It is arsenic boiled in milk, and can be used to kill flies. He also recommends a mixture of white lime, opium and black hellebore painted on the walls to the same purpose. This preparation ... ' He took one of the jars from the table, and lifted the lid, showing it to Saphira. '... This is the herb henbane which Pliny says can be used to cure earache. Though he does warn it can cause mental disorders.'

A month or so ago, Saphira would have gone to touch the contents of the pot. But now she knew better, and recited what she had learned about henbane.

'It is well to beware. Four leaves only will induce the sleep of drunkenness from which you may never awake.'

Samson patted her arm proudly. Since starting her studies, she

36

had found herself wanting to know more and more, until the lectures had lasted into the early hours of the morning. More than once Samson had fallen asleep over the big kitchen table, and she had quietly let herself out of his house, and crossed Fish Street to return to her own home opposite, magical words echoing in her head.

'Mercury, gypsum, copper, iron, lapis lazuli, arsenic sublimate, lead.'

These were all powerful, strong words for materials with powerful effects. But she preferred the names of the herbs and insects.

'Usnea, hellebore, bryony, nux vomica, serpentary, cantharides .... cateputria.'

As these words circled round her head, and Samson stirred his arsenic and milk mixture, there came a thunderous knocking at the front door.

Chapter Five

'Listen,' said Aldwyn, opening the book at a page marked with a piece of cloth. '*"The Red One will grieve for what has happened..."* That's the levelling of the mountains, and the rivers running with blood, as I explained before.'

Falconer sighed, knowing he would have to indulge the old monk in his fantasies, if he was ever to learn more about the fate of his mother.

'Yes, I recall all that. The Red Dragon being the royal house of Wales, and the White Dragon being King Henry and his son. But I don't think the Welsh rivers ran with blood. And what were these "mountains" that were levelled?'

Aldwyn grumbled about Falconer's carping criticisms, explaining the words away as mere poetic license by Geoffrey of Monmouth.

'King Henry almost defeated ap Gruffyd's grandfather, his namesake, Llewellyn the Great, in Snowdonia. In so doing, he could be said to be levelling the great mountain. And the river running with blood could be, in the historian's mind, the ancient ford of the River Severn where princes of Wales have traditionally met kings of England. It was there young Llewellyn had to bend the knee to Henry more than ten years ago. A sort of bloody submission.'

Falconer was minded to mention that, if this poetic view of history was the best Geoffrey could do, then the rest of his fanciful book was not to be trusted. He recalled another more down-to-earth chronicler, who had called the Welsh no more than Trojan debris swept into the wooded savagery of Cambria under the guidance of the devil. But he could see Aldwyn's blood was up already, and didn't want to provoke him further. The old man was intent on continuing his exposition.

'*"The Red One will grieve for what has happened, but after an immense effort it will regain its strength."* That's the rise of Llewellyn, do you see?'

Falconer was about to question this, but was stopped by Aldwyn holding up a cautionary finger. With Falconer thus silenced, he read on.

'*"Calamity will next pursue the White One, and the buildings in its little garden will be torn down."'* Before Falconer could query even this, Aldwyn interpreted for him. 'That is metaphorical, explained by the next line. *"Seven who hold the sceptre shall perish."'*

He looked at Falconer in triumph.

'You see? It's clear to what that refers. The "little garden" is a reference to Edward's line – the Plantagenets, named for the common broom his ancestor wore in his cap. Merlin's prophecy says seven of his brood will die, and already six have perished including young Henry, the one-time heir to the throne, just last year.'

Just like everyone else in England, Falconer knew of the succession of children given birth to by Queen Eleanor, two of whom were stillborn or died almost at birth, and four others dying in childhood. Of course it was not unusual for children to die in those perilous early years of life, but Edward and Eleanor did seem prodigiously unlucky. Was there something in Merlin's prophecy after all?

*

Saphira and Samson were transfixed by the thunderous knocking on his door. When you were a Jew in a Christian world that blamed you for all sorts of misdemeanours from drinking Christian babies' blood to the murder of their Messiah, you didn't open your front door without finding out first who was knocking. There had been plenty of times in Oxford in recent years when you would have found a mob outside. Indeed, it had not been long since Saphira's own front door had nearly been cleft in two with a hatchet. William had been with her then, and she wished he were around again now. It was all very well being an independent woman, running the family business of wine shipping, and keeping unruly and thieving sea captains under her thumb. But a man did come in useful when you were faced with physical force. A woman and an old man like Samson could be easily overwhelmed. Fortunately, this time William's strong arm was unnecessary. Samson cautiously slid back the panel in the upper part of his stout oak door, and peered out to see who was knocking so peremptorily. He breathed a sigh of relief, turning to tell Saphira who it was.

'It's Peter Bullock, and he's alone.'

The old man began to slide back the bolts that secured the door. As he bent down to open the lower bolt, Saphira could see the constable's face through the barred hatch. He looked pale and worried, and a pang of anxiety shot through her. She instinctively felt that something was seriously amiss for Peter to announce himself so noisily. The constable knew only too well that his loud hammering on the old man's door would create a mood of fear amongst the Jews. Seeing Saphira's look, Bullock spoke quietly through the hatch.

'Forgive me if I alarmed you, but there is an urgent problem, and I need Samson's help.'

Saphira pulled a face, and chided Peter nevertheless.

'What could be so important that you risk scaring half the neighbourhood to death?'

Samson pulled the door open far enough for Bullock to slip through. Then he closed it behind him, and made sure he threw the top bolt again before turning to his visitor.

'And what is so urgent that you risk falling dead at our feet in your haste.'

Saphira noticed for the first time what Samson had seen immediately. That the constable was breathing heavily, and that his face was as grey as a pewter tankard. It had taken the physician in Samson to notice the symptoms of someone who could the next moment fall sick of the half-dead disease, or even worse. Saphira silently cursed her own poor observation, and led Peter to a chair. Bullock was about to protest, asserting there was no time, but suddenly his legs felt like jelly, and he slumped down in it gratefully.

'Thank you. I will just take a moment to catch my breath. I have been tired lately ... can't sleep.'

Samson hurried off, his sidelocks swinging as he shook his head in annoyance at Bullock's stupidity. The constable would not admit he was not the man he had been when he had fought as a mercenary forty years ago. Appointed by the aldermen and merchants of Oxford to keep the peace, he still took on too much work associated with his role as constable. When Samson came back, he was carrying a glass bottle with a blood-red, cloudy potion in it.

'You should get some of your minions to do the fetching and carrying. And the running around. Now drink this.'

Bullock balked at the command, but Samson was insistent, and he tipped back the small bottle, swigging down the reddish-coloured contents. Saphira quietly asked Samson what the potion was.

'It is an essence of hawthorn berries. It relaxes the body and helps in situations where ...' He lowered his voice so that Bullock might not hear. '... where the heart is threatening to stop.'

Bullock pulled a face at the taste of the potion, but Saphira could see he was already beginning to breathe more normally.

'In future I might indeed get a man to be my runner, Samson. But in this case, the fewer people who know about the situation the better.'

Bullock pushed himself out of the chair and back on to his feet, his face once again stern.

'You must come with me now.'

'And why is that, Master Bullock? It is getting late, and I would prefer to retire to my bed soon. I know when an old man must rest, even if you don't. That potion will help you, but its effects are slow-acting. I would recommend ...'

Bullock grabbed Samson's arm to stop him, and Saphira could see the anxiety expressed in his look. She laid a hand on his shoulder.

'Tell us, Peter. What has happened?'

Bullock took a deep breath.

'There is a man in Dagville's Inn who is ill with some sort of pox. I am afraid it may be a plague of some sort. I would have got Will Spicer the apothecary to take a look, but I fear he would refuse. He does not have a stout heart when it comes to the pox. Besides, you have a far greater knowledge of such ailments.'

Samson knew what Bullock said was true. He would not entrust any sick person to the care of Spicer the apothecary if he could help it. He equally knew he would need help, if he were to care for this man over a long period of time. He looked at Saphira hesitantly, not sure whether he had the right to ask it of her. She saved him the pain of asking by nodding.

'I will help you. It will be a good way of learning about diagnosis and treatment.'

Bullock was not happy at this turn of events. He recalled the phlegm that had landed on his sleeve, and rubbed at the spot nervously.

'No, Mistress Le Veske, you cannot come. The very air of the room is dangerous to breathe.'

Samson, who was already gathering some instruments and vials and thrusting them into a pouch, snorted in derision.

'So you are now a physician as well as a constable, Peter Bullock.'

The constable face turned red, and he began to wave his arms.

'No. But that room is no place for a woman just now. Besides, Falconer will never forgive me if ...'

Samson took Bullock's wind-milling arm.

'Stop, stop, or I will have to give you another dose of hawthorn berries. Mistress Le Veske and I will protect ourselves. Depending on the cause of this man's illness, I believe the danger is going to be from contact with the bodily fluids of the patient. We will be rigorous in avoiding them. But ...'

He stopped Bullock's new protest with a raised palm.

'But, we will also wear a cloth across our mouths and noses, if that will please you.'

'And a nosegay of sweet flowers and herbs. I have heard that that will protect you from the plague.'

Samson nodded patronisingly at the constable as if to a child.

'And a nosegay too, though we have not yet decided if it is the plague. And may the Name protect us, if it is.'

Samson came as close to naming God as a Jew may, and Saphira had a sense of the perils they were about to encounter. She shivered but, determined to assist him, she picked up Samson's pouch, which clinked with the bottles he had placed within. Grimfaced, the three of them went out on to Fish Street. Though it was late, there were still people walking around, blissfully unaware of the horror that was about to engulf them.

*

The next part of Merlin's prophecy made Falconer's blood run cold.

'Say that again, Brother Aldwyn.'

The old monk looked solemnly at Falconer, knowing what the line he had just spoken implied.

'It will have nothing to do with your birthing, as that took place so long ago.'

Falconer pulled a face.

'Not all that much in the past, Aldwyn. I am only in my fifties. But read the line again.'

Aldwyn sighed, and shifted his gaze from the regent master to the writing on the page.

'"The bellies of mothers shall be cut open, and babies will be born prematurely." They do say the queen is pregnant again, and so this may refer to her next child.'

Falconer shook his head.

'It says "bellies" and "babies" in the plural. The cutting was unusual in my mother's day. You said so yourself. But this is a time when this operation has become more commonplace, is it not?'

Falconer couldn't believe what he was saying. He, the great sceptic,

41

was himself finding facts to fit Merlin's prophecy. What was he thinking? Saphira and Peter Bullock would not believe their ears, if he told them what he was contemplating. And all because he had been persuaded to learn about his own past. He had spent fifty years neither caring about his ancestry, nor believing that his unknown parents could have any effect on the way his life developed. Yet now, on having been given the smallest clue about how he came into the world, he was imagining that some mythical being living in the mists of time, could predict the future. He laughed out loud at his own gullibility.

Aldwyn frowned, and closed his precious text, seeing he had lost Falconer's attention. He made to rise from his chair.

'I must go. It is getting late, and I have to get back to Oseney before dark.'

Falconer, regretting his rudeness, placed his hand on Aldwyn's knee.

'No, stay a while longer and have some food with me. The evenings somehow get longer when you are on your own, so I could do with some company.'

That was the truth, because he had recalled that Saphira, with whom he might have otherwise spent the evening, was now engrossed in her studies of potions and poisons with old Samson in Jewry. He all too often neglected his duties attending to the needs of the students who lodged in Aristotle's Hall, preferring the womanly charms of Saphira Le Veske instead. Their relationship was an unusual one, being both across religions, and also flouting Falconer's supposed celibacy as a regent master in holy orders. Their time together was snatched at moments when Falconer chose to ignore his duties and when Saphira's maid, Rebekkah, had returned to her family for the night.

Tonight though, Falconer would attend to his proper duties, and be a true host to the old monk, who had given him some confirmation of the first splinter of information about his parentage. He knew Saphira would be safe behind the heavy oak door of Samson's house, even if a riot broke out in Oxford that very night. Reassured, he called for one of his students to bring Aldwyn something to eat.

Chapter Six

Inside Dagville's Inn it was eerily quiet, with the everyday noise from the street muffled by the closed door of the inn. That of itself made Bullock feel a cold shiver run up his spine, although he already knew what lurked behind the door. Every inn in the town would normally have its doors thrown wide open to welcome new customers. For this one to be firmly closed gave a clear sign of something seriously amiss. Saphira and Samson must have had the same feeling as he did, for they stood uncertainly in the open courtyard beyond the street door. With no soul to greet them, Saphira and Samson were not sure which way to turn. So they looked to Bullock for guidance.

'This way.'

He led them across the hard, beaten clay of the yard and through another door on the opposite side. Beyond, stood a staircase, which creaked ominously as Thomas Dagville descended towards them. He frowned at the sight of the two people who accompanied Peter Bullock.

'What's this? What use to us are a woman and an old Jew? Where is the apothecary?'

The only answer from Samson was a faint frown and a lowering of his eyes to the ground. He would have turned to leave had not Saphira grasped his sleeve. Her flame-red hair, unruly strands of which escaped from her snood, should have been a warning to Dagville of her temperament. He ought to see that she would stand no nonsense from such a bigot as the innkeeper. But Dagville's mind was closed. She stepped close up to him, hissing a warning in his face.

'If you want to save the life of your customer, and with it the reputation of this excuse for an inn, then you will stand aside and let this expert physician ...' She gestured at Samson. '... get on with his work.'

Dagville was about to bring a retort to his tight-stretched lips, when a woman spoke up from behind him.

'Thomas, don't look any more foolish than you normally do. Let the Jew pass. It was he who saved my life when our little Robbie refused to come out into the world. He was here to help when you were too drunk to even notice what was going wrong.'

Grace Dagville stepped out of the shadows, and took Samson's arm, ignoring the expression of pent-up fury on her husband's face.

'Hello Master Samson. Come this way, and I will show you the patient.'

She led Samson up the stairs, and Saphira and Bullock followed, grinning at the tavern-keeper's discomfiture. Dagville for his part

43

kicked at the doorpost, and stormed across the yard to take out his anger on the young lad who looked after the stables.

The upper floor of the inn was even quieter than down in the yard. It was evident that nobody else was left in the rooms rented by travellers for their overnight stay. Grace saw the look on her visitors' faces and explained.

'There's no-one else here to worry about. It is indeed fortunate that the knight was our only customer yesterday. He ate downstairs of course, but must have been feeling ill already. He kept to his corner, and was not bothered or intruded upon except by me. Since then he has been in his bed through there.'

She indicated a half-open door at an angle to the small landing at the top of the stairs. Darkness was falling outside, but the gloomy section of the room that could be seen appeared darker still. The air looked thick with vapours like an anteroom to Hell. Everyone present could feel this oppressive atmosphere leaking out from behind the door, and even Samson hesitated to enter. Saphira fumbled in the shoulder bag she was carrying, and produced two linen strips. She gave one to the old man, and began to wind the other round her nose and mouth. Samson just stood holding the cloth in his hand.

'You know, my dear, I think I am too old to be worrying about all this. Besides, the poor man may be afraid if two masked robbers burst into his room.'

Grace Dagville, who was instinctively now holding a hand to her mouth, mumbled some fear-filled words to Bullock. The constable patted her shoulder, and guided her to the top of the stairs.

'You go downstairs, Grace, and calm Thomas down.'

Relieved to be excused, Grace thanked Bullock with a look, and scurried down the stairs. After she had gone, the constable turned back to Saphira, who by now had enveloped her lower face in the linen cloth. But he could still see from her eyes that she was wondering what Grace had said.

'She said the poor man is too far gone to be aware of anyone in his room, masked or not. So ...' He held out his hand to Samson. '... if you are not wearing that cloth, I am not too embarrassed to use it. I may be old too, but I don't want to catch what he has got.'

Samson shrugged, and handed over the linen strip.

'You don't need to come in the room though, Peter.'

Bullock began binding the cloth around his face, but still his voice rang out harshly.

'I am the representative of law and order in Oxford, and I think I do need to be there. So let's get on with it.'

Saphira had never heard the constable be so abrupt, and guessed it had to do with the grave nature of the situation. They were all on edge, if not a little fearful, and the sooner they faced their fears the better. Samson recognised this too, and stepped resolutely round the half-open door. When his old eyes had adjusted to the dim light, he saw on the bed the figure of a half-naked man wrapped in a tangle of bedding. The fever was high and the crusader had been writhing around as he tried to toss off the linen from his burning body. Samson grimaced at the sight, and there were gasps from both Saphira and

44

Bullock. The muffled voice of the constable spoke in Samson's ear.

'He's covered in spots. When I saw him not so long ago, he had no more than a rash on his face.'

Samson's only reply was a low groan. He knelt down beside the bed to examine his patient more closely. By now, even he was shocked, and he held a hand over his nose and mouth. After a moment he beckoned to Saphira.

'Look, Mistress Le Veske, but do not come too close. See how the lesions are flat not raised.'

He stroked the knight's mottled skin, causing Bullock to gasp in horror.

'It is alright, constable, there is no danger to be had from touching his skin. All the same it would be wise for you to stay back.'

Bullock wasn't too sure about the lack of danger, and when Saphira stepped forward to touch the lesions too, he growled out a warning. Saphira looked over her shoulder at him.

'Don't worry, Peter. I will be careful.'

As she touched the spots, Samson continued his lecture, apparently oblivious to the peril facing him.

'See how the spots are flat and buried in the skin. How do they feel to you?'

Saphira continued stroking the man's feverish skin.

'They are soft and ...' She sought the right word. '... velvety to the touch.'

Samson sighed.

'Yes, just so. It is as I feared.'

With the aid of Saphira's arm, he rose to his feet, his old bones creaking at the abuse. The old Jew shook his head and stared Bullock in the eyes.

'It is the red plague, as you might have guessed. Some call it the small pox.'

Bullock pulled a face that was not seen behind his linen mask.

'That's bad. How many will die who catch it? One in three?'

Samson looked at the floor, and paused before replying. When he looked up again, there were tears in his eyes.

'That would be a correct estimate, if it were the ordinary type of pox. But this is the malignant form of the red plague.'

'And?'

'It is nearly always fatal.'

Bullock stared at the figure on the bed, knowing that some hard decisions were coming his way. Covered as the body was with red spots, he was suddenly struck by the idea that the man looked as though he had been standing in a rain of blood.

*

He gasped on seeing the tomes that filled the chest before him. Earlier, he had once again prostrated himself before the altar, letting the chill of the stone slabs strike through his thin robe. He had felt it cool the fever that burned within his body, but it did not affect the heat in his brain. He was afire with righteous anger, and God's words still rang in his ear. It was the name of Regent Master John Bukwode that he had been told, and it moved him. He had risen to his feet, his brain dizzy with exultation, and plunged out into the night. The streets were dark after curfew, and the only people he had seen were some drunken students skulking back to their hall under cover of night. On an impulse, he had followed them at a distance, and it came as no surprise to him that they led him to where he was intent on going. Corner Hall at the end of Shidyerd Street was ruled over by Bukwode, and that was where the students were returning. He took it as a sign of the righteousness of his actions that they had led him straight there. Trailing in the wake of the roistering boys, he hailed the last one through the front door of the hall.

'Leave it open for me.'

The boy was too drunk to question who it was who was following him, taking him for a laggard amongst his band of fellow revellers. The door was thus left ajar, and he had entered Corner Hall with ease. Now he knelt in front of the book chest where Bukwode's treasures were stored. One by one he lifted them out, shocked by their perversity. He mouthed their names like awful spells.

'*The Prophecies of Merlin*, the *Polychronicon*.'

These he lay to one side, and delved further in the chest shocked at finding books of magic. These too he named in horrified undertones.

'*De pentagono Salomonis, Vinculum Salomonis, Sapientiae nigromanciae.*'

The three books he removed were also laid aside with the first two tomes. He would be pleased to purge them from the collection. He began to delve for more abominations, but heard a noise from somewhere. The creaking of floorboards or perhaps a door told him he should be satisfied with his haul and leave. So content with enough books to cope with in one night, he gathered the five works up, and slunk back towards the street.

The reason that Regent Master John Bukwode's students had been revelling in the lowest of taverns was that he himself had been in one of the whore-houses in Grope Lane. Unfortunately, he had not had enough coin to engage the services of one of Sal Dockerel's sluts any later than the tolling of the curfew bell. It was doubly unfortunate for Bukwode that, once he had been forced to leave the warm embraces of Peggy Jardine, he had come back to Corner Hall just as the book thief was leaving. They encountered each other on the threshold. Bukwode was the first to react, and he hissed a warning to the intruder.

'Who are you? And what are you doing with those books?'

He made to snatch the collection of heavy tomes from the thief, who reacted instinctively. He was holding one book in his right hand, with the others balanced precariously in the crook of his left arm. He lifted up the book in his hand, and brought the edge of it down on Bukwode's skull. *The Prophecies of Merlin* had been well-bound with brass at the corners for protection. This sturdy chunk of metal stove in the regent master's skull, and he fell to the floor as if poleaxed.

*

Peter Bullock left Dagville's Inn resolved on carrying out an essential but contentious task. If he did as he thought he must, he would face censure, disapproval, and outright rebellion. But he knew he would have to hold fast. He stood at Carfax, the crossroads of the town, where the north-south and east-west thoroughfares intersected. It was dark, and he slowly turned a full circle, taking in the whole of Oxford. Strangely, no sounds disturbed the peace of the town. Even the noise of riotous students, so common to his ears usually, failed to breach the silence. It was as though every person in the town had had an awful presentiment of impending doom, and had retreated inside, barring their doors against the unknown horror. The town constable stood still for a moment savouring the silence. Soon there would be clamour aplenty to deal with. He struck out for North Gate first as it was the closest to where he stood. And the man on the gate was Thomas Burewald, his most calm and reliable right arm. But even he paled when Bullock announced his intentions.

'Lock up the town?'

Bullock nodded grimly.

'Let no soul in or out?'

'Exactly.'

Burewald shook his head.

'For how long? A day? Two days?'

Samson had told the constable that the pox festered for twelve days before it showed itself. If Sir Hugo de Wolfson had wandered around Oxford since his arrival, then anyone who had caught the disease from him would not know for that length of time. He paused before breaking the bad news to Burewald, then took a deep breath.

'Two weeks. We cannot allow the pox to spread any further. God knows, some who have caught it may have left the town already. There is nothing we can do about that. What we can do is prevent it going any further.'

Burewald felt as if he had been punched in the stomach and all the wind knocked out of him.

'Two weeks! There will be riots. Recall what happened ten years ago when just Smith Gate was locked.'

Bullock knew exactly what his watchman was referring to. In 1264 in the confusion over his and William Falconer's search for a murderer, he had been persuaded to lock the small gate that gave students access to fields outside the town walls. It had caused a riot, the consequences of which were only offset by the pleasure of a murderer being caught. Burewald pressed home the point still more.

'Now you are saying we should lock all the town gates for two weeks. It's impossible.'

But Bullock was adamant.

'Not if we explain our purpose.'

He clutched Burewald's arm, squeezing it hard.

'Do this for me, Thomas. I need your support, and all will be well. Inge and all the others will fall in line, if you are with me.'

Burewald grimaced, but eventually nodded. Bullock thanked him, and went on his rounds to pass the news to all those who guarded the other gates of the town. Tomorrow, Oxford would be a town sealed off from the outside world.

47

Chapter Seven

Though he had eaten well and it was now quite late, Brother Aldwyn insisted that he should return to Oseney Abbey forthwith. Falconer found he could not persuade him otherwise.

'What I insist on doing then, Aldwyn, is accompanying you to the South Gate. Oxford evenings can be quite rowdy, I'm afraid.'

The elderly monk, who was actually fearful of a chance encounter on the streets of the university town with drunken youths, expressed his gratitude. Old bones, once broken, took a long time to mend, and he would rather avoid any confrontation.

'Thank you, Master Falconer. I will not refuse your kind offer.'

Aldwyn clutched his precious volume of Merlin's prophecies to his chest as they emerged from Aristotle's Hall. But in the end, their walk through the back lanes of the town, past St Frideswide's Priory, coming out opposite St Aldate's Church, was uneventful. To Falconer's ears, the town was unusually silent, but he wasn't going to complain about that. He was glad that, for once, peace reigned in the turbulent town. However, his comfortable feeling did not last long. As the two men approached the southern gate of the town, they could see the main gates were closed. Even so, there was nothing unusual in that, as men on horseback or driving carts were forbidden to enter or leave so late. The small wicket gate set to one side could be opened to let travellers on foot through. But suddenly a nervous figure stepped out of the darkness, calling out to them.

'Stop there, and return home. You cannot leave by this gate tonight.'

Falconer recognised the voice of Will Sekyll, a dull and somewhat dim-witted young fellow, whom Peter Bullock had employed as night-watchman the previous year. It had been a kindness to his family, who couldn't find him any other work. Falconer smiled and took another step forward.

'Will, it's me, Master Falconer. Don't you recognise me? I have Brother Aldwyn with me from Oseney Abbey. He is anxious to return there tonight, so be a good fellow and open the side gate.'

The youth frowned, clearly perplexed by this conundrum. Constable Bullock had told him expressly that no-one was to enter or leave by the South Gate only a short time ago. Now Master Falconer, whom he knew was a close friend of Peter Bullock's, was telling him otherwise. In the end, his fear of Bullock's anger was greater than Falconer's, whom he knew as an amiable man, who would understand his orders. He pulled a face, but stood his ground.

'I'm sorry, Master Falconer, but I have my orders. The constable said I'm not to let anyone through this gate tonight. Not until I am told otherwise.'

It was Falconer's turn to be puzzled. This was a most unusual situation, and he assumed that Will Sekyll had got his orders wrong. However, from the set of the young man's face, Falconer knew it was pointless arguing. He turned to Aldwyn, and shrugged his shoulders.

'It would seem that you can't use this gate. I have no doubt that young Sekyll has his orders mixed up, but there is no use in disputing it with him. Let us go to the castle, and find Peter Bullock. If nothing else, he will be able to let you out the postern gate.'

Though most people used the four main gates to get in and out of Oxford, there were two more means of passing through the fortified walls. One was within the confines of the Franciscan friary that straddled the walls just below the castle. And the other was close by the castle itself, where there was a small postern gate in the walls that debouched on to the marshy ground leading to Oseney Abbey. This latter was the one that Falconer proposed that Aldwyn should use. Once he had made Peter Bullock aware of the problem with Will's misunderstanding at South Gate.

Oxford was a town of churches with thirteen within its walls alone. So the two men's route to the castle could be navigated by some of those churches. Passing St Michael's at South Gate, they walked up the quiet thoroughfare of Fish Street to St Aldate's, where they turned left. Passing St Ebbe's, they hurried on in the near dark along Freren Street to end up crossing the castle moat. Having entered the castle gate, they passed into the vast courtyard dominated by the old keep. St George's Church stood to one side of the open space, and half-hidden by it was St George's Hall, the quarters of the constable of Oxford.

The door to the hall stood half open, and Falconer could hear raised voices coming from inside. One of them was that of Peter Bullock, and he sounded very weary.

'It is impossible, Master Sparrow. You cannot leave and there's an end of it.'

The other voice was redolent of good wine, and a well-filled belly, its tones being rich and meaty.

'I find I must remind you, Bullock, that as an alderman of this town, it is I who appointed you in the first place. I can as easily rescind your appointment, and put someone more sensible in your place.'

'That's as may be, *alderman*.' Bullock placed a mock obsequious stress on Sparrow's title. 'But until such time as I am replaced, what I say goes, and I say no-one enters or leaves this town for two weeks.'

Falconer heard Aldwyn gasp at this confirmation of Will Sekyll's statement, knowing the monk must be as shaken as Falconer himself was. What was going on that required the whole town to be so sequestered? And for two weeks at that. Falconer marched towards the open door, only to be barged aside by a fat and very red faced man. Alderman Sparrow strode off across the courtyard, muttering dire threats about the intransigent constable. Falconer and Aldwyn stepped cautiously through the doorway, half expecting more angry people to fall upon them. Inside, a bright fire in the centre of the old hall lit the outline of a droop-shouldered Bullock. His back was to his new visitors, but even this aspect of the constable told a story of heavy burdens bearing down on the man. Falconer tried to put some joviality into the question burning on his lips.

'Whatever has happened, Master Bullock, that requires such dire action?'

Falconer was shocked by Bullock's savage response. The constable half turned, already cursing him.

'Don't you dare question my decision, William Falconer.'

Falconer raised his hands in submission, and Bullock's face suddenly fell, embarrassed by his outburst. He scratched his balding head, and sighed.

'Forgive me, old friend. But tonight is not the night for levity.'

At Falconer's side, Aldwyn coughed anxiously, nudging the master with the edge of his tome. He clearly wanted the situation resolved and his return to Oseney Abbey expedited. Falconer gave him a warning glance, and walked over to the troubled Bullock.

'We have only just heard from Will Sekyll at South Gate. So you can imagine that we thought he had his orders all wrong. What else would anyone think when told the gates are to be closed for two weeks.'

Bullock grimaced.

'At least two weeks.' He looked past Falconer at his companion. He could tell from his robes that the monk came from Oseney Abbey.

'So I am sorry, brother, but you are trapped here as we all are for a while.'

As he said these words, Bullock made a gesture with his hand taking in another person, who had been lurking in the shadows beyond the glow of the fire. A swarthy man stepped forward and bowed rather awkwardly, a hank of long black hair falling over his shoulder as he did so.

'This is Isaac Doukas. He is secretary to Robert Burnell, who was here on business in Oxford. His master was fortunate to have left earlier, his business done with Chancellor de Bosco. Unfortunately, Isaac remained to complete some notes, and was caught in my trap.'

A man less like a secretary Falconer could not imagine. Doukas was dark-skinned, stocky, and well-muscled, his bare arms betraying someone who habitually wielded a sword rather than a pen. But then Falconer had to remind himself he had been a mercenary soldier in his younger days, and was now a regent master of the university. Perhaps this Greek had made the same transition. He returned the man's bow, and then picked up on something Bullock had said earlier.

'Two weeks, you say?'

Bullock pulled a face, and nodded. Aldwyn, having been a monk who had worked at Bartlemas hospital was beginning to understand. The definitive period of time alluded to by the constable could only have one meaning.

'Two weeks? Is there some infection in the town?'

'Yes. I fear it is the red plague, or small pox, as some call it.'

'Are you certain? It could easily be something else far less dangerous.'

The shaking of Bullock's head made Aldwyn shudder.

50

'I am afraid it is confirmed by the Jew, Samson. He is knowledgeable in such matters, and says it is the malignant form of the plague. Inevitably fatal in most of those who catch it, he says. The man who has it is at Dagville's Inn. They are caring for the poor fellow now, but his fate is sealed, I fear.'

Falconer's heart pounded in his breast at the implications of Bullock's incautious words.

'*They*, did you say, Peter? Saphira was supposed to be with Samson this evening learning about medicines. Don't tell me she is with him at the bedside of this man?'

Bullock looked sheepishly at the floor.

'I am afraid she is, William. She ...'

He could hardly get the words out his mouth before Falconer gave him a hard look and spun on his heels. His reproof was thrown over his shoulder as he ran out of the hall.

'Damn it, Peter, could you not have stopped her? She is risking her life.'

Bullock called after him in exasperation born of his sense of guilt.

'I tried to stop her, but you know what she is like. She's more stubborn than you.'

But Falconer wasn't listening, he had already gone. The constable slumped in his chair, speaking to himself now his friend was out of earshot.

'You can't ever stop her doing just as she wishes. What chance had I?'

*

John Peper was regretting bringing the small band of jongleurs back to Oxford. In better days, they had travelled around in their own wagon, which also served as a place to sleep. But recently the troupe had fallen on hard times and were reduced to pushing the tools of their trade around in a handcart. In the countryside they could always find a barn to lay their heads in. But in a town like Oxford, patrolled by watchmen at night, they couldn't even find a corner to rest that didn't involve paying for it. Last night, Peper had dug into the shrinking contents of the communal purse to pay for a room at the Golden Ball Inn. It had been just about big enough for the four of them. Their purse would need to be replenished before they tried to find accommodation again.

So earlier today, they had entered a nameless tavern in Grope Lane, and Peper had begun his patter.

'Friends, I come to bring you pleasure.'

In truth, he was not as good as their old barker, but that man was dead and gone. John did his best, and though his voice was loud, it didn't seem to penetrate the buzz of conversation in the tavern. Undeterred, he had pressed on.

'I am Master John Peper, and I bring you jongleurs who have performed before kings, and at a private audience with the Pope. Tonight, however, we perform not for the idle nobility, but for you.'

At last, a few curious looks were cast his way by drinkers who were not yet so far in their cups as to be oblivious to him. Before their attention could drift away, he lifted the black cloak he was wearing with one outstretched arm.

'I bring you the sinuous Margaretha.'

He waved his arm to reveal his wife in a thin brown shift and tight hose. Margaret bent over backwards at her waist until her hands were on the ground behind her feet. The crowd gasped at the seemingly impossible feat, as she held her stance for a moment, then flipped over backwards twice, landing on her feet just in front of a red-faced silversmith who dropped his tankard of ale in the rush-strewn floor in surprise. The crowd shouted their approval, though John imagined it was more to do with the exposing of Margaret's limbs, still trim after all the years she had been a saltatore, than with any amazement at her dexterity. Next, Simon Godrich essayed a ballad, but the moment had been lost when Margaret had finished her routine. They had all beaten a hasty retreat when the cat-calling had begun.

Now, John turned to his wife and asked how much they had collected at the tavern they had performed in. She pulled a face, and tipped a few small coins on to palm.

'Not enough to even cover the cost of our room here for another night.'

She waved her hand in the air, taking in the low-ceilinged cramped quarters that huddled under the very roof of the inn. It was the cheapest room they could find at short notice. Robert Kemp the juggler cursed their fifth, missing member roundly.

'Where the hell is Will? He was to go ahead to drum up trade, and make sure we had somewhere to stay between Wallingford and here.'

Peper sighed. He had been wondering where Will Plome had been for the last week. As Kemp had stated, he was supposed to have gone from village to village announcing the arrival of the small band of jongleurs. But wherever they had stopped, they couldn't find anyone who had seen him.

'Damned silly boy. I knew he was too stupid to trust with such a task. And after he had learned his letters from that priest too.'

Will Plome was actually more than a boy. At twenty-six, he should have been considered a man, but was so slow-witted and so innocent of visage that most people still treated him as a boy. In Wallingford, where they had over-wintered the previous year, he had fallen in with a priest, who taught him his catechism for the first time. Then Will had been so eager to learn to read, that the priest had agreed to try and teach him. To the surprise of everyone in the troupe, he had picked up reading well enough to decipher some of the play texts that John Peper kept carefully stowed away in their cart. But trusting him with travelling ahead of the troupe had proved disastrous, and now Peper had taken a decision.

'We will leave Oxford tomorrow early, and try our luck towards Woodstock. They do say the king is there at the moment.'

Kemp and Godrich grunted their agreement, and settled in the far corner of the room, leaving what privacy they could to the Pepers. None of them knew their plans would fall apart the following morning.

Chapter Eight

The streets of Oxford were deserted with not a glimmer of candlelight coming from any of the houses Falconer ran past. As he reached Fish Street, he could smell the stink of the open drain that ran the length of it. He had never noticed it before, not during the day, when all the bustle and noise seemed to drown out the odours. Now, the stench of human ordure seemed to reflect the dark underside of the town, and the vile infection that must already be running through its alleys.

He shivered at the thought of it taking Saphira away from him. It cost him so much to have the life they did have together. Canon law sought to discourage any sort of intimacy between Jews and Christians, including dining or bathing in the company of Jews, consulting Jewish physicians, or taking medicine compounded by a Jew. Though these laws were commonly ignored – Grace Dagville had had good reason to be grateful for the services of Samson when her child refused to come forth into the world – there was a peculiar loathing of deeper intimacies. And secular laws had sanctions for anyone violating the ban, ranging from fines and confiscation of property to castration and death by burning. Falconer's life with Saphira was therefore secret for good, practical reasons even leaving aside his supposed celibacy. The effort of hiding this intimacy, was all the more reason for him not to lose her to the plague.

He hurried along the High Street and towards Dagville's Inn. Ominously, the door was closed, and when he pushed against it, he realised it was bolted also. He beat with his fist on the weathered surface, in his anxiety skinning his knuckles on the studs that reinforced the door. He sucked the blood off his damaged hand and, hearing no sound from behind the obdurate door, beat again with the flat of his palm. Suddenly, the door opened, but only a crack, allowing Thomas Dagville to press his face to the opening.

'We are closed. It's the middle of the night. Besides, we've had a family bereavement.'

He went to close the door again, but Falconer grabbed the edge of it with his bleeding fist.

'I know what is afoot here, Dagville. And if you don't allow me in, I shall let all your neighbours know of the infection that lurks here.'

Dagville's face turned ashen, and he grabbed Falconer's arm, dragging him inside the inn. He slammed the door and threw the bolt again. Leaning back against it for support, he stared at Falconer wide-eyed.

'What do you want with us?'

'I want to speak to the lady who is in attendance on the man who is infected. Is she still with him?'

Dagville nodded his head.

'Yes. And the Jew is there too. They both must be crazy.'

'Take me to them.'

Dagville sighed, and crossed the courtyard of his now deserted inn. He took Falconer through a door, and stood at the bottom of the stairway beyond. He pointed up it.

'They're at the top. The room on the left. But if you take my advice, you won't go up there. The air is bad. I don't know how I'm going to make it clean ever again.'

Falconer ignored the disconsolate inn-keeper and his problems, and hurried up the stairs. They creaked ominously under his feet, the sound seeming even louder in the stillness. At the top of the stairs, he saw the flicker of a candle beyond the half-open door before him. A shadow moved across the opening, and a strange apparition appeared in the crack. The figure's head and lower face was covered with white linen, leaving only a pair of eyes peering out from the wrappings. They were green, and Falconer recognised them immediately. He stepped through the doorway, and hissed out indignantly.

'Saphira. What in God's name do you think you are doing?'

Saphira looked his way, then stepped up to him, and pushed Falconer through the doorway back on to the landing. Pulling the linen mask from her mouth, she hissed back at him.

'Making a dying man comfortable. What would you have me do?'

'Bullock says he has the red plague. And that he can pass it on to anyone close to him.'

She could see the terror in William's eyes, and knew it was not because he feared for his own life. She forced down the tempest that had brewed up inside her at his unmannerly reaction. Taking a deep breath, she calmly explained Samson's observations on how the plague might only be spread by phlegm and other bodily fluids.

'And so, what I am doing is perfectly safe. The clothes I am wearing must be washed, or even burned when I return home. But the loss of a dress is a small price to pay, if I am to learn what can be done to prevent this pox.'

Falconer pointed at the cloth in Saphira's hand that had formerly covered her face.

'Then what is that for, if the very air you are breathing is not infected?'

She blushed, and looked away momentarily.

'I admit I was not entirely convinced by Samson's assertions. Even he may be wrong. But tell me, what has Peter Bullock done about the problem?'

Falconer pulled a face.

'He has ordered the town gates locked. None can enter or leave until this is over.'

'Thanks be for that.'

It was the voice of Samson from behind Saphira that called down praise for the constable's actions. Falconer went to shake the old

54

man's hand, but Samson held him back with a gesture of his upraised palms.

'You should not touch me, as I may pass on the noxious effluence by doing so. You should leave, and now you can take Saphira with you.'

She tried to protest, but Samson was adamant.

'You have done enough here. The man is dying, and I can see this through by myself now. Go home and cleanse your clothes and yourself. Use the mikveh in the tunnels.'

Samson was referring to the ritual bath down under the ground in Jewry. Several cellars of the houses along Fish Street had been linked as a refuge and escape route in times of trouble. Falconer knew of the tunnels because they had once saved Saphira's life when some violent men had broken into her home. She could access the tunnels by raising a slab in her kitchen floor. In the catacombs, the ritual bath was fed by an underground stream, and was reached through a low archway and down a flight of stone steps. It was deep enough for total immersion as required by the Jewish law, and Samson was recommending it for both ritual cleansing, and for the wholly practical purpose of washing away any evil taint from the dying man.

Saphira nodded her acquiescence, and followed Falconer down the stairs. Dagville let them out into the street, and they heard the bolt sliding back behind them. It completed the image in both their minds of the inn being a prison. Indeed, Oxford itself had now become a prison for every soul who dwelled there, who were all sentenced to a term the length of the red plague's life.

Numbed from lack of sleep, and the seriousness of the situation, Falconer and Saphira Le Veske trudged back to the house on Fish Street that she rented from a cousin. The journey was completed in silence, neither knowing what to say to the other. And because of Samson's warnings about Saphira's clothes, neither one of them touched the other. At her front door, Saphira raised her hand to stop William following her.

'The ritual requires nakedness, and separation of men from women. Go back to your students. They are going to need your guidance over the next few days.'

Falconer grimaced, and nodded his acknowledgement of Saphira's good advice. The young students under his care in Aristotle's Hall would no doubt react badly to being locked inside the town. In fact, once the circumstances were known, the whole town would be seething with anger and fear. They would all be incarcerated cheek by jowl with the small pox, not knowing where it might be lurking, and who might already be infected with it. Peter Bullock would have his work cut out keeping a lid on the bubbling stew that mixture would cause. He looked Saphira in the eyes.

'I know it is useless of me to ask you not to get close to another infected person again. Your skills and Samson's knowledge will save someone's life, I am sure, even if the man at Dagville's Inn is doomed. But please take care of yourself.'

Saphira smiled, and closed the door. Falconer put with his ear to the scarred timbers that still bore the mark of the axe that had nearly killed Saphira and himself during the recent riot. He could hear on the other side of the door the swish of Saphira's dress against the stone floor as she walked to the kitchen and the secret tunnels. He stood there long after the sound had disappeared, praying to a God he was not sure of for her safety. Finally, he turned away and walked through the silent town towards Aristotle's Hall.

*

Dawn, the Feast of St Adam, 15ᵗʰ September.

Peter Bullock had spent a restless night tossing and turning on his straw-filled pallet pulled close to the open fire in the great hall of St George's castle. He kept to the old ways of communal sleeping arrangements for servants. Though only he lived in Oxford castle, he did not feel like the lord of St George's. His master was the town in general, and so he still avoided sleeping in the solar that was by rights the private room of the master of the castle, especially as a fire always burned in the great hall. This past night, however, he wished he had usurped the position of lord of the castle. The problem had been his sharing of the open space of the great hall with his two guests. One – Isaac the Greek – had been acceptable despite his snoring. It was Brother Aldwyn who had prevented Bullock from sleeping well. The monk had kept to the offices that governed his daily life at Oseney Abbey.

In the middle of the night, just as Bullock had been dozing off, he had become aware of a murmuring from across the other side of the fire, now reduced to glowing embers. He prized open an eye, and in the reddish light observed Aldwyn on his knees praying. But even as he opened his mouth to protest, the monk completed his devotions and settled back down on his rough bed, soon joining his snores to Isaac's. Bullock, however, lay awake for some time, his mind racing with thoughts concerning the events of the day just ended. So he was not aware of falling asleep, but must have done, because the next thing he knew was that he was again being woken by a quiet voice. This time he could see more, as a pale dawn was illuminating the hall. Having previously disturbed Bullock with Matins, Aldwyn was now observing the liturgical office of Lauds. The constable groaned for he knew it would not be long before his sleep would be disrupted by Prime, the first office of the day proper, and then after that by Terce. Sleepless, he lay back until the monk did in fact begin the Prime liturgy, and then rose, his limbs creaking with the cold. He threw a log on the embers, and went to fetch some stale bread from from the bin, and a jug of weak ale.

When he returned, Aldwyn was seated close beside the revivified fire. He held open on his lap the book he had kept close to him all the night. He looked up at Bullock as he returned.

'Listen to this. *Then the Red Dragon will revert to its true habits and struggle to tear itself to pieces.* What can that signify but the events of last November, when Prince Llewellyn's own brother, Daffyd, conspired against him along with the Lord of Powys? The prince prevailed – thank the Lord – and the conspirators fled to England. But it weakened the Red Dragon of Wales even further.'

56

Bullock, unaware of Merlin's prophecies, wasn't sure what the old monk was maundering on about, and limited himself to a grunt. He passed his guest a piece of bread and poured him some ale into a goblet. Crossing the hall to his customary chair, he saw that the Greek was stirring, and went over to him with his meagre breakfast. Isaac sat up and thanked him. Aldwyn had not finished his diatribe, however, and his piping voice carried across the hall.

'And then listen to Merlin's next prophecy. *Next will come the thunderer, and every one of the farmer's fields will be a disappointment.*'

He stabbed his bony finger at the text on his lap.

'Do you see? That fixes the time of the unravelling of the prophecy precisely.'

Bullock sniffed disdainfully. He was disinclined to believe in vague prophecies that told of events that happened time and again.

'Crops have failed before. I recall in the year of the great comet ...'

'Ten years ago, as I recall.'

Bullock acknowledged the monk's erudition.

'Yes, the year before King Henry's fiftieth year on the throne. Crops were poor and some starved because of it. Why could not that have been the time referred to in the prophecy?'

'Yes, tell us, priest? And who is this Merlin you speak of.'

Isaac was now joining in the debate, as he flattened his greasy, black locks over his skull and dusted off the rushes that had stuck to his tunic in the night. Aldwyn stared at him, as if realising for the first time that someone else was present.

'Where are you from that you do not know of Merlin? You have the dark looks and build of a Welshman like myself. But you cannot be one, if you have not heard of King Arthur's great priest and helper.'

Isaac pulled back his shoulders, and adopted the wide-legged stance of a warrior.

'I am Isaac Doukas, descended from the kings of Pafos in Cyprus, servant to Robert Burnell, Chancellor of this kingdom.'

Aldwyn was clearly not impressed, and sniffed.

'A follower of the Byzantine heresy, then. That explains why you have not heard of Merlin. Nor can understand the prophecy so clearly laid before you.'

He turned to address Bullock directly, ignoring the Cypriot.

'The more important part of the prophecy concerns the *revenge of the thunderer*. On the Feast of St Protus there was an earthquake felt south of here, was there not? Do you not recall it?'

Bullock recalled it. How could he not? It had happened only a week ago, and though it had not been felt in Oxford, news had reached the town the next day. The constable was beginning to feel uneasy.

'What does the prophecy say next?'

Aldwyn stared him in the eyes, reciting from memory.

'*Death will lay hold of the people, and destroy all the nations.*'

*

Having lifted the flagstone in her kitchen floor, Saphira descended the stone steps to a world the Christians of Oxford were unaware of beneath their feet. At the bottom of the steps, the walls either side were built solidly of good ashlar, and arched over her head. It could have been a simple cellar, but this was more than that. For as she walked through this first arched room and on into another, she finally found herself in a low tunnel at a junction of arches. She held a small lamp in her hand to give her light. The air down here was cool, and she could hear the sound of water dripping further off. Right now she was underneath Fish Street. Many of the cellars on either side of the road in the houses owned by Jews were linked together. It was here that those of the faith had a mikveh – the ritual bath for cleansing after certain defilements such as a woman's monthly flow of blood. Saphira had once assumed the only one in Oxford was by the river near the Jewish cemetery. After all, dead bodies as well as living men and women needed ritual cleansing. But she had been wrong, and was finally let into the secret of the tunnels. She stepped through a low arch, and now stood at the top of a flight of stone steps that led down into a crystal-clear pool of water. Having shed her dress in the house above and thrown it into the fire to burn, she was dressed only in her shift. She pulled it over her head and stood naked at the top of the steps. She removed her snood and shook out her hair to ensure it too would be properly cleansed. Slowly she walked down the steps into the chill waters, sucking in her breath. At first cold, the waters seemed to envelope her like a balm, until she stood up to her shoulders in the cleansing pool. Shivering a little, she took a deep breath and ducked her head under the waters. Her red hair spread out above her like a bloody stain on the pool's surface.

Chapter Nine

John Peper crept down the stairs of the inn where they were staying just as dawn was breaking. As soon as he saw that the courtyard of the inn was clear of people, he hissed up the stairwell, and Margaret tripped lithely down, followed by the more rotund and uncertain Simon Goodrich. Halfway down, he trod on a loose step, and it gave a crack that could have woken the dead. He clutched his pipe and tabor to his chest and froze. John Peper scowled, and motioned Margaret back into the shadow of the stairwell. They held their breath for an age, but the sound had not aroused the unsuspecting innkeeper apparently. The troupe's escape without paying the bill was still possible. Simon managed to reach the bottom of the stairs without further mishap, and Robert Kemp quickly followed him, avoiding the traitorous step. Outside the inn, Agnes Cheke, who had gone ahead to muffle their cart's wheels with rags, was already waiting for them in the street. As the darkness of the night gave way to a grey morning, they hurried towards South Gate. The wheels of their cart made little noise due to Agnes's attentions, but they stopped close to Torold's Lane to remove the rags. Otherwise the gate keeper might guess why they were abroad so early, even though they had chosen this gate because of Will Sekyll. They knew him from previous sojourns in Oxford during their annual circuit of the country as a callow youth with not much brain.

As they approached the gate, John noticed it was not yet open, and assumed they were earlier than he had imagined. Robert Kemp, juggler and occasional fool, surreptitiously pulled a carved mask out of the cart. It was painted white with two dark holes for eyes and a row of bare teeth. He fixed it on his face and pulled his hood well forward obscuring his features. As Sekyll emerged from his little box beside the gate, Kemp hovered behind John Peper, who advanced on the gate-keeper. He gave him a jovial welcome.

'Good morning, Master Sekyll. I hope we are not to be kept waiting too long. We have an engagement in Abingdon this very day, and must be on our way.'

Before Will could say anything, Kemp raised his head and stared through the eye-slits of the skull mask at the gate-keeper. He uttered a low moan to add to the impression. Will Sekyll took one look at the spectre on Peper's shoulder, and fainted straight away. Peper, who had been unaware of his companion's performance, looked behind him and growled at the apparition.

'You fool, Robert. This was supposed to be a quiet escape from the town. Now the gate-keeper is swooned away at our feet, and a crowd is gathering.'

He was right about his last statement. Already, several townsfolk, who were clearly about their business early, were gathering round the strange scene. With a laugh, Kemp pulled the mask off and tossed it in the cart. Margaret knelt beside the prostrate Sekyll, and slapped his cheek.

'Will? Are you all right?'

Sekyll groaned, and as he came to, gazed fearfully around him.

'Where is the ... the ... skeleton?'

Margaret patted his arm comfortingly.

'It's nothing, Will, just Robert playing the fool. Now get up and open the gate. Look there's a gaggle of good citizens waiting on you.'

Will scrambled to his feet, still casting around for the apparition with a death mask. He already had an inkling why the constable had told him to bar the gate to anyone. Gossip flew fast, even in the night hours, and it was being said that plague stalked the streets of Oxford. So the appearance of a skeleton before his eyes only served to confirm what he feared. And it seemed that one or two of the people waiting anxiously for the gate to open had also heard something. Saul Shoesmith was a pot-man at Thomas Dagville's inn, and often drank the dregs from the jugs he collected. Some nights he was too drunk to drag himself back to the stews of Beaumont where he rented a room. So he slept off the effects of the bad ale Dagville served in the stable block. Last night had been a particularly bad night, and he had retired to the hayloft early. Dagville had assumed he had gone home to Beaumont, outside the town walls, and hadn't even come to seek him out in his usual lair. Shoesmith had therefore still been inside the inn when all the comings and goings had roused him. Though his head throbbed unmercifully, overhearing the merest whisper of the word *pox* from his master's lips as he spoke to his wife was enough. He had tied up his belt, and sneaked away. Realising North Gate was still barred and bolted, he had scurried down Fish Street, fearful that the pox was on his heels. He knew Sekyll as a dimwit, who always opened South Gate if a tale of woe was spun to him. Now these stupid jongleurs were holding him up.

Before even Shoesmith could urge Sekyll to do his duty and open the gate though, another figure entered the fray. Dressed in the fine robes of a merchant and atop a rouncey laden with saddle-bags, sat Alderman Robin Sparrow. Behind him, and with a look of fear on her face born of the hatred of being on horseback at all, Mistress Sparrow clutched at her palfrey's neck. The gawping crowd parted to allow the horses to the fore, and the alderman called out irritably to Sekyll.

'Open this gate, damn it, or you shall be a night-soil collector by tomorrow morning.'

Sekyll blushed, but ever fearful of Peter Bullock, stood his ground.

'You must speak to the constable, master. I have my orders, and they are not to open the gate or to allow anyone in or out until I am told otherwise.'

This statement from the gate-keeper's own lips caused a buzz of fevered conversation amongst those standing around South Gate. It was the first many of them had heard of the town being cut off from the outside world in this way, and the implications were worrying. Without even considering the reason behind it, some men, who had jobs to go to outside the walls, became annoyed. They now were wondering if the work they were going to would be there when the gate was finally opened. A pair of women put their heads together and exchanged opinions on whether there were enough food supplies in the town to last out more than a few days. After all, there were reckoned to be some two thousand souls in the town with all the students swelling its numbers as they did. John Peper and his troupe were merely left wondering how they would now avoid the inn-keeper they had swindled out of rent.

Saul Shoesmith could restrain himself no longer.

'You've got to open the gate. There's pox in the town, and I'll be damned if I'm going to catch it.'

There was a collective gasp from the assembled crowd, and all eyes turned to the finely-dressed Alderman Sparrow. Someone shouted from the back of the restless mob.

'Is this true, alderman?'

Sparrow's face flushed red, and at first he was inclined to deny the pot-man's statement. The entire town knew Shoesmith was a drunk, and that his word couldn't be trusted. But he wanted to escape as much as the next man, and reckoned that, if he confirmed what he knew to be true, Sekyll would be forced to open the gate.

'Yes it is. There is the red plague in Dagville's Inn.'

He turned in his saddle to address the gatekeeper.

'So you should open the gate, man, and save yourself as well as all these good citizens.'

Will Sekyll's face paled, and reluctantly he pulled the large key, fixed on a ring, from the hook on his belt.

'Stop right there, Will Sekyll.'

Peter Bullock's authoritative voice rang out over the murmur of the frightened mob. The constable gave thanks for the monk's mutterings that had awoken him early, and which had occasioned his early patrol through the town. He had decided to check on South Gate first, knowing that Sekyll was the weak link in the chain that held Oxford secure. He shouldered his way through to the front of the assembled townsfolk, seeing men and women who were his neighbours, and the fear that was in their eyes. He knew what he was asking of them, and hoped they would comply if reasoned with. He picked on a few whom he thought he could enlist on his side. He would need all the support he could get over the next few days.

'Walter Felde, John Doket, Andrew Bodin. Good morning to you.'

The men he had addressed nodded, and muttered a greeting. In their returning his gaze, he knew he could trust them to back him up. He stared at them unblinkingly as he explained the situation.

'What you have heard is true. The red plague, that some call the small pox, has visited the town. So far, there is only one case, though.'

A man's voice called out from the back of the crowd.

'It's the Jews, isn't it? They brought it here with their filthy ways. They mean to kill all us good Christians.'

Someone else took up the theme, eager to blame the traditional scapegoats.

'Yes, we should burn them out of their houses while we can.'

Bullock stood firm, his voice harsh and firm.

'Shut your mouth, Peter Glover. The man who is dying of the pox is a Christian knight returned from Outremer. It was he who brought it from over the seas himself. So let's hear nothing more of Jews from you.'

He could have said that it was the knowledge of the Jews, and Samson in particular, that would save lives over the next few days. But like everyone, he knew of canon law that forbade Christians, amongst other things, from taking medicines compounded by a Jew. So though Samson was already deeply involved and he was grateful for it, it was another matter to refer to him publicly. Besides, Glover was quite capable of suggesting that, if someone died despite the attentions of Samson, the fault lay with the Jew. Instead, relying on threat rather than reason, he eased his trusty old sword in its scabbard, and told the crowd to disperse.

'Go home, and stay indoors. You will all be safe, if you avoid contact with anyone who already has the plague. The crusader was only in the town for one day before he succumbed. With luck not another soul will have been infected by him, but only time will tell.'

Walter Felde frowned, thinking about how long he could survive without work.

'How long is that, constable?'

Bullock hesitated, not wanting to tell everyone what Samson had told him. If they all knew they had to wait out the disease's passage for two weeks, he could lose control of the situation right at the start.

'A few days will be enough to know the worst.'

Thankfully, no-one asked what happened if the worst did come about, and others fell ill. Muttering amongst themselves, the people began to disperse. Even Sparrow and his wife turned their mounts and plodded back to their home. The only people left at the gate were the small band of players, who huddled round their cart. Bullock breathed a sigh of relief, and patted Will Sekyll on the back.

'You did well, Will. Just stick to it and you will be fine.'

Sekyll had the good grace to lower his gaze to his scuffed boots, knowing he had almost broken. But the constable's praise left him with the resolve to do better next time. Bullock carried on his patrol, bearing the bad news to each of his gatekeepers and the town as a whole.

*

Robert Burnell, unaware as yet of his timely escape from the confines of Oxford, had returned to Woodstock and the king's presence. He would have informed Edward of what he had discovered in the university town, but the king was in a bad mood once again and not inclined to listen to tales of his chancellor's machinations.

'That bastard prince of Wales has been playing me for a fool again.'

Edward's normally serene and manly features were contorted with fury, his face red, and his actions agitated. Burnell pursed his lips and enquired what Llewellyn had been up to now.

'And how may I serve my Lord in this matter?'

'It seems that he thinks he can revive the Barons' War by marrying that de Montfort girl, after all.'

'Ah yes.'

On his return to Woodstock, Burnell had been swiftly apprised of the series of events concerning Eleanor de Montfort, daughter of the late Earl Simon, the man who had stood against Edward and his father ten years earlier. His daughter had set out in secret from France, where she had been living in exile, on board a ship stuffed with the arms and banner of the de Montfort family. The exercise had been so inept, however, that the king's agents had easily learned of it, and had stopped the ship on the high seas. Eleanor was now a prisoner, and Burnell reassured Edward that all was well.

'I have arranged for her to be safely locked away in Windsor, where she can stay as long as you wish, my Lord. Forever if need be. Though I do think that at some point, when you have suitably subdued Llewellyn, you can show your magnanimity and permit the two to be married.'

Edward frowned at his chancellor.

'Allow Llewellyn to marry a de Montfort, when that family's treason still smoulders in the hearts of some people in my kingdom?'

Burnell was unconcerned by Edward's apparent intransigence, and began to insinuate his ideas into the king's head.

'Once you have conquered Wales, both Llewellyn and his supposed bride will be spent forces. Your giving permission for them to marry will only grind your heel into the prince's face. A worthless bride for a worthless prince.'

Edward could see the benefit of such an act, and began to pace up and down the room.

'I have been thinking about the military campaign. It will be hard for our forces to defeat the Welsh on their own territory. They are so well known for sweeping out of the hills, hitting hard and disappearing again. My father suffered from such tactics, and dreamed of cutting off their supplies by taking Anglesey, that they call Môn, but drew back from doing so because he lacked the resources.'

Burnell smiled coldly, knowing that Edward had been led along the right path.

'The island is the bread-basket of Wales, as you so rightly identify. But you are also wise to see that we do have the men and the ships that your father did not. Now we are in a position to take it.'

Edward grinned rapaciously, convinced that he had known all along what Burnell had suggested. He knew now that his course of action was set. Wales, in the shape of Llewellyn, would soon be kneeling at his feet. For Burnell, any thoughts of Oxford, and the course of action he had set Roger Plumpton on, were driven from his mind.

*

The flapping of wings woke Falconer from a deep and exhausted

63

sleep. He looked up into the roof timbers over his head, and saw Balthazar settling on his perch like a pale ghost. This was the fourth or fifth reincarnation of the first barn owl that Falconer had tamed. He couldn't recall precisely, as all were named the same and behaved in quite the same way. Come the evening, Balthazar drifted out of the solar's window on silent wings to hunt across the marshes south and west of Oxford. With the arrival of the dawn, today as on every day, he returned. The only sign of his success or failure was the regurgitated pellet of small bones and fur that the owl later coughed up. He and his predecessors provided Falconer with a silent companionship, and a worldly-wise stare in response to the regent master's idle ponderings. Falconer now gazed up at the white apparition.

'Tell me, Balthazar, will I outlive you, as I have done several of your ancestors? Or will the red plague gather me in?'

The owl's round eyes stared down at Falconer, and his only response was a slow winking of his eyelids.

'Not telling, eh? I should have eaten you while you were still an egg. Well, as ever I am in God's hands.'

He rolled to the edge of his bed, and persuaded his aching knees to take his weight. At the door to his little private room in the eaves of the great hall that was Aristotle's stood the pitcher of water that one of his students drew for him every morning from the well in the rear courtyard. He splashed the cold water over his head, and donned the plain black robe that was his everyday wear. Sitting back down on the bed, he eased on his worn and comfortable leather boots, thinking that he must at least make a start on de Bosco's problem. The book thief's deeds paled in significance next to the threat of the red plague. But if the normal commerce of the university was to be interrupted by the disease and its consequences, then he would have time on his hands. And the chances were that the perpetrator was now locked inside the town along with his hunter.

Hearing movement down in the great hall, he made for the door. He would have to give his students the news about the pox, and ensure they did not leave Aristotle's while it stalked the streets of Oxford. He sighed at the thought of ensuring their enforced imprisonment, and of keeping them occupied. Even he would have to take care to avoid close human contact for a while, which may in turn hamper his investigation. Suddenly there was the thunderclap of a door being flung open, and the noise from downstairs got a whole lot louder. He heard his name being called.

'Master Falconer, a body's been found.'

Chapter Ten

The body lay just inside the threshold of Corner Hall, and when Falconer arrived, the young students were huddled round the fire almost as far from their former master as they could get. The boy who had fetched Falconer, stood at his shoulder staring at the congealed black blood that ran from Bukwode's head in straight lines along the cracks between the slabs of stone at the entrance. The youth had explained as he led Falconer along St John's Street that he had come to Aristotle's because he didn't know what else to do. And everyone knew Master Falconer's interest in dead bodies. The boy knew that a hue and cry should be initiated, and that as first finder, it was his duty to start the process. However, all the clerks who studied at Oxford University, knew of the tensions between the town and the university authorities. Lines were jealously drawn between the spheres of influence of the town and the gown, hence the students' uncertainty. The boy gazed anxiously at the body.

'Did I do the right thing, Master Falconer? I sent Jack to bring the constable too.'

Falconer patted his arm.

'I know he will be busy at the moment, so you did well to fetch me.'

He knelt down, careful to avoid the blood in its grid-like pattern across the floor slabs. Someone else had not been so careful. The blood was smeared in two places, suggesting a person had stepped in the blood and slid in their haste. A head wound always bled out terribly, and was often worse than it looked. However, in this instance it was clear Bukwode was dead, and had been so for some time. His skin was stone cold, and flies were beginning to settle on the blood and on the man's unseeing eyes. Falconer waved them away, and turned the head to examine the site of the wound that had caused so much mess. There was a jagged tear to the skin of his scalp on the left side, and beneath it the bone of the skull was cracked. Gritting his teeth, he poked at the wound, and behind him he heard one of the students gag, and rush outside to retch in the street. He could feel the pieces of broken bone giving way under the pressure of his finger. Bukwode's skull must have been quite thin at that point to have given way so easily. He wondered what the weapon could have been that had had such a devastating effect.

He was suddenly aware of a dark shape filling the doorway and obscuring the morning light. He called a warning.

'Be careful where you tread, Peter. His blood is everywhere.'

An unfamiliar guttural voice responded.

'It is Isaac Doukas, Master Falconer. The constable is busy just now.'

Falconer looked up and saw the stocky Greek, who was Robert Burnell's private secretary.

'I am surprised to see you here, Master Doukas. What has brought you from the comforts of the castle to observe a dead body?'

Isaac Doukas chuckled throatily.

'I could have said the same about you, sir, except your reputation for being present at the scene of murders extends beyond this small town.'

He peered more closely at the body, being careful to avoid the blood.

'It is a murder, I take it?'

Falconer pointed at the wound on the skull.

'There is no doubt about that, I fear.'

'And there's the mark of someone's foot in the blood. Was that you?'

Falconer looked into the man's dark brown eyes.

'Of course not. Nor could it have been the murderer who made it. Unless he chose to wait until his victim had first fallen and bled profusely, and then fled.'

Doukas squatted on his haunches, making the hard muscles of his legs even more prominent. Falconer guessed he hadn't always been some lily-livered clerk in Burnell's service. He watched carefully as Doukas stroked his black, bristly chin.

'Of course, if he was intent on stealing books and was disturbed by the regent master, he might have killed him and still carried out his task of taking what he wanted, walking in the blood as he left.'

His statement intrigued Falconer. How did this man know of de Bosco's little problem with the book thief? Was that his real reason for being here? Of course, his proposition could be true, and the thief could be the most cold-blooded of individuals with nerves of steel. Then as he re-examined the body, he saw close to Bukwode's feet, and half hidden by the folds of his robe, that a book lay on the floor. He pointed it out to Doukas.

'What you say would be possible, if it were not for that. I would estimate that the thief was already on his way out, when he encountered Master Bukwode.'

Gently he lifted the book up, and saw that there was hair stuck in the brass furniture on the corner. From a cursory glance, he thought it matched Bukwode's hair. Moreover, there were traces of blood on the brass and the tooled leather cover. He had found the weapon, and probably the reason for Regent Master Bukwode's murder. The book thief had been caught in the act, and had finally turned to killing. Idly he flipped the cover open, and saw it was a copy of Merlin's Prophecies, quite like the one in the possession of Brother Aldwyn that he had been looking at yesterday.

*

'Are you crazy? The castle?'

This was Robert Kemp's judgement on Peper's suggestion as to where the players might stay during their enforced sojourn in Oxford. They had debated where they might go after being turned back at South Gate, knowing that an irate inn-keeper would be seeking them out for skipping without paying their bill. So obviously, they could not go back to the Golden Ball Inn. Equally, if they stayed at another inn, the word would have got round eventually, and they would be traced. The inn-keepers might all be in competition, but they always pulled together when it came to welshers. Godrich had suggested seeking sanctuary in one of the numerous churches in the town, or even St Frideswide's Priory. But John Peper was reluctant to rely on the church, where priests would badger them about their errant lives. Goliards and jongleurs did not have the best of reputations with the clergy. So he had suggested falling back on the assistance of the secular authorities.

'We should go to the constable, and ask him for a place to stay. It's his fault we are in this fix, anyway.'

That had been when Robert Kemp had made his outburst. Peper was ready to argue, but Agnes Cheke stepped in quickly. She was the oldest member of their troupe, and acted like a mother to them all.

'I think it's a good idea. Sometimes, when you need to hide, it's best to do so in the least likely place they will look for you. We will go to the castle. There's an old chapel in the courtyard that is no longer used. Do you remember when we put on the miracle plays, when de Askeles got killed, we stored some of the play scenery there.'

Of course they remembered the time. De Askeles had been their leader then, an overbearing man, who got all he deserved. They had been glad to be rid of him, but it had to be said that times had been very lean for them since his demise. In those days, they had travelled in a large cart containing props and scenery pulled by a good nag, and had performed outside churches. Now they were reduced to a handcart, and performing in taverns with Margaret doing her tumbling and letting old drunkards imagine how she would perform in their beds. Agnes could see that her words had got them all thinking of the good times, and so distracted them with another problem.

'And maybe Will Plome will have the good grace to come and find us out, and apologise for disappearing.'

'Ah, yes. Wandering Will,' muttered John Peper. 'Where do you think he could have got to, Agnes?'

The old woman shrugged her scrawny shoulders.

'Lord knows. I just know since he learned his letters, he's not the same simple Will Plome I knew. That priest never should have opened his eyes to what's written in those lines of the plays we used to perform. He believed every word in them.'

Robert Kemp laughed contemptuously.

'But they were all tales from the Bible. Are you saying that God's word isn't true?'

'God's words? It was man's words that scared poor Will to death.'

She began to recite from memory a short piece familiar to all the players.

"Solomon said, for he foresaw, that whoever enters Hell within

Shall never come out, the scholars know. And therefore fellow leave this din.

Job, your servant, also, thus, in his time, did tell
That neither friend nor foe should find a release from Hell."'

Peper knew the words, though he rarely performed them, being no good at reciting.

'The Harrowing of Hell. Yes, I remember Will hiding under the old wagon when he first heard those lines. He thought he was doomed to an eternity in Hell. That's what the priests want from such words. To scare the witless into obedience to the church.'

His wife, Margaret, clutched his arm.

'And to bring them to God, John. Come on. Let's see if we can find somewhere to stay at the castle.'

Downcast by their own sober thoughts, the little band gathered up their possessions and walked up an eerily silent Fish Street. To bolster his own fears, Simon began to put some words together, singing out to fill the void left by the lack of traders calling out.

'Wandering Will, I'm feeling hungry,
So where'er you are, I'll kill and eat thee.'

Agnes nudged him to stop, but had to suppress a laugh.

*

The body was removed to St John's Church nearby, and Thomas Symon, Falconer's former pupil and now regent master in his own right, agreed to examine it more closely. Symon had turned himself into an excellent anatomist, but because the church disapproved of cutting open God's work in the form of a human body, he worked cautiously and discreetly. And usually on convicted murderers who had forfeit the protection of the church. A good and devout Christian, Symon had reconciled himself to the requirements of anatomy, seeing it as a way of understanding God in His shaping of a human body. In the case of John Bukwode, however, there would be no need for an intrusion into the carcase that lay in a side chapel of the church. Falconer had simply asked him to examine the wound on Bukwode's head and compare it with the book he now held in his hand.

'*Merlin's Prophecies*, I see,' Symon muttered, flipping through the stiff vellum pages. 'What a shame Master Bukwode didn't see his own end prophesied in it.'

He looked at the brass corner that William had indicated, observing the hair wedged in the book furniture. And the bloodstain on the worn leather cover. Bending over the body, he aligned the edge of the book with the caved-in area of Bukwode's skull. It was a perfect match. Looking over his shoulder to make sure the priest who had brought him to the dead body was no longer in evidence, Symon slyly pulled a small but very sharp knife out of his purse and pared away the skin around the wound. Then he used the tip of the blade to prise some of the bone out of the indentation. One look at its unusual thinness told him all he needed to know.

'You didn't stand a chance, did you, John Bukwode? He hit you in just the wrong place.'

He slid the knife back in his purse, his work done.

*

With the body of their master out of sight, the clerks of Corner Hall were a little less on edge, so Falconer began the task of examining them one by one. He had hoped that Doukas the Greek would get bored with what he was doing and leave. But he showed every indication that he intended to remain, and even produced a small quill, a pot of ink and a used piece of parchment from the satchel slung over his shoulder. In response to Falconer's questioning look, he explained what he was doing.

'Chancellor Burnell will want to know everything eventually.'

He seated himself at the table set at the end of the gloomy great hall, and laid out his tools. The students stared at him nervously, and Falconer knew that he would need to reassure them that they were not under suspicion, or he would learn nothing. He turned to the youth who had summoned him from Aristotles'. He looked older than the others, and a little more in control of himself.

'Tell me your name, boy.'

Doukas lifted his quill up in anticipation, and seeing the look of fear in the boy's eyes, Falconer laid a firm, restraining hand on the hand holding the quill.

'It will not be recorded, only the facts as you tell them to me.'

Doukas sighed and laid his quill down again. With a final glance at the scribe, the boy licked his lips and spoke up, the tremor in his voice belying his bold demeanour.

'My name is Alexander Leys. I am in my third year of study. What can I tell you, master? We were all in our beds last night and heard nothing.'

Unseen by anyone Doukas quietly pick his quill up and begin writing as Falconer pursued his investigations.

'You heard nothing despite the fact that there must have been a struggle?'

Falconer did not know if such a struggle took place, but he wasn't about to make his enquiries that easy for the students. Alexander Leys examined his shabby shoes for a considerable time before answering.

'We had been revelling, and I suppose we had drunk too much. When we got back last night, we all just flopped in our respective beds.'

Falconer could see, as in Aristotle's Hall, that one end of the great hall had been partitioned off into cubicles rather like in Bartlemas hospital. Each student had his own pallet and it was obvious that, from there, no-one would have been able to see someone entering Corner Hall.

'And Regent Master Bukwode allows such dissolution?'

Leys looked furtive.

'The regent master was not in his solar last night.'

Someone whispered something from the back of the bunch of clerks by the hearth, and a spotty-faced youth at the front giggled. Falconer strode over, and grabbed his arm, pulling him from the group.

'And what have you to say, boy?'

69

The youth squirmed in Falconer's vice-like grip, but spoke up defiantly.

'Master Bukwode was in Grope Lane.'

Falconer grimaced. While his students misbehaved, Bukwode was paying a whore to service him. He felt some indignation, until it occurred to him that he was little better. He often stayed late with Saphira Le Veske, at the expense of the students in his care. Looking over at Doukas, he saw the scribe shake his head slightly, his quill hovering above the parchment. At least he had the kindness to not record the reason why Bukwode was abroad last night. Falconer took a deep breath, and carried on.

'So you all came back late in the night, not knowing if your master had returned or not, and simply climbed into your respective beds. There you slept the sleep of innocents, not hearing your master return, nor even his murder. Was there nothing unusual that you can tell me of.'

He watched as the clerks, abashed by his tirade, look at each other and shake their heads.

'There was something, master.'

It was Alexander Leys who spoke out, and Falconer turned back to him.

'What was that?'

The youth screwed up his face, trying to bring some vague recollection to mind.

'When we came back, I was sure I was at the back of the group – making sure none of the kids got left behind.' He tipped a thumb at his comrades. 'Anyway, these all ran ahead of me, and I couldn't keep up. But when we got to the door, someone called out from behind me to leave it open. I didn't think anything of it at the time, but now I think about it, I am not sure who it was.'

Doukas butted in with a question before Falconer could.

'Can you describe who you saw?'

Falconer glared at the Greek, but let it go. It was what he would have asked. The boy thought for a moment.

'I can only say that he had a cloak or a long robe on – grey, with the hood up.'

He looked pleadingly at Falconer.

'I was drunk. It was all unclear to me, and still is, even now.'

Falconer knew he would not get much more from him or any of the others.

*

'I questioned the others, but it was no use. They didn't see the intruder either, nor heard the confrontation with Bukwode that led to his death.'

Falconer was in the hall of the castle, apprising Peter Bullock of what he had learned. Doukas sat in the background, his record of the interrogations firmly stowed in his satchel. He was offering no opinions of his own, and Falconer wondered whether he was saving his thoughts for his master, the Chancellor of England. Brother Aldwyn sat in the shadows apparently immersed in his copy of *Merlin's Prophecies*. The constable stomped back and forth in front of Falconer unable to contain his agitation.

'Damn it. This is the last thing I need at the present. I have a town full of people afraid to show their noses outside their front door in case they get the plague. And now I have a murderer running amok.'

Falconer tried to calm his friend down.

'Hardly running amok. If it is the same person who stole the other books, this is the first time he has killed, and that is only because he was caught in the act. Besides, on the other matter, you should be glad everyone is staying indoors. Better that than hammering on the town's gates demanding to be let out, and spreading the pox across England.'

Bullock sighed, and dropped into his favourite chair. He felt an ache in his chest, and his left arm tingled. Absently, he began to rub away the pain in his arm.

'You're right, William. I only wish that I knew who this thief was. A grey cloak is all you have as a description?'

'Yes, it's not much to work on but ...'

As Falconer expressed his fears about the poor scraps of information he had to work on, Aldwyn's voice piped up from the other side of the hall.

'Could it have been a grey habit, not a cloak?'

Bullock frowned, peering into the shadows where the old monk sat.

'The grey habit of a Franciscan, are you saying?'

By way of reply, Aldwyn pointed a finger down at the book in his lap.

'Listen to this. It comes a little later in the prophecies, but it may be relevant.'

He began reciting in a low, sepulchral tone.

> "*Piety will frown upon the man who has inherited goods from the impious; that is, until he takes his style of dress from his own father. Girded around with a wild boar's teeth, he shall climb over the mountain summits and higher than the shadow of the Helmeted Man.*"

Bullock growled in frustration.

'You'll have to explain that to me, brother. I'm only a simple warrior and constable, and it doesn't make sense. What has that to do with our murderer being a Greyfriar?'

Falconer, who had understood Aldwyn, intervened in order to help.

'I think Aldwyn is suggesting that the book thief is a pious man who has set his mind against those who have garnered their books and learning from the impious. Mathematics learned from the Arab Al-Khwarizmi, for example, or medicine from the ancients who lived before Christ. I can understand that, but the stuff about wild boar's teeth is beyond me.'

Aldwyn leaned forward into the light of the fire.

'It may be a simple mistake on the part of whoever wrote down Merlin's prophecies. The text calls for the impious to adopt the dress of his father, which is girded around with wild boar's teeth. Now

Saint Anthony tamed a wild boar during his temptations. So you could say the reference is to St Anthony, who was a Franciscan.' He stopped a moment and frowned. 'Except it was another Anthony – St Anthony of Padua – who was brought into the order by St Francis himself. That is why I say it may merely be a mistake in the text that still identifies the book-thief and now murderer as a Franciscan.'

Chapter Eleven

The Feast of St Edith of Winchester, 16ᵗʰ September.

Saphira Le Veske walked through a deserted Oxford towards Dagville's Inn. Before she had even reached the crossroads however, she saw Samson wearily dragging himself back to Jewry. His shoulders were slumped even more than was usual in a man of his advanced years. His grey side-locks half-covered his face, but she could see his features were the colour of ash. She raised a hand to touch him, but looking up and realising she was there, he held both his hands up. Warding off her attempt at comfort, he told her the bad news.

'The crusader is dead, and I have wrapped him in a nightgown Dagville provided. You should not touch me before I have removed these clothes and washed. I have told Grace Dagville to burn everything he possessed, and all the bedding he lay on. I must also arrange for the body to be buried.'

Saphira stood as close as she dared to the disconsolate physician, wishing to ease his burden.

'Let me do that. I will tell the constable what he must do.'

Samson nodded, and turned back towards Fish Street. Saphira posed a question.

'Will there be more, do you think? How long will we have to wait?'

Samson paused before answering.

'It could be another ten days before we know for sure if he passed the disease on to others.' He looked around him at the desolate street. 'At least Peter Bullock has done what he can, and fear is very useful in these circumstances. If people stay indoors, whoever might have been infected by the crusader will not pass on the pox themselves. Did you wash?'

Saphira nodded her head, recalling her ritual cleansing the previous day and the good feeling it gave her. She had held her breath under the waters of the mikveh for as long as she could, dragging her mane of red hair under with her. Emerging from the waters had felt like a rebirth, and she had sat by the fire in the hall of her house drying her hair and warming the shivers away from her body. She had busied herself for the rest of the day, and had longed for the closeness of William, but knew he had to be with his charges in Aristotles' Hall.

Even so, she longed for their intimacy to be renewed, but then laughed quietly, recalling what he had said a few weeks earlier about Christian exhortations against fornication. He had sat up in her bed, counting off on his fingers the number of reasons given by the church not to have intercourse.

'Never during Lent, Advent, Whitsun week, or Easter week. Nor on feast days, fast days, Sunday, Wednesday, Friday, and Saturday.'

She had been astonished, but he had not finished.

'Not during daylight, or if you are naked, if you are in church, or at all unless you are trying to produce a child.' He grinned. 'St Augustine, poor soul, failed to see what use a woman could be to a man, if one excluded the bearing of children.'

She remembered fondly what he had then done with her in her bed, with no intention of producing a child, and with both of them naked. Indeed, it had been a Wednesday too, if she recalled it correctly. So many laws broken all at once and so sweetly.

This new morning, she now had more serious matters to deal with. After her meeting with Samson, she hurried to the castle to speak to Peter Bullock. Leaving the unnatural quiet of the streets and entering through the gates, she was surprised to see an encampment in the castle's courtyard. One brightly dressed man was dextrously juggling three coloured balls in the air, and another was tuning a rebec, making the stringed instrument produce strange wails and screeches. From behind the old chapel, a slim figure in tight hose appeared, walking on his hands. Saphira gasped as the saltatore lithely bent backwards, placing his feet on the ground behind him, forming an almost backbreaking arch. The rebec player made his instrument emit a howl of admiration. Saphira was even more surprised when she realised 'he' was a woman, who proceeded to perform three back flips across the courtyard to land on her feet in front of her.

'Mistress, are you seeking the constable?'

Saphira saw that the slender woman was older than she had thought, with crow's feet defining the edges of her grey eyes. She was not much younger than Saphira was, and suddenly, Saphira felt even more envious of her suppleness and slim figure.

Margaret Peper saw the admiration in the red-haired woman's eyes as she looked her up and down. She picked up a modest skirt from the ground, and wrapped it round her hose-clad legs, pulling a face.

'I could bend my body much further than that ten years ago. And what I can do now is bought with endless, grinding exercise. Don't envy me that, mistress.' She cocked a thumb at the building behind her.

'The constable has allowed us to rest here, as we cannot leave the town. He is in the great hall.'

Margaret slid gracefully away, to help an older woman who was breaking some bread up for the troupe of players. Saphira carried on her way towards Peter Bullock's spartan quarters. Inside the great hall there was almost as strange an assembly as out in the courtyard. Close by the fire that glowed dull red in the centre of the hall sat an old monk in black robes, his head bowed over a leather tome. He was reading to a stocky, black-haired man with the swarthy skin of someone from the Mediterranean. As she entered, this man's black eyes swivelled in her direction. She felt a shiver run down her back from the cold, calculating look. Peter Bullock descended the stairs from the solar that he rarely used in normal times. Perhaps having unwelcome guests had driven him to the retreat. He lumbered across the hall with that familiar gait of his that brought comfort to the minds of the citizens of Oxford. He was a big, elderly bear of a man keeping calm and good sense in the streets at night. Today, he looked more pleased than usual to see Saphira.

'Mistress Le Veske, you are well I hope?'

The question would have been only a minor courtesy at any other time. Today, it was full of meaning. Saphira smiled reassuringly, and squeezed the old man's arm.

'I am very well, thank you, Peter. Both refreshed and cleansed.'

She drew him aside, away from his involuntary guests, and lowered her voice.

'Unfortunately, the same cannot be said for the man resident at Dagville's Inn.'

'Ah, he is dead then? Well, it was to be expected. Is Thomas Dagville burning everything?'

'I am not sure. I met Samson on the way back to his house. He has given the Dagvilles instructions, and the body is wrapped in a shroud. I said I would tell you, so that you could ensure it is disposed of properly.'

Bullock puffed his cheeks out, his face a mask of indecision.

'Should I have the body burned also?'

Brother Aldwyn must have heard the conversation between Saphira and Peter, because at this stage he spoke up.

'You cannot burn a Christian. His body must be interred like Christ's body after the Crucifixion.'

Bullock looked from Saphira to the old priest and back.

'Can we safely bury him without catching the red plague ourselves?'

Everyone looked uncertain, and it was left to Isaac Doukas to resolve the problem. He rose from beside the fire, where he had been perusing the book put down by Aldwyn.

'I think I can help you out. I have had the small pox myself many years ago.' He pointed to some small scars on his cheeks. 'It was the mild form, and though I would guess what you have to contend with here is more virulent, I believe that I cannot catch the pox in any of its forms again.'

His cold, dark eyes scrutinised Saphira again.

'You are a Jew, and this Samson of whom you spoke also is a Jew?'

Ready for some criticism of her people being involved in the care of Christians, Saphira clenched her teeth.

'Yes.'

Doukas nodded briefly.

'That is good. Eastern physicians and Jews know more about the plague than here in the West.'

He looked at Bullock.

'I will move the body tonight, when there is less chance of being seen. Where will it be buried?'

'Bring it here – he can rest in the chapel. Then we can bury him in the grounds.'

Saphira had hoped she might find Falconer in the castle, so she had a question for Bullock.

75

'Have you seen William? Is he all right?'

*

Falconer, in fact, was very far from all right. His unease had nothing to do with the red plague, however. He had left his students with an injunction not to the leave the confines of the hall, and was on his way to the Franciscan friary on the edge of the town. In fact, strictly speaking, the friary was outside the town walls, but only because of a peculiarity of its construction. The few Franciscans who had arrived in Oxford in 1224 had found adequate lodging at the house of Robert Mercer in the parish of St Ebbe. Twenty years later, their growing needs had been met when they had the King's permission to demolish a section of the town wall between Little Gate in the east and the castle in the west. This gave them access to an island in the Thames where they built their friary. The gap in the wall had been filled with their church constructed on an east-west axis so that the very body of the church formed the new wall. The choir of the church was devoted to the friars for worship, and the nave was a preaching hall.

It was this hall that Falconer now entered, and he crossed it to go into the friary. He was seeking out Friar Gualo, to whom he had spoken about the woman who had given birth fifty years earlier in Bartlemas hospital. But this time he didn't want to investigate his own ancestry, but the vexed question of the book-thief and murderer possibly being a Franciscan. What he wanted to find out was the attitude to books of the Franciscans currently in the friary at Oxford.

Falconer knew all about the Franciscan ambivalence to learning. The Ordo Fratrum Minorum had come into being to act as a counter-balance to the cloistered orders of monks. The new order of mendicant friars preached in the rural communities and growing towns of England. They had a simple creed in consequence, and when in the universities, translations of Aristotle into Latin were challenging Christian scholarship, they took up the opposing cause in the name of the Christian church. But for Falconer there was a more personal reason to be wary of the mendicants. His long-time friend, Roger Bacon, was a Franciscan friar, but of a very different stripe. Bacon was a scientist who worked on the principles of optics, and he made burning glasses and magic mirrors. He searched the stars and their influence on the lives of men. He delved into alchemy, averring that it taught the generation of things from their elements. Ten years ago, with the then pope on his side, he had compiled in three volumes an encyclopaedic collection of knowledge. Unfortunately, Pope Clement had died, and Bacon's works had been locked away. Now, Roger Bacon was also hidden away in a Franciscan friary somewhere unknown to Falconer. Scientific enquiry was forbidden by the order, and deemed heretical. Falconer hoped that Friar Gualo, as a man who took an interest in medicine, would be more open-minded, and put a name or two to the more severe Franciscans in Oxford. Though he hardly dared tell Gualo that he was also trying to get him to put a name to a murderer.

The preaching hall was quite empty, and Falconer could hear the ending of the midday prayers – sext – being sung in the choir. He waited patiently until the prayers finished, then watched as the grey-clad friars dispersed. Seeing the bent figure of Gualo limping towards the door that led into the friary proper, he called out.

'Friar Gualo, may I speak with you?'

The old man looked over his shoulder, and squinted in Falconer's direction. His frown told Falconer that the friar's eyesight was worse than his own. Falconer had a fine pair of eye-glasses ground for him by an expert on lenses. He rarely used them, though, as their heavy metal frame gave him the appearance of a half-blind owl. He strode over to Gualo, until he was close enough to be discerned clearly.

'It is I, William Falconer. We talked about the past recently, and of Bartlemas hospital.'

The old friar smiled in recognition.

'Ah, yes. The unfortunate matter of the serving girl ... I am afraid I still can't recall whether she lived or died, though.'

Despite his wishes to know the fate of the girl, who could have been his mother, Falconer had to put this hunt aside.

'It is not that business that I come about, Friar Gualo.'

He saw that the friar was shuffling back and forth, and realised the old man had difficulty standing for any length of time. Sext would have tired him out. He indicated one of the benches in the nave of the preaching hall.

'Let us sit down here. I could do with a rest.'

After they had settled down side by side, Falconer gazed towards the choir aisle and the altar. He formed his first question carefully.

'I wanted to ask about my friend, Friar Bacon. I have not heard from him for some time.'

Apparently, Gualo was not perturbed by being asked about such a controversial figure.

'Yes, Friar Roger. I believe he is devoting his time now to the study of Christian doctrine in Paris. He is a wild thinker, our Roger, and needs some ... discipline applied to his waywardness.'

The old man patted Falconer's leg reassuringly.

'Have no fear, though. He is well and hearty, I am certain of that.'

Falconer didn't think so. If Roger had been deprived of access to scientific experimentation, he would be a very distressed and frustrated man. However, he wanted to put Gualo at his ease, and he laughed softly.

'Yes, Roger was always very ... wayward in his thinking. I suppose he might have annoyed some of his brothers here in Oxford because of that.'

Gualo shook his head slowly from side to side.

'Indeed, there were those who opposed him when he was teaching here.'

Falconer felt he was beginning to tease out of Gualo something that might be useful to his search for the murderer. But he still felt he had to skirt around the subject, or the Franciscan might balk at revealing names of fellow members of his order.

'It is the same in the university. Recently we have had a book-thief stealing contentious works. I fear he has even threatened the life of those he steals from.'

Gualo shook his ancient head sadly.

'There is no accounting for the perversity of man. But those who opposed Friar Bacon were all honourable men. They would merely invoke the words of St Francis, who warned a novice that "when you have got a psalter, then you will want a breviary; and when you have got a breviary, you will sit in your chair as great as a lord, and gape after knowledge."'

A sharp voice echoed down the aisle, cutting into the conversation.

'Wise words, brother. Books and learning have no place in Francis's scheme.'

Gualo groaned quietly, glancing sideways at Falconer. He whispered a warning under his breath.

'Fulbert is one of those who would do more than merely incarcerate Roger Bacon.'

Falconer watched as the same severe young man who had interrupted his conversation with Gualo last time, hurried towards them. His sandals slapped ferociously on the cold stone floor. Falconer wondered how long he had been standing close by, and if he had heard his words about the book-thief. Friar Fulbert was obviously Gualo's keeper, and had a face like thunder having found his charge talking with the regent master again. Standing stiff-backed before them, he rounded off his homily.

'Our founder's sole aim was the practical imitation of Jesus. He told his first followers that a day would come when men would throw their books out of the window as useless.'

His sudden, cold words filled Falconer with dread and foreboding.

Chapter Twelve

That night, Isaac Doukas slipped out of the castle, and silently made his way to Dagville's Inn to recover the crusader's body. Falconer, meanwhile, was telling Bullock what he had found out about the Franciscans.

'The young friar fills me with dread, Peter. If Fulbert can yearn for a time when books are thrown out of the window, he can be the one who is stealing them in the first place.'

'And murdering the owners of the books also.'

Falconer signalled his agreement with a nod of the head. He and the constable were closeted in the upper room of the tower that Bullock was using to escape his unwelcome visitors. Through the narrow window slit of the room, he could see across the marsh lands transected by streams that sparkled in the moonlight to Oseney Abbey in the distance. Since locking the gates, he thought the outside world seemed almost unreal. An impression rendered even starker by the ghostliness of the full moon. He turned back to Falconer, and slumped down into his chair.

'Two days since I closed the gates, and we have at least ten more to wait to see if we are free of the pox. Now we have a murderer running around killing scholars. Chancellor de Bosco must be tearing his hair out.'

Falconer smiled wearily, thinking of William de Bosco's bald head, and the impossibility of what Peter had suggested.

'Actually, he is remarkably calm and well-organised. He has decreed that no lessons take place until the problem is over in order to avoid contagion. I think he is relieved that our self-inflicted incarceration gives him respite from having to answer to Robert Burnell and the king about the thefts.'

'Then you will have to come up with a solution before I reopen the town, or our guest, Doukas, will be reporting failure to his master as soon as he can.'

Falconer pulled a face at the thought of the Greek. When he had come to the castle that evening, Isaac Doukas had wanted to know all that he had been doing. The swarthy man had insisted that Falconer sit down and tell him, while he noted down what he heard in his crabbed hand. If nothing else Doukas was meticulous, but made no comment as Falconer told him of Friar Fulbert's words, and his own suspicions.

'Where did he go, by the way? Doukas, I mean. He made his notes and then said he had business to attend to.'

Bullock waved a hand indicating the night outside the tower.

'He is making himself useful collecting the crusader knight's body. He says he has had a form of the small pox when he was a youth, and will not be able to catch it again.'

'Can that be true?'

Bullock gave Falconer a steely look.

'Frankly, I don't care. Let him die, if it's not true. Though I would be grateful if he didn't bring it inside the castle. I have that motley band of troubadours to consider as well as my own well-being.'

'Yes, I saw them in the courtyard as I arrived.'

Falconer had spoken to Margaret Peper as he crossed the yard, asking about Will Plome, who he had recalled seeing in the town earlier. Curiously, Margaret had told him that no-one in the troupe had seen Will for days. She had explained.

'Since learning his letters, he has been obsessed with reading anything and everything he could find. Now, he has disappeared entirely.'

Falconer could understand Margaret's concern. Will Plome was a simpleton, who needed someone to look after his interests and ensure he didn't get into trouble. He had reassured her that he had seen the fat young man in Oxford two days before, and that he must now still be in the town.

'Nobody can escape Oxford for the time being.'

Margaret had nodded, but clearly was still worried, and Falconer had carried on his way to speak to Bullock.

'Why have they set up camp in the castle courtyard, Peter?'

Bullock smiled wearily.

'I think they are avoiding a bill for accommodation at the Golden Ball Inn. This morning, Gil Sexton accosted me in the street accusing some wandering players of skipping without paying. I told him I would look into it, but that they may have gone before the gates were closed. What with all the other business, I haven't yet taxed them on their misdeed.'

Falconer recalled the threadbare nature of the jongleurs' clothes, and the fact that their once commodious wagon had been reduced to a handcart.

'I doubt whether they have enough to pay for a night at Dagville's, let alone the Golden Ball. Even with a pox-ridden body lurking in the next room. Talking of which, I wonder if Doukas is back yet.'

Falconer pushed himself up and out of his chair, and crossed to the window that overlooked the courtyard. By the silvery light of the full moon, he could tell that the jongleurs had all retired to wherever they had found to lay their heads. The yard was empty save for their handcart, on the top of which lay a hideous Devil's mask with long curly horns. The moonlight shone on the jagged white teeth in the mask's mouth giving the impression that the castle yard was the gateway to Hell. But if it was, and the dead crusader was bound thence, there was no sign yet of Doukas and his grisly burden.

*

80

When Will Plome woke up, he was astonished to hear no movement above him. Even in the evening, the church was normally bustling with pilgrims who came to obtain a remission of sins committed or a miraculous cure. The bones of St Frideswide were still a popular draw for pilgrims, even though more recent relics such as the blood of Saint Thomas Becket at Canterbury attracted many more sinners seeking pardons. But as he wriggled out of where he was hiding, he saw that the church was empty. Even the feretarius or guardian of the shrine, Richard Yaxley – a man well known to Will – was not in evidence.

Before daring to set foot in the town, Will prostrated himself on the cold slabs of the church as he had seen pilgrims do, and prayed to God for guidance. Since learning to read, he had found himself lost in the realm of words that enveloped him. Each book he read puzzled him more, and he feared he could not discern the truth from lies – God's words from those of the Devil. In the peculiar stillness of the church, God was silent, not responding to his muttered prayers. And he pushed himself up to his feet, and went out into the town.

There, he was even more astonished to find the streets deserted. Scuttling from street corner to doorway, always keeping out of sight – though of whose sight he knew not – he soon found that not a soul existed in the town. Suddenly, he was fearful that the Day of Judgement had come while he slept. He recalled the words from the play about it that the troupe he once belonged to had performed often. He could read the words now, but they were emblazoned on his memory anyway.

'On earth I see sin everywhere,
And therefore angels I shall send,
To blow their horns, that all may hear.
The time has come: I'll make an end.
Angels, blow your horns and strive,
That every creature you may call:
Learned and lewd, husbands and wives,
Receive their doom, this day they shall.
Every soul that ever had life:
Let none be forgotten, great or small.'

He wondered if he could find more books while they were unguarded by their normal keepers. Perhaps the black-clad scholars who jealously hoarded them had been consigned to Hell. Behind the looming mass of St Frideswide's, he surveyed the short row of four narrow-fronted houses at the end of Shidyerd Street. Each door he knew led into a place where masters lived with their students, some poor and dressed in grey drab like himself, some rich in fine robes. He had seen their comings and goings from the shadows often. He scuttled across to the first door, and tried the latch. It clicked up and he pushed the door open. He was uncertain about entering, but then he heard the clatter of a horse's hooves on the cobbled surface of the street behind him. To avoid being seen, he pushed on the door, and slid in through the opening.

81

Robert Chetwyn was having a restless night, what with the threat of pox, and the proscription by the chancellor on giving lectures. He was a regent master whose life was ruled by orthodoxy and routine. He had few students lodging at Nevill's Inn in Shidyerd Street because students were generally an unruly bunch with no regard for regularity. They didn't care for a master who demanded order. In fact he only had three clerks lodging with him at present, and his income was suffering. But better that his purse was light than his temper was taxed overmuch. Now, he could not even give lectures, and the boys lodging with him were already getting restless at being kept indoors. He lay perfectly still on his back, his arms at his side and his eyes closed, praying for sleep. Then he thought he heard the latch on his front door being lifted. Or was it next door? His door was hard by that of Beke's Inn, and visitors often mistook the one for the other. He wasn't sure even if he had heard the sound, but then it didn't matter all that much for it was overtaken by the clatter of horse's hooves on the street outside. Who could be riding around Oxford so late, and on a night when movement had been forbidden by the constable? He might have got up then, and been a better witness later, but curiosity was not in his makeup. He merely cursed the transgressor, and pulled the bedclothes up around his ears. Then just as he was dozing off a loud thumping sound from Beke's Inn roused him again.

This time he sat up in bed.

Listening, he wasn't sure if he could hear a human cry or not from the other side of the wall that divided Beke's from Nevill's Inn. Then there came another loud thump. Like a body falling to the floor. He could ignore the sounds no longer, and got up. He padded barefoot across his solar to the shuttered window that looked out on to the street. Though it was still quite dark, he saw a shadowy figure crossing the street.

Will Plome was shivering as he dragged open the door, and peered out into the narrow street. What was inside the house scared him nearly to death, but what was outside was almost as fearful. The horse he had heard earlier stood like a statue at the corner, its head bowed to the ground. It was a monster of a horse that glistened like silver in the light of the full moon. He glanced nervously up and down the street, mortally afraid of what else he might see. A rustling noise from somewhere behind the church made him gasp, his indrawn breath like the last rattle of a dying man. Flattening himself against the door, he pressed his hands on the rough surface as if trying to sink into the oak and disappear. He only began to breathe again when a rat scuttled out of a heap of rubbish that had been piled against the church wall and off along the open drain that ran down the lane. The horse made a faint whinnying sound, and raised its weary head to stare incuriously at him. A cloud of steam issued from its nostrils, and he imagined he saw the Devil breathing smoke and fire. He suppressed a squeal of horror.

The night had turned into a scene from one of those plays he had seen performed so often. The Harrowing of Hell.

Then afterwards he harrowed hell,
And took those wretches from within;
Fought worthily with fiends so fell,
For souls that sunken were in sin ...

The words rung in his ears like the bells of the church across the lane. What had happened in that house that night would remain with him forever. Fear of it finally propelled him forwards. He pushed himself away from the door, and made a dash for the sanctuary of the church. He left two bloody hand-marks on the surface of the oak.

*

It was almost dawn and Bullock had received an urgent message to go to some incident at the back of St Frideswide's Church. The details were unclear, and Falconer would have gone with him, but the constable asked him to stay and wait for Doukas.

'If it is a matter concerning the university or your book thief, I will send for you.'

Falconer reluctantly agreed and waited. And waited. He had almost dozed off when he saw a shadowy figure move slowly across the castle courtyard. It seemed to be a strange humpbacked apparition with its head set to one side. The moon had fled behind heavy, dark clouds and the monster was at first indistinct. Then, as it got closer, Falconer made it out. Doukas had returned, and he was bearing a shroud-covered body over his left shoulder. A lesser man might have been weighed down by such a burden, but Doukas walked easily. He crossed to the patch of beaten earth beside the old chapel, and laid the body down on the ground. Quietly, Falconer slipped out of the room, and descended the stone steps to the ground floor. Aldwyn was sleeping soundly, so Falconer carried on out to where Doukas was already toiling with a spade, making a hole in the ground to accept the crusader's body. The Greek grunted in acknowledgement of Falconer's presence, and carried on digging.

'I thought it best to bury the body while it was still dark. The jongleurs ...' He tilted his head towards the chapel, where the Pepers and the rest of the troupe had made their beds. '... they might get a bit skittish seeing the cause of the pox right before their eyes.'

'Bullock didn't tell them he was bringing the body here?'

Doukas shook his head, his tail of hair swishing round his shoulders.

'He doesn't want anyone to know. Few in the town know it was a crusader brought the pox to Dagville's Inn. And the innkeeper will be guaranteed to keep his mouth shut, if he values his future business.'

He paused while he relentlessly made the hole deeper. Then he looked up at Falconer again, wiping the sweat from his brow.

'Myself, I would tell them the truth. There are those who will jump to conclusions, and find scapegoats for the outbreak. Foreigners will have a bad time.'

Falconer knew exactly what the Greek was saying. There were plenty of people in England, and in Oxford indeed, ready to blame the Jews for any disaster that occurred. It did not matter if it were a national catastrophe, or the mere breaking of a valuable possession in someone's house, there would always be a person ready to point a finger at the Jews because of it. On the other hand, he suddenly remembered that the Dagvilles knew Samson and Saphira had attended to the crusader before he died. It would be so easy to twist the truth, and despite Samson's brave efforts, somehow accuse him and Saphira of colluding in his death at the very least. If not that, then of infecting the town deliberately themselves. If the facts of the crusader's last hours were known, blame could be shifted to the Jewish community anyway. It would be better to cover up the cause of the pox's arrival in Oxford while people still felt vulnerable and afraid.

He gave Doukas a helping hand in scrambling out of the makeshift grave.

'I think on balance it is better that we bury the evidence for the time being. The Jews here are used to being blamed for all sorts of ills. They have sturdy stone properties and good oak doors, and are used to keeping their heads down in times of trouble. Come, let's get this body buried.'

Doukas shrugged his shoulders, and took one end of the linen-shrouded body. Falconer stooped and lifted the other end. Together they heaved the crusader into his grave. After he had made a perfunctory sign of the cross in the Greek way, Doukas began back-filling the hole. The dry earth pattered down on the grey linen cloth that was Sir Hugo de Wolfson's shroud, and soon his body was covered over.

Chapter Thirteen

The Feast of St Hildegard, 17ʰ September

Bullock stared down at the bed and the bloody mess that was Edmund Ludlow's head. He had sent for Falconer almost immediately, but so far there was no sign of him.

'Jesu Christ, where is William, when you want him?'

He prodded the point of his sheathed sword into the floorboards, and using it as a support, eased his creaking body down. Kneeling uncomfortably over the body, he poked at the man's greyish linen night-shirt, lifting it from the body to see if anything was hidden under it. He saw the edge of a crushed parchment roll beneath the man's chest, and teased it out. Pressing out the creases against the floor with his palm, he was disappointed to see only gibberish. He started to get up off his knees, but they protested, and he groaned. He felt a hand grab his arm, and he looked round, surprised that Falconer had crept up on him without him hearing.

'There was a time when a man who sneaked up on me like that would have had a knife in his belly.'

He grumbled, but was grateful for his friend helping him back on to his feet. He pointed at the body.

'We have another one.'

When Bullock had arrived at the scene of the reported incident that had taken him away from the castle, he had been confronted by a whey-faced regent master. The man rented a small hall at the back of St Frideswide's, where he had the care of three scholars of the university. Nevill's Inn was in the middle of a row of properties opposite the corner of Frideswide's Lane and Shidyerd Street. Though the small community was keeping indoors because of the fear of pox, Master Chetwyn said his attention had been drawn to the horse loose on the street outside their hall. He didn't suppose his neighbour, Edmund Ludlow, had a visitor himself and the man had only one young boarder in Beke's Inn. So the presence of such a large destrier, undoubtedly the property of a knight, had filled him with curiosity. Venturing out on to the street, he had noticed that Ludlow's door was ajar. Uncertain of what he might find, and fearful that the plague had visited his neighbour, he had walked up to the door. He had pushed it wide open, and was horrified to find blood on his hand. He had called out, and had heard a low moan like someone in extremis. Stepping over the threshold, he had seen blood dripping through the ceiling.

Even as he had later babbled out his story to a weary constable, who had hardly got any sleep, he was still not sure if it was murder or small pox that had struck Ludlow down. Bullock now knew for sure which it was. The man's brains were all over his bedding.

Now it was Falconer's turn to crouch over the body, which he did with greater ease than Bullock.

'He has been hit several times with a club or some such heavy object. This is different from the other death. It looks more deliberate rather than done on the spur of the moment by a thief caught stealing books. Are you sure this is our book thief striking again?'

Bullock grunted, and pointed out the open chest standing at the back of the solar.

'It's been rifled of all its contents, I would say. At least, there are no books in it, and I would expect that to be the place where Ludlow kept what he had.'

Falconer rose and walked over to the dark, polished chest. The large metal lock had been forced, and shards of fresh wood showed through the otherwise deeply coloured surface. It was empty, so whatever books Ludlow had cherished were gone.

'All taken, then.'

'Except for this.'

Bullock held out the crumpled roll of parchment that he had discovered under the regent master's body.

'It lay underneath him, as if he was trying to hide it from the thief's clutches. But I can't read what it says.'

Falconer took the scroll from Bullock's outstretched hand, and opened it out. Frowning a little, he scanned the lines of text. It was a while before he recognised it for what it was.

'It in Greek, and is some old poem about a hero called Digenis.'

He pointed at the lines not obscured by Ludlow's blood.

'This bit reads - *Blood flowed down over their horse-trappings, and their sweat ran out over their breastplates.*'

'Curiously apt, isn't it? Especially as there was a horse standing out in the lane. A knight's horse with all its barding on – great plates of bronze. As if it was going into battle.'

Falconer could not immediately figure out what all this meant, if anything at all.

'I saw an empty chamber downstairs. Was there someone else in the house?'

'Yes, a student of some means. He is next door now.'

'Hmm. And where is it now, the horse?'

'I had it taken back to the castle.'

'Then let's go back there, and see if we can puzzle it all out.'

He looked down at the dead man.

'Ludlow wasn't known as someone who harboured controversial texts like the other masters who have suffered thefts.'

He waved the scroll.

'This was more in his line. Old manuscripts that none could find bothersome.'

Bullock couldn't see that the type of books taken mattered one jot. But he understood that his friend knew more than he did about the book thefts, as Falconer had been charged by William de Bosco to ferret out the thief. He agreed to meet Falconer at the castle shortly, and set about arranging the disposition of the body.

It was Falconer's intention as he left Beke's Inn to visit Saphira. Even though assemblies of people were forbidden in Oxford for the time being, he did not think there would be any danger in his meeting her. Both of them had been in contact with the same people and the same risks already. But as he left Ludlow's house, he was hailed by a slight, stooped man standing just inside the door of the next house. Without his eye-lenses, he couldn't make out who it was, so he approached him closer. But his action caused the man to rear away, and he even made to push the door closed.

'Don't come any closer, Master Falconer. The pox is abroad and I don't want to catch it.'

Falconer recognised the voice more than the features of the man. It was Regent Master Robert Chetwyn, a timid man at the best of times, who taught the seven disciplines with a strict adherence to orthodoxy. He held up his hands, palm outwards, in a propitiatory gesture.

'I am coming no closer, Master Chetwyn. What is it you wanted to say to me?'

Relieved that Falconer was now keeping his distance, Chetwyn pulled his door open again.

'It was I found the body, and at first I feared it might be the plague. I have three students here, and their safety is my responsibility. If this is murder instead, and is to be laid at the door of the book thief, then you should look in St Frideswide's for him.'

'And why should I do that?'

'I heard a noise last night. Well, a lot of noise actually, and it woke me. First there was the sound of a horse's hooves clattering down the lane, and then later I heard some sort of thumps from next door.'

Falconer assumed that those sounds had heralded the ending of Edmund Ludlow's life.

'Thank you, that is very interesting.'

Falconer started to turn away, thinking that the man's observations were of little consequence. Chetwyn, however, had more to say.

'I was wary of looking out at the time, because of the pox, you understand.'

Falconer thought it was more likely that Chetwyn had been scared to do so in case he put his own life in danger, and he met the same fate as his neighbour.

'Is that all you can tell me?'

Chetwyn screwed up his face in annoyance.

'No, of course not. I was telling you how I found the body. I didn't look out immediately, as I said, but the continuing sound of the horse was too much to keep me in bed. I resolved to complain to Ludlow, and got up. When I saw his door ajar, I began to be concerned, especially when I saw the blood.'

Chetwyn's voice broke at his recollection of the scene, and Falconer thought he was about to faint. But then he rallied and carried on.

'And then after a few moments I heard another noise. It was a sort of moan, and it put me in mind of someone with the plague. I was all for leaving, but then I saw Ludlow's boarder huddled in the corner of the hall looking quite distraught.'

'Who was this student?'

'Why should you wish to know?'

'Just for information. I might need to talk to him later.'

Chetwyn growled disapprovingly, as if he deemed divulging the information was unnecessary.

'He has seen enough horror tonight. The sight of blood coming through the ceiling would break anyone. I brought him to Nevill's Inn and tried to calm him.'

Falconer imagined Chetwyn had to calm his own fears too. He persisted with his enquiries though.

'And this student's name?'

'If you must know, it was Geoffrey Westhalf. But I don't want you talking to him. His father is a very influential man.'

Falconer wasn't sure what relevance the wealth and power of Westhalf's father had to do with it, other than he might object to his son being questioned about a death. But anyone was subject to the rigours of the law when a murder was being investigated.

'Thank you for the information. But now I must get on.'

Chetwyn's next words were full of mockery.

'Don't you want to know what else I saw?'

Falconer sighed, not wishing to play the man's games, but knowing he would now have to ask.

'What else did you see?'

'Before I went next door, I was at the solar window up there.'

He pointed up above his head to the small window in the house's frontage.

'It was from there that I observed the horse. And then beyond it in the shadows I saw him.'

Falconer was getting impatient.

'Who?'

'Why, the book thief, of course. Book thief and murderer, it seems. He was bent over picking up an armful of books from the ground where he must have dropped them. Then he scuttled around the back of the church and under the archway over there.' He pointed again. 'It leads straight into the priory grounds.'

Falconer turned to look, and he heard the door behind him slam. Chetwyn was taking no more risk with the murderer or the plague. So he followed the narrow passage that ran along the northern side of the priory church and out to beneath the eastern façade. He could still not get over the quietness of the normally bustling town. It was only a few days since Bullock had imposed the stringent controls on the inhabitants, and de Bosco had agreed to suspend classes. But it was not enough time to have become accustomed to deserted streets, and empty churches.

Falconer stood hesitantly at the west door, then strode inside and up the nave of St Frideswide's. The sound of his feet echoed up into the soaring arches over his head. The interior was gloomier than usual as no candles were burning on the tall holders that stood at intervals along the length of the nave. Falconer heard a rustling sound and thought he saw a movement from behind the high altar. It was there that the shrine of the saint was located. He called out instinctively. Though, if the movement had been caused by the murderer lurking there, it was an incautious thing to do.

'Hello?'

A monkish figure in black emerged from behind the high altar, and came forward until he stood with one hand on the arch of the rood screen. Cursing his poor eyes, Falconer approached cautiously, not wishing to scare off the man as he had done with Chetwyn. This man stood his ground, however, though he looked anxiously at Falconer's approach. As Falconer got closer, he saw the pale, ethereal face of Richard Yaxley, the feretarius or guardian of the shrine. The Augustinian monk, the waxy cast of whose features were a result of a life spent inside the church, spoke up.

'Perhaps we should keep our distance from each other, master.'

Falconer stopped in his tracks for the second time that morning.

'Perhaps so, brother.'

'Do you come seeking solace in the Lord for the horror inflicted on us? I am afraid the prior is not here, though you are welcome to pray alone.'

Falconer, who had long since ceased praying to God for anything, shook his head.

'Thank you, but that is not the reason I have come here now. I wonder. Have you seen any sign of disturbance in the church? Anything that would suggest an intruder has got in?'

Yaxley waved a dismissive hand, while still keeping his distance from Falconer.

'The church is still open for worship, even in these uncertain days. Why should anyone need to break in?'

Falconer looked around, imagining he had heard another noise, but the church was empty still. Fleetingly, he wondered if Richard Yaxley was the thief and murderer. But if so, where had he hoarded the books Chetwyn had seen being carried off? And what about all the other stolen texts? The church was vast and full of secret corners, so it was possible to hide away any number of volumes. Suddenly, Yaxley's nervousness at his presence seemed to have another cause than fear of contagion.

'I was not imagining someone breaking in, but perhaps hiding away in here.'

Yaxley gave a little laugh.

'There are many nooks and crannies, it is true. And you may have read my mind. I was thinking the very same thing, and that is why I am here. I have had the feeling for a few days of a ...' He hunted for the appropriate word. '... a presence in the church. I am frequently here on my own carrying out my duties as the guardian of St Frideswide's remains. But it has only been recently that I have thought someone was watching me.'

Falconer was curious to learn more, though he remained cautious in case the man was the killer he sought, and was merely leading him astray. He took a step forward.

'Explain to me what you mean.'

89

Yaxley disappeared behind the rood screen, and Falconer darted forward in case the monk was fleeing. But as he too went behind the wooden screen, he saw that Yaxley was walking past the high altar. The monk called out to him and went behind the altar.

'It's in here, by the shrine that I feel it.'

Falconer came up close beside him, neither of them thinking any more about the plague and its transmission. The vicinity of the shrine did feel strange, but Falconer thought that was only to do with the sanctity of the place. St Frideswide's coffin was located in the feretory – the area behind the high altar – on a raised platform and enclosed by stone. He looked at the stone tomb, peering through one of the narrow apertures in the side which were cut in the shape of an ornate cross carved within a circle. There were three such openings set evenly in each side of the shrine intended for pilgrims to put their arms through in order to touch the coffin. Even as he looked, he thought he saw a movement inside the shrine.

'What was that?'

Yaxley, who had been looking at Falconer, turned to look.

'What did you see?'

Falconer hesitated, knowing that it was impossible for anyone to be inside the stone tomb. The apertures were too small to allow anyone other than a small child to squeeze in. But he had seen something, and he pointed.

'There, behind the coffin.'

Yaxley's face darkened like thunder clouds.

'Not again.'

'Again?'

The monk was already bending down trying to get his fingers under one of the slabs close to the shrine.

'Help me with this. We have to lift it.'

Falconer saw that the slab was loose and scrabbled to get a grip on its edge. Slowly it shifted, opening up a dark hole below. The monk explained.

'In years gone by, pilgrims were allowed closer proximity to the saint by crawling from the retro-choir here and under the reliquary. There, they could get into the shrine itself through a so-called Holy Hole in the shrine's floor. It has been eighty years since its usage was stopped due to the damage caused to the saint's coffin. Too many hands rubbing away the gilded ornamentation, you see.' He peered down into the darkness. 'But a few years ago some halfwit found this way in, and crawled into the shrine. It caused quite a stir, and nearly had me dismissed from my post.'

Falconer smiled, suddenly recalling the event. He had been present at the time. Why had it not occurred to him? Especially bearing in mind who he had seen in the street the other day.

'I remember now. It was Will Plome, wasn't it? From the troupe of players?'

Yaxley grimaced at the recollection and nodded. He called down the hole.

'If you are there, Will Plome, come out this instant.'

A muffled cry came from the hole, but not a soul emerged. The monk made to climb down, but Falconer stopped him. It would be better if he went into the Holy Hole, rather than the angry Yaxley. The monk shrugged and stood back, and Falconer went down the worn stone steps one at a time. The dim light from above hardly allowed him to see clearly in the chamber below. But when he got to the bottom, he saw the fat shape of Will Plome cowering in one corner. And in the other lay a disorderly pile of books.

Chapter Fourteen

'He said he found the books in the lane.'

Bullock snorted at the presumed naivety of Falconer's comment. They were back in the castle, where Falconer had brought Will Plome. He would have trusted the lad to stay with the other players, but Bullock had insisted on locking him in the crypt of the disused chapel. Now, Falconer and Bullock were once again disagreeing with each other.

'Of course, he would say that. He had a pile of books in his possession that were taken from Edmund Ludlow's chest on the very night the regent master was bashed on the head and killed. And he had blood on his hands. Will Plome has a child's brain. But physically he is a big man, and has the strength to overpower another easily. His thefts have been progressing to towards murder for some time. The death of Bukwode might have been unpremeditated, but once he had the scent of blood in his nostrils, he couldn't stop. Ludlow was hunted out in his bed, and deliberately killed.'

'But why?'

'How do I know? You told me that the books the thief has stolen up to now were contentious books. Magic and science, you said, which are one and the same thing to me. Perhaps not content with merely stealing the books and disposing of them, Plome wanted to destroy the men who had read them. Both Bukwode and Ludlow had their brains bashed in.'

'An interesting theory, Peter, and one that has passed through my mind too. But I just can't see Will Plome hatching it.'

Bullock growled his impatience at Falconer's pedantry. He could never understand why his friend didn't just accept the obvious once in a while. He suddenly felt weary, and slumped down in his chair. With a wave of his aching arm, he questioned Falconer's alternative.

'You would put your money on the disappearing horseman, then?'

Brother Aldwyn, who had been along with Isaac Doukas, silent witness to the debate so far, perked up.

'A horseman, you say?'

He fumbled through the pages of the book he kept constantly to hand. Finding his place, he read out the lines under his finger.

'"Men will suffer most grievously, in order that those born in the country may regain power. He who will achieve these things shall appear as the Man of Bronze, and for long years he shall guard the gates of the town upon a brazen horse."'

He slammed the tome containing the Prophecies of Merlin shut.

'When I saw you bring back that destrier, constable, I was reminded of those lines. With all that armour on it had to be the brazen horse.'

Bullock frowned.

'And the man of bronze? Who is he?'

'The prophecies do not make it clear. It is only later that the 'Prince of Brass' is referred to again. Here ...'

Once more he delved into the tome in his lap.

"Once again the White Dragon shall rise up and will invite over a daughter of Germany. Our little garden will be stocked again with foreign seed, and the Red Dragon will pine away at the far end of the pool. After that the German Worm shall be crowned, and the Prince of brass will be buried."'

Falconer couldn't help but laugh at the nonsense, causing Aldwyn to scowl furiously.

'So you are telling me that my book thief is a chimera, who will guard England for years until the throne is occupied by Germans. I can never imagine that happening.'

It was Doukas's turn to offer a suggestion.

'I think you are right about that. My master – Robert Burnell – is the king's right-hand man, and I don't imagine him recommending that Edward's children be married off to some minor German princeling. But what of the simpleton Constable Bullock has locked away in the chapel? Why do you not think he did it, Master Falconer?'

Falconer looked out of the window on the troupe of players in the courtyard of the castle. Robert Kemp was juggling with three daggers, always neatly catching each one by the hilt. Simon Godrich was sitting with his back against the cart that held all their possessions scratching out some words on a scrap of parchment. Penning a song about Will Plome and murder, perhaps. Margaret and John Peper squatted by the chapel door, deep in discussion. Occasionally, John Peper got very loud and agitated, and Margaret stroked his arm and calmed him again. They would be debating the same thing that Falconer and Bullock were. The culpability of Will Plome. Unfortunately, his interrogation of Will Plome had proved quite unsatisfactory. The simpleton had been quite uncommunicative, and Falconer had got the impression he was afraid. But of what or whom he could not divine, and he had finally given up. Aware they were expecting an answer from him, Falconer returned to the people in the great hall.

'I have known Will a long time. Or more precisely, I met him a long time ago, and have seen him from time to time since, when the players return to Oxford on their tour of the region. He is simple by nature, and I don't believe he could have conceived of such a deeply evil plan.'

Doukas and the priest looked at Bullock for confirmation of Falconer's estimation of the man held in the crypt. Bullock, his head aching, was feeling stubborn, and would not let the matter go, however.

'He is not as you knew him, William. He has learned to read, and has had his head crammed with knowledge too deep for him to fully understand. It has addled his brains.'

He looked his old friend in the eye, harsh thoughts playing in his own head. He allowed himself to give rein to them for once in his long and presently tiring life.

'There are those in the town who believe that too much knowledge can turn a head. That some of the great minds of the university consider themselves able to fathom the workings of God. And there are some who think they are above God in their understanding of the world.'

Falconer knew that the constable was referring to such people as his own dear friend Roger Bacon. The Franciscan friar had immersed himself in the study of astronomy, botany, mathematics, chemistry and even alchemy, the mysterious science that awed and fascinated thinkers. In the end, he probably knew more than any man alive. But all his knowledge had done him no good. He had been locked away from communication with his fellow men by his order, which feared his ferocious intellect. Falconer knew Roger had not accumulated all that knowledge to challenge God, but simply in a burning desire to know all there was to know. He knew the friar's faith in God was not broken by it, but stimulated. It was Falconer himself, with his faulty understanding of the world, who lacked the faith that sustained most of his contemporaries. He realised that that the other three men were still staring at him, expecting some rebuttal of Bullock's accusations. But he had nothing more to say in his defence. He held his hands up in defeat.

'At least Will is safe where he is, innocent or guilty. I suppose I should pay attention to my own obligations, and see that the students in my hall are safe and well.'

Leaving an embarrassed and awkward silence in his wake, he left the castle and walked through a still and quiet town.

*

As darkness fell, he once more prostrated himself before God. This time he knew he had no need to wait for God to speak to him. He had seen Him for himself. His hot and fevered mind was awhirl with images from the previous night. The removal of blasphemous books from the hands of evil men had been until now carried out by his own agency at God's behest. Now God himself had appeared to spirit them away from right under his nose. If he needed a greater confirmation of his actions, he couldn't imagine what it might be. And God had smitten the evildoer into the bargain. His very body burned with righteous fervour, and his throat was dry as dust. Lying face down on the floor making the shape of the cross, he once again marvelled at the mark of favour granted him. He had seen God.

*

Falconer didn't return immediately to Aristotle's Hall, as he said he would. Instead, he sought the opinion of the person he trusted the most when he was perplexed and frustrated. Saphira le Veske was

94

the most unusual woman he had ever met. While being utterly bound up in her Jewishness, she was completely open-minded about the world and all it contained. Falconer often wished the Christian world was as welcoming as hers. Once, Saphira had reminded him of the exhortation in Exodus. He remembered her words now as he walked through Carfax.

'"Thou shalt neither vex a stranger, nor oppress him: for ye were strangers in the land of Egypt.",' she had said. 'We are expected to show hospitality to all, and that doesn't only mean other Jews.'

He had joked then that she had shown him especial hospitality. At the time they were lying together after indulging in that greatest of intimacies that the Church frowned upon when between Jew and Christian. But she had been deadly serious, and didn't rise to his humour.

'I mean it, William. That is why I wish to learn about medicine from Samson. We must share with non-Jews all the benevolent works of a community, including supporting the poor, and visiting the sick.'

Those words came back to him now with a vengeance. He was still afraid that Saphira had put herself at risk in ministering to the crusader, who now lay dead of the pox and buried in the confines of the castle. He knocked on her door, and experienced a momentary shiver up his spine when there was no response immediately. Then he heard her soft tread behind the door, and the swish of her robe. A bolt slid back inside and the door opened. He slipped through the opening, admonishing Saphira.

'You should have asked who it was before unbolting the door.'

Saphira smiled and stroked Falconer's cheek.

'Who else knocks so gently on my door so late at night? Especially on a night when only those on a special mission are stirring because of the pox. But I thank you for your concern.'

She took his hand and led him to the kitchen at the back of the house, where she began to prepare some food for him. It was a house she rented from a cousin, and she had never really made it her own home. She disliked the large great hall, and spent most of her time in the cosier confines of the kitchen, where a fire always burned. It often niggled at Falconer that she gave the impression that Oxford was only a temporary home for her. She had spent most of her life in Aquitaine, where she had effectively run the wine business that was her husband's by right. Her elusive, and by now deceased, husband had been more immersed in the esoteric study of Kabbalah than in his trade, or his wife. Saphira's son, Menahem, now ran the business, though he himself had been drawn to Kabbalah by his father at first. When his father had died, Menahem had disappeared, and Saphira had come to England in search of him. It was then that she had met William Falconer, and eventually settled in Oxford. But in Falconer's mind the state of the house in Fish Street gave the lie to her settling down at all. He kept imagining that one day he would knock on her door, and she would be gone. He would have understood, of course, for what could he offer her other than clandestine trysts and illicit conversations? He was a regent master and nominally celibate and in holy orders.

'What are you thinking, William?'

He realised she had asked him something, and he had not replied. Sitting down close to the fire, he sighed and stretched his long legs.

'Of people and how little I really understand them.'

She looked up from the platter of cold meat and bread she had put together, and pinioned him with her green-eyed gaze.

'That is a very philosophical statement. Who are you thinking of?'

He chose to lie to her, and led his thoughts away from his concerns about her and on to the matter of the murders.

'I thought I knew a young man — a simpleton, but harmless and quite guileless in his way. Now he stands accused of vile crimes that I hardly imagined him capable of.'

He began to lay out before Saphira the complicated tale of the theft of rare and sometimes dangerous books that had escalated into deliberate murder. He explained the theory that the murderer was someone who wished to rid the world of books that in his eyes challenged faith in God. And that in the process he had perhaps progressed to erasing the same knowledge locked in the minds of the owners of those books also.

'Will Plome was discovered in St Frideswide's Church with the books from the last theft, and blood on his hands.'

'But your instinct tells you that he was not the murderer?'

Falconer nodded in reply to Saphira's enquiry, and took the food she had prepared.

'I knew him as a person who cared for the horse that the troupe had to pull their cart in better days. And he took great care of a little monkey he called Ham. I cannot see him beating a man's brains out.'

'Then you should trust your instincts and seek out the real killer.'

Falconer had known that she would cut through the obscuring fog of Bullock's stubbornness and Aldwyn's prophetic maunderings. Though, concerning the latter, he thought there might be an inkling of truth in them. He smiled ruefully.

'All I need to do is find a prince of bronze, who will stand guard at our gates. We have his horse, so perhaps he will come to retrieve it.'

He broke some of the fine white bread and laid a slice of beef on it before hungrily putting it in his mouth. Saphira poured him some of her own red wine, and then sat down opposite him with her own goblet. She took a deep draft, and sighed. Falconer was aware for the first time that she appeared distracted. He wondered if she was feeling ill, and he felt a hand clutching at his heart. He leaned forward in his chair, putting the pewter platter down on the floor.

'Is there anything wrong, Saphira? You're not feeling ... ill, are you?'

She looked at him, at first puzzled by his enquiry. Then she laughed gently.

'No, there is nothing to fear on that matter.' She pulled a face. 'But there is a rumour going around concerning the parliament the king has just called.'

Falconer knew immediately that she meant a rumour circulating amongst the Jews of Oxford. King Edward had shown himself to be, if not exactly an enemy of the Jews, then certainly not a friend. And Jews relied on the king for protection. Many years ago, they had been accepted in England because of their ability to lend money with interest – a practice which was forbidden Christians. Barons, needing to finance armies and go on crusade, made use of the Jews, sometimes to immoderate levels. More recently though, Jewish bonds had been changing hands as richer men bought up poorer landowners' debts with the aim of ousting them from their lands. Edward needed to tax these very men who were being bankrupted to pay his own debts to Italian moneylenders such as the Riccardis. It wasn't difficult to see where the king was proposing to go, and Saphira explained her fellow Jews' worries.

'It is thought that Edward will abolish all the debt, and even stop Jews from lending money altogether. If so, it will be impossible for many to make a living in England.'

The implication for herself and Falconer hung in the air between them like a dark storm cloud. What he feared the most seemed to be coming to fruition. He hesitated a while, but then asked the question foremost on his mind.

'What will you do?'

Her face took on a solemn cast.

'It may come to the point where what I wish to do is irrelevant. If we are no longer of use to the king, we may be expelled from England.'

Chapter Fifteen

The Feast of St Hygbald, 18th September

Whenever Edward was vexed he resorted to his precious copy of *"The Histories of the Kings of Britain"*. And he was particularly vexed right now. Robert Burnell had nothing to report on the situation in Oxford due to its self-imposed isolation. Burnell's creature was supposed to resolve the problem the king had with all due haste. But the outbreak of pox had thrown a veil over the proceedings. Eleanor was avoiding him, as she always did when she was big with child. Not that she was all that large yet, being no more than three months gone, if the physicks were to be trusted. He suspected she was just keeping out of his way because of his bad mood, not realising she was making matters worse by doing so. No, he had to admit the root cause was firstly the problems with the Jews, and secondly his confrontation with Llewellyn and the Welsh nation generally. So he had shut himself away in his private solar at Woodstock and placed Geoffrey of Monmouth's book on his reading stand. Four lit candles cast an extravagant light on the pages. He first opened it at one of his favourite passages describing tourneys and games such as he used to indulge in himself. He traced his finger along the page, which was already stained with this repeated act, and read out loud Geoffrey's description of King Arthur's tourney.

> *'Presently the knights engage in a game on horseback, making show of fighting a battle whilst the dames and damsels looking on do cheer them on for the sake of seeing the better sport. Others elsewhere spend the day in shooting arrows, some in tilting with spears, some in flinging heavy stones, some in putting the weight.'*

Earlier that year he had taken part in a tournament in France that some had dubbed the "Little Battle of Châlons". A French count had all but tried to murder him during it, and the courtly battle had degenerated into a full skirmish. Even the thought of it now stirred his blood, and he turned the pages to read another favourite passage – Arthur's encounter with a giant. Once more the stain of his passing finger marked the passage.

> *'Arthur, swiftly bestirring him with his sword, hacked the accursed monster first in one place and then in another, and gave him no respite until at last he smote him a deadly buffet on the head, and buried the whole breadth of his sword in his brain-pan.'*

Mimicking Arthur's action, Edward swung his sword arm down in the killing blow. He almost felt the judder up his arm as the sword's arc was stopped by the giant's skull. He gasped in satisfaction.

'You know, my Lord, that scholars say that Geoffrey's book is mere fancy. A fantasist's desire to raise his fellow Welshmen up from their lowly and ignorant status to the heights of founders of Britain. That he should portray Arthur as a Briton who fought against our Anglo-Saxon forefathers was unforgiveable.'

Edward hadn't heard his chancellor, Robert Burnell, entering his chamber. The damned fellow sneaked hither and thither without even disturbing the air he breathed. Indeed Edward wondered if he even did that as breathing was the pursuit of a normal man. Burnell appeared to be a wraith.

'Yes, yes, I know. William of Newburgh was at pains to say so fifty years after the book became known. But his opinion matters not a jot. Too many people wanted it to be true for any petulant scholar to ruin its appeal. But that is why I wanted to talk to you, Burnell.'

For once his chancellor was confused.

'What is, my Lord?'

Edward smiled easily at the thought he had kept Burnell on the hop.

'I want to go to Glastonbury before I take any action against the Welsh.'

Edward's intentions appeared to dawn on Burnell, who smiled.

'Ah. Just as your great-grandfather, Henry, saw a benefit in the monks at Glastonbury finding the skeletons of Arthur and Guivenere, you too wish to lay the ghost of the legendary king.'

'Yes. Henry had his own problems with the Welsh at the time, and a skeleton of Arthur was proof positive that he was dead, and could not rise again as the legend goes to help the Britons or the Welsh in their hour of need. I need to do the same.'

Edward closed his favourite book firmly and doused a couple of the candles with the flat of his hand. No point in wasting good candles on Burnell, who could probably see in the dark anyway. The two extinguished wicks streamed smoke for a while, leaving the distinctive smell of wax in the air of the room. Burnell remained standing by the door through which he had entered, his hands clasped over his stomach. His voice, when he spoke, was quiet and unemotional.

'If you ordered Arthur's tomb to be opened, you would reveal the wondrous large bones of the king, and those of Guinevere of marvellous beauty. I suggest it be done at twilight to heighten the dramatic effect. Then you and the queen could wrap the bones in silk and have them reinterred, leaving the skulls on permanent display outside the tomb on account of popular devotion.'

Edward paused a moment, seeing how perfect such a ceremony would be. Then he sighed. Burnell's account of what could be done at Glastonbury was so clever, he realised that his chancellor had planned it long ago. Long before Edward had even thought of the ploy. He had not caught Burnell out after all, and would have to find some other way of disconcerting the man.

'Tell me about matters in Oxford.'

*

Eventually, Falconer managed to have a talk with Geoffrey Westhalf concerning what he might or might not have heard on the night Edmund Ludlow was murdered. He had been surprised to discover that the youth had returned to his lodgings in Beke's Inn. He had at first knocked on the door of Nevill's Inn next door, expecting Westhalf to be there still. He had half assumed he would have to badger Chetwyn into allowing him to see the boy. The last time they had spoken, Chetwyn seemed to think Falconer should not bother Westhalf due to the moneyed nature of his father. The shutter at the upper window of Nevill's Inn opened in response to his knocking, and he squinted upwards. The head of Robert Chetwyn hung out of the window staring down suspiciously at him.

'What do you want, Falconer?'

'To speak with Geoffrey Westhalf, if I may.'

'You know my opinion on that. However, the decision as to whether you can speak to him or not, is no longer in my hands.'

'Oh, why is that?'

'Because the boy no longer resides in Nevill's Inn.'

Without further explanation, the head bobbed back inside and the shutter slammed to. With no more information as to Westhalf's actual whereabouts, Falconer resorted to the only other option he had. With the town gates closed, Westhalf could only have gone to one other place, even if it was a bizarre relocation. He walked the few paces to Beke's Inn, and once again knocked. After a short silence, he heard the sound of booted feet approaching the other side of the solid door. A voice called sharply out.

'Who is there?'

'Geoffrey Westhalf? It is Regent Master Falconer. I have come with the agreement of the constable to speak to you about the other night.'

There was a long pause, and Falconer was just about to speak again, when he heard a bolt being withdrawn, and the door creaked open. Westhalf looked pale and he glared at Falconer suspiciously.

'What do you want ... sir?'

He added the final word almost as an afterthought, and Falconer reacted to the insolence.

'I am here to seek the truth concerning Edmund Ludlow's murder, Westhalf. Which you would do well to remember.'

The young man's eyes glittered with the heat of some inner passion.

'Which truth is that, master? The conjunctive or disjunctive truth?'

Falconer was disconcerted for a moment, until he recalled his last encounter with Westhalf in his class on *sophisma*. So much had happened since that he had forgotten the confrontation between Westhalf and Peter Mithian. The intellectual puzzle set by Falconer had resulted in Westhalf being called a donkey. Clearly the young man before him had taken the joke to heart so much that it had seethed in his breast and grown to something unbearable. But Falconer was not to be diverted from his task by the feelings of this overwrought youth.

'A sophism is merely one way to come to the truth by examination. So let us examine the facts about Master Ludlow's death.'

Westhalf pulled a sneering face, but stood his ground at the half-open door. He clearly had no intention of allowing Falconer in, so the regent master continued the conversation from where he stood. If Westhalf was fearful of being in close proximity to another person, it was not an uncommon feeling at present.

'What did you hear the night that your master was murdered?'

The youth's eyes were cast down, as if he was plundering his memory and trying to dredge up whatever he could. He held back so long that Falconer thought he had decided not to speak. Then he raised his red-rimmed eyes to the regent master and replied.

'I heard nothing until I awoke, and then I heard horse's hooves in the lane. I thought it was perhaps the sound that had awoken me. With the plague abroad, it was odd to hear anything outside at all, and I got up.'

He paused, and Falconer urged him to continue, though the look in the boy's eyes as he recalled that night was of fear. No, perhaps not fear but awe.

'I sleep at the back of the house behind the hall. I heard another sound like the passage of angels, and got up to see.'

'Angels? What sound do angels make?'

Falconer was beginning to be sceptical of the youth's account. He was clearly overexcited still, and ascribing the most mystical of causes to the sound of the fleeing murderer. Westhalf's look hardened at the obvious expression of disbelief from the regent master. He blushed and muttered his reply.

'A whispering sound that no earthly step could imitate.'

Falconer thought that in his experience a good thief could glide over strewn floor rushes and not disturb them much. But he did not say as such, and Westhalf concluded his account.

'I peeped through the archway into the hall, but there was no-one to be seen. It was then I saw the blood dripping from above. A rain of blood from the solar where Master Ludlow was sleeping.'

He glanced nervously over his shoulder back into the darkness of the hall behind him. He must have been remembering the sight of the blood, and thinking of angels. In his present condition, Falconer doubted that the youth should be staying where he was. But when he offered to take Westhalf to the castle instead, the youth went pale and clutched the frame of the door.

'No! It is not safe. I saw ...'

'You saw what?'

Geoffrey Westhalf lowered his eyes, and shook his head.

'I saw nothing.'

Then the door was closed, and he was gone.

*

'He sounded afraid to be where he was, and yet more afraid to come out into the streets. And who could blame him at the moment.'

This was Bullock's sensible comment on hearing Falconer summation of Westhalf's story. Doukas laid his quill down, and pushed his parchment aside for the ink to dry. He had made careful note of

Westhalf's evidence as he had done with everything that had happened since his enforced incarceration in the town. He had asserted that his master, Chancellor Burnell, would wish to know everything concerning the thefts and subsequent sequence of murders. But as Falconer scanned the spidery script of the Greek, he wondered what story would emerge from the series of notes. Doukas was offering no opinion on who might be the killer, though he already had a pouch full of scribbled interviews. Perhaps William de Bosco's tenure at the university was due to come to a close soon. That thought reminded Falconer that he owed the university chancellor an update on what he had discovered about the spate of thefts and murders. Even if the only fact was that Constable Bullock suspected a simple-minded member of a troupe of actors, acrobats and musicians of being the perpetrator. He wished he had more to tell de Bosco, and slumped by the fire in Bullock's great hall.

The shadows of evening stretched across the rough stone floor, and Doukas turned to Aldwyn, who sat beneath the west-facing window to catch the last rays of the setting sun.

'What do the prophecies tell us, brother monk?'

Doukas's rough, accented voice roused the elderly monk from his reverie, and he eagerly flicked the heavy pages of Geoffrey of Monmouth's tome.

'I had been pondering that question, master scribe, and seeking to interpret the riddles Merlin presents us with. The Man of Bronze has put in an appearance, and none can deny the probable truth of the line, *"Death will lay hold of the people and destroy all the nations"*. Some in the past thought that referred to the end of the world, but we can now see it is specifically about Oxford. The nations that the students at the university divide themselves into stand to be destroyed, if the plague takes a hold.'

Falconer interrupted the monk's doom-laden maunderings.

'But it has not yet happened, thanks to Peter's actions.'

He glanced over at Bullock, who appeared to be asleep in his chair. Aldwyn waved aside Falconer's protests, however.

'We shall soon see about that.' He tapped a bony finger on the page of the book. 'Each prophecy has come true so far.'

Doukas chuckled.

'Then read on, Aldwyn, and tell us what is to come next.'

'That is what I was about to do, Greekling. And it has come already, if I read the meaning right.'

Falconer was becoming increasingly frustrated at these mystical pronouncements of the monk's.

'What has already come about?'

Aldwyn lowered his eyes to the book in his lap, and by the red glow of the dying sun recited the next lines.

"The North Wind will rise, snatching away the flowers which the West Wind has caused to bloom. There will be gilding in the temples ..."'

'What on earth does that mean? It's gibberish.'

Aldwyn glared at Falconer.

'It is obvious that the North Wind represents the cleansing air of piety that is blowing away the growing evil of spurious knowledge that certain minds have nurtured in order to challenge God's creation.'

Falconer thought of Fulbert's condemnation of people like himself and Roger Bacon and their thirst for empirical knowledge. He wanted to challenge Aldwyn, but the monk was in full flow.

The gilding of the temple refers to this wrapping of alchemy and science in appealing garlands. But the next prophecy is to be heeded well.' He took a deep breath. ' *"But the sword's cutting edge will not cease its work."* '

*

The crypt was cold place at night, but Will Plome was used to hiding away in the Holy Hole in St Frideswide's Church, so this was like home to him. He lay curled up in a corner on a sack of straw that the constable had thrown in after him. Then the old man had locked the door. Since then, only Agnes had come to see how he was. She told him that John Peper and the others were angry with him for not doing what he had been sent to do.

'But I was busy, Agnes. I had other things to do.'

'Like stealing books?'

Agnes couldn't bring herself to say the other word expressing what Will was also accused of.

'I found them, Agnes. Really I did. I couldn't leave them on the ground where they were.'

Agnes's sigh from the other side of the solid door made Will realise that even she didn't believe him. And soon she wasn't there any more, and he was alone again for a long time. He dozed off, but then a sound woke him up. He listened for a while, imagining he could hear rustling outside the door. He tried a little whisper, scared of who it might be.

'Is that you, Agnes?'

There was no reply, and he was going to call out a little louder, when he heard a creaking sound. He looked, and saw the door swing slowly open. He clutched his knees and hugged them up to his chest. He was mortally afraid now. But no-one came in, and soon he was emboldened enough to crawl across the damp floor of the crypt. He peeped around the door, and saw a pair of legs at the top of the stone steps that led down to where he had been imprisoned. They were encased in sturdy boots with mud on the heels. He couldn't see the body that was atop the legs, and he crawled through the open door to get a better look. As he did so, the person turned and moved away, so all he could see was still the booted legs. He felt impelled to follow, and cautiously got to his feet, and made his way up the steps. At the top of the steps stood another open door, which he knew led out into the castle courtyard. He ventured up to it, and risked a glance out. A dark figure stood with its back to him on the other side of the yard, close to the gate that led out into the town. Clouds scudded across the moon, and made it difficult to see who it was. He rubbed his eyes, but when he looked again, he couldn't see the figure at all. He tiptoed across the yard towards the open gate, not sure if he should take advantage of his freedom, or stay safely in the crypt. Then he heard a low moan from behind him.

Swinging round, his heart in his mouth, he saw that the same figure had somehow got to his back. A silvery beam of light shone through a break in the cloud, and he saw a face at last. Dark, with staring eyes and exposed teeth, it made him shudder with half-recognition. He hesitated, but the outline of the horns sticking out from its forehead made him certain it was the Devil that was calling him onwards. His heart pounding, he took to his heels and ran.

Chapter Sixteen

Early hours of the Feast of St Theodore, 19th September.

Master Gerard Anwell felt his full seventy years. The night was chill, and his bones ached at the very thought of another winter. He no longer taught at the university, finding the task of plodding through the basics of the trivium – grammar, logic and rhetoric – with dull, young clerks tedious in the extreme. The quadrivium was only marginally less excruciating. Arithmetic, astronomy, geometry and music could be worthwhile topics to study, but not with the stumbling idiots who seemed to populate the schools of the university nowadays. No, he had given all that up to devote himself to the study of pure knowledge. In his tiny back room that he rented with his dwindling funds from Mistress Dockerel who ran the brothel next door, he surrounded himself with texts that few could decipher. No longer content with the stilted Latin translations of Aristotle and the like, he had taught himself Greek, Hebrew, Chaldean and Arabic. Now, he read texts where he could get them in the original. Even then, he eschewed the authorities approved by the church, confining himself to reading such esoteric texts as he could lay his hands on. These included such nonreligious authors as Galen, Maimonides, Ptolemy, Hippocrates, Abraham ibn Ezra and Samuel ibn Tibbon.

Recently the Jewish Kabbalah intrigued him, but he dare not tell anyone of his interest. Studying Hebrew texts was frowned upon by the university and the church both. He had made some indirect approaches to scholars who also were of an enquiring nature and might have helped him trace the works he sought. Edmund Ludlow, a fellow Welshman, had promised to find out more for him, but had not come back to him for a few days. He wondered why that was, and cursed his one-time friend for ignoring him. As Anwell rarely left his room, and had certainly not stirred himself in order to attend the Black Congregation, where his joints would have ossified with the cold, he was quite unaware that Ludlow was dead. Or that a thief was plundering texts of the very sort that Anwell himself cherished. He had barely acknowledged the pox that ran through the streets of Oxford. He didn't have contact with a soul from one day to the next, other than with Sal who collected his rent weekly and brought him some food at the same time. He was content to immerse himself in scholarship, and especially liked the ornate decoration of some of the Christian texts he owned, where the rich reds, blues and yellows were offset with lettering in gold leaf. Some of his precious Arabic and Hebrew texts were similarly decorated with geometric patterns in gold.

As the cold of the night set in, and he remained unable to sleep, he wrapped his fur-trimmed gown around him, lit another candle, and opened his favourite work, Maimonides's philosophical treatise, *Guide to the Perplexed*. As the candle grew lower, and the wax dribbled over the base of the pewter stick that held it, Gerard Anwell's eyes began to tire. The Arabic text on the parchment began to swirl and stretch so that it became a long, undecipherable string for a while. He screwed up his eyes and when he looked again, the text had returned to legibility. But then it happened again, only this time Anwell's weary, old eyes drooped and refused to focus.

He awoke with a start, not sure if he had slept for long or merely dozed off for a moment. He looked at the candle, which was still alight but was no more than a blackened stub of wick in a misshapen mass of wax dribbling off the edge of the table so that it resembled the hand of an old man with long fingers dangling down to the floor. He estimated that he must have slept for some time. Then he heard a noise, and realised that it had been a similar sound that had awoken him. He shook his head to clear his senses, and he looked round behind him where the noise had come from. He heard a door creak open, felt a breeze on his cheek, and the remains of the candle guttered and went out. He thought the intruder might be Sal Dockerel come to collect the rent, but then remembered she had only done so a couple of days earlier. Fear gripped his heart and he tried to call out, hoping that his landlady might hear him. But that was a forlorn hope, and his throat was dry anyway. All he could manage was a croaking sound.

'Who is that?'

The dark shape loomed over him, and he saw the silver light of the moon catching on a blade that swung towards his neck. The blow, when it came, made him choke and gurgle. But only for a moment, then he was dead.

*

Having spent a celibate night in Aristotle's Hall with his mind tossing backwards and forwards theories of Will Plome's guilt or innocence, Falconer was anxious to talk to Bullock again. As he entered the castle courtyard, he was surprised to find a scene of some confusion. The members of the players' troupe were standing in a group debating anxiously amongst themselves, while the constable was poking at their possessions with his trusty sword. As he prodded the cart in which were piled all their precious props for mounting scenes from morality plays, John Peper jumped forward.

'Take care, Bullock. There are irreplaceable items in there.'

Bullock snarled, and continued to poke away. Peper was so anxious he tried to stay the destruction by grabbing the constable's arm. Bullock, despite the disparity in their ages, easily threw the actor off. Peper fell back on his arse complaining.

'How could Will be in there? It's too small to hide him.'

The other members of the troupe were aghast at their leader's treatment, and Robert Kemp was emboldened enough to step forward. But Falconer strode across the courtyard and interposed his body between the protagonists. He threw a warning look at Kemp, and then turned to address Bullock.

'What is going on here, Peter? Why should Will Plome be hiding somewhere in the yard?'

Bullock scowled, casting a look around the group of players.

'Because someone released him from the crypt last night, and I don't doubt it was one of his friends here.'

This accusation raised a howl of protest from Peper's troupe, words that were cut across by a harsh but controlled voice with a foreign accent.

'If you didn't free your friend, then why not show your allegiance to the law and go and find him.'

Isaac Doukas strolled out of the shaded archway leading into the stronghold that was the tower. He stuck his thumbs in his broad leather belt, and tossed his head in the direction of the gateway to the town.

'Go and find him before he gets into any more trouble.'

John Peper picked himself up off the ground, and looked to be ready to attack Peter Bullock again. But the wiser head of Agnes Cheke prevailed. The old woman screwed her wrinkled face up in what passed in the circumstances for a grin, and diverted Peper's attention.

'The foreigner is right, John. We can best help Will by finding him before either he does something silly, or ...' She stopped and stared hard at the constable. '... or the real murderer kills again, leaving Will accused of a new crime.'

Bullock growled, but sheathed his sword, and the tension in the air eased. Simon Godrich strolled casually away from the constable singing gently under his breath.

'He that courts a pretty girl, courts her for his pleasure.

He is a fool, if he marries her without store or treasure.'

Robert Kemp linked arms with him and joined in the second verse.

'He that drinks strong beer, and goes to bed mellow,

Lives as he ought to live, and dies a hearty fellow.'

Peper was still red-faced and angry, but followed his compatriots, and the awkward moment was over. The troupe of players gathered by the castle gate, and planned their search of Oxford. Falconer looked at Bullock, who shrugged his shoulders and signalled for his friend to follow him into the castle keep.

*

The next few days witnessed a strange revival in the life of Oxford. Not that anything returned to normal – such a rebirth was not yet possible. The whole town knew – because the rumour had spread like wildfire – that the red plague took ten days before it might reveal itself again. The cursed evil was seen to linger in doorways, and trickle down drainage gulleys. It hovered in the very air, and would sneak in open windows, if it were allowed. Then the rumour was somehow

107

born that it was a Jew who had said all this. And if he knew how long it took to fester before it broke out again, then he must be responsible for its existence in the first place. From that surmise it was only a short step to the conviction that it was all therefore a Hebrew plot to ruin the business of the town, cutting off the market from its customers, and starving the population. On Saturday – the Jews' holy day – Peter Bullock had to use force to disperse a gang of four men, who had broken the curfew and taken it into their heads to try and break into Simeon's house on the corner of Fish Street and Jewry Lane.

Martin Durham, the ring-leader of the gang that was made up of his three sons, had been convinced that Simeon was hoarding food. He knew that the Jews went to the synagogue on Saturdays because he rented his house at the other end of the lane from Jacob and Cresse. It would be a perfect time to break in and steal the food. Unfortunately, Simeon, like all the other Jews, was observing the proscription on assembly, and was at home with his family. Martin had got no further than damaging the sturdy lock on Simeon's front door, before Samuel across the street had seen the rumpus and raised the alarm. His own boy was despatched secretly but with speed to fetch the constable.

Bullock, together with Isaac Doukas, who had offered his help, was soon on the scene. He threatened to lock the whole Durham family up, if they did not return to their own home. Durham, faced with the constable and some swarthy individual with authority written all over his face, backed down, and then complained about their straitened circumstances.

'We are starving and have nothing in the larder.'

Bullock knew that the main reason why Mistress Durham had nothing in reserve was that her husband, Martin, drank away most of the money he earned as a mason. His wife had precious little food to last them from one pay day to the next, let alone during a siege laid by an invisible enemy like the pox.

'Go to the bakery at the other end of this street. Simon will let you have a loaf on the promise of payment. Tell him I sent you. Then get home and stay home.'

Durham slouched away grumbling under his breath, and was followed by his three growing and pinch-faced sons. Bullock hoped the man would pay his dues afterwards, or Simon would be complaining to him soon enough about the mason's arrears. As the constable and Doukas walked back to the castle, it became evident that others were running out of food. Shadowy figures lurked in doorways, waiting until they had gone past before sneaking out to buy what provisions they could find. As they went down Pennyfarthing Street, a woman approaching them crossed to the other side of the street to be as far away from them as possible. She nervously nodded her head at the constable, held her hand to her mouth, and scurried on past. On any other day, Bullock might have been hailed, and drawn into a conversation. Today he, like any other person abroad, was shunned for fear of being a bearer of the pox.

And so it was for the next day and the next. Fearful figures sneaked along lanes, carefully avoiding anyone else in a terrible parody of the crowds that would normally have filled these streets. A few days ago, people would rub against each other, shoulder to shoulder, not caring one bit if they were jostled. Now, the widest berth was afforded, and if there was no reason to be outside, everyone stayed indoors. And even there, a sneeze was viewed with suspicion, and the offender was ostracised as far as the narrow confines of the houses in Oxford permitted. Families lived cheek by jowl, so a wife could not avoid her husband, or a father his children. But any sign of illness in anyone was occasion for the victim to be closely watched from a distance. The mood in every single home was therefore tense, and it was no surprise that such circumstances bred resentment and a need to apportion blame.

Chapter Seventeen

The Feast of St Maurice, Sunday, 22nd September

Saphira was at the home of Samson, and Falconer had joined them. Will Plome had not been found, and his hunt for an alternative suspect had got him nowhere. So when Saphira had asked him to join them to talk about a suitable strategy in their combating the pox, he had readily agreed. He was fascinated that the doctor's room was filled like his with vials and pots, and a mixture of sweet scents overlaid with a faint, but still noisome, stink. Samson, more so than even the ever curious Falconer, obviously distilled various preparations, for stained glass alembics stood beside a small furnace with its own set of bellows. But all these possible distractions did not at this time divert Falconer from the task in hand. It was less than ten days since Hugo de Wolfson had been found by Thomas Dagville, and examined by Samson and Saphira. That was a fixed point in the calendar of the development of the red plague in Oxford. Much of the rest was uncertain, however. Where de Wolfson had gone, and whom he had come into contact with was unclear. But the exact date of the crusader's arrival in Oxford could be verified by Falconer.

'He almost ran me down at East Gate. It was the twelfth day of September.'

Samson frowned.

'You can be certain it was him?'

'Yes. It's not every day that a well-built knight with a tanned face that has been exposed to the sun of Outremer comes to Oxford. Besides, I saw his horse at close quarters. It is the same one that was found wandering the lanes close to Beke's Inn the other night.'

Saphira laid her hand on his arm.

'The one that convinced the monk staying at the castle of his Prince of Bronze prophecy? But how did it get free?'

Falconer shrugged his shoulders.

'It was the very same. But I can't answer your other question. Dagville says it was still in his stable after de Wolfson's body was removed. He had intended to sell it to defray the costs incurred by the knight. How it got dressed in all its armour and set free in Shidyerd Street is a mystery.'

Samson made a suggestion.

'Perhaps the monk did it to help fulfil this prophecy you mention.'

'It's possible. But Aldwyn is quite old, and truly believes in Merlin's Prophecies. He wouldn't have need to create proof — it would be manifest as far as he was concerned.'

Samson peered at Falconer, a sceptical look on his face.

'Like the miracles of Christian saints, and the ... the discovery at Glastonbury nigh on a hundred years ago of the bones of King Arthur, just when King Edward's great-grandfather wanted to show that the mythical king was dead and would not return to aid the Welsh?'

Falconer laughed out loud.

'You are right. And in the same circumstances as now, for it is just at a time when Henry was trying to crush Welsh ambition. But to get back to the point, you may be right. Aldwyn may have helped his prophecies along a little.'

Saphira was frustrated by all the wild speculation. She was more anxious to get back to the reason for their meeting that morning.

'If the crusader knight arrived ten days ago, then he could have passed on his pox to others in the town soon after that. If he did then some will show signs from tomorrow perhaps.' She turned to Samson. 'What will they be – these signs?'

Samson began to explain.

'Ten days may be a little early, but the signs are fever, headaches and muscle pains. The victim will also feel nauseous and will vomit. Quite soon after that, visible lesions will appear in the mouth and on the tongue and throat such as you saw with the crusader. That is what we must look out for.'

Falconer wondered if anyone in the town would reveal to Peter Bullock a member of their family showing those symptoms. Or if they would keep it quiet. Nobody wanted their house marked as a plague house.

'I questioned the Dagvilles concerning de Wolfson's movements, but I fear I could not get much information from them. When he was in the inn, he kept pretty much to himself, which is lucky for the drunkards who usually frequent that place. But Thomas Dagville did say that de Wolfson was complaining of aches and pains, and he told him to consult Will Spicer in Kepeharm Lane.'

Samson grunted in a way that showed his low opinion of the apothecary.

'I would rather suffer in silence from whatever ailment had cursed me than ask Spicer for a cure. I have seen some of his work brought me by his long-suffering patients. One who complained of shortness of breath was told to put the lung of a fox in sweetened wine and drink it. He was sick. Another had a pricking sensation in his left eye and consulted Spicer. As a result, he walked around for days with a left eye plucked from a dog bound to his own. It took a lot of ointment to salve the resultant soreness. Spicer is such a danger that I might even have hoped that de Wolfson did infect the man to rid us of such a fool.'

Falconer shook his head.

'He didn't. I spoke to Spicer, and he couldn't recall anyone like the crusader coming to consult him recently.'

'A pity.'

'The only thing that Dagville could tell me was that de Wolfson returned to the inn later in the day, and made a contented comment about ...' Falconer glanced at Saphira furtively. '... about satisfying his lusts in Grope Lane.'

111

Saphira grinned at William's obvious embarrassment. But Samson was not happy about the revelation.

Then not only could he have spent the day wandering around the market passing on the red plague to almost anyone, he is sure to have given it to a poor doxy in one of the establishments there. Such an intimate contact would be certain to pass on the disease. We should get the constable to check with all the brothels for signs of illness. If men are still going there, the pox could easily be passed on again and again.'

Falconer nodded in agreement.

'I will see Peter immediately. We should have thought to have him close such places down straight away, but we only thought about public places not such houses of personal contact.'

Saphira rose from her chair.

'I will come with you, and perhaps Peter will allow me to examine the women for signs of the disease.'

Falconer's lipped tightened, but he knew there was no use in forbidding such a dangerous act. Saphira was a woman who knew her own mind, and they had argued before about his protectiveness. He could only hope that Bullock would forbid her, or that the brothel-keepers would deny her access. No madam would want her place to be seen as a home of the pox. Leaving Samson to plan what could be done should the red plague spread, Falconer and Saphira Le Veske hurried through the quiet streets of Oxford towards the castle.

*

Inside St George's Tower, which was hardly illuminated by the fire and a few candles even though it was bright daylight outside, Aldwyn knelt in prayer. His book of prophecies was close at hand still. Doukas was sitting at the large table that he had appropriated for making his notes. When he saw Falconer and Saphira enter, he dipped his quill in the ink pot, as if making ready to record the events of the morning. Bullock stared at him, a defeated look in his eyes. Whatever the outcome of this strange time in the life of the town, he had a feeling in his bones that it would not be a good one for him. In fact, he saw no future for himself – nothing but a dark, yawning pit. He closed his eyes and wished it all would just disappear – his worries, his fears, the town and all the responsibilities it loaded on his shoulders.

'Peter, did you hear what I said?'

Bullock sighed, and turned to Falconer, who had been telling him something that he felt sure he didn't want to hear.

'Something about the brothels in Grope Lane.'

Falconer's face had a look of deep concern.

'Yes. We think that de Wolfson went to one of them the day after he arrived in Oxford. If so, there could be a woman there who will pass on the plague to any other man who lies with her.'

'I don't think any man has been down Grope Lane since I set the curfew. Anyone with a wife would not be able to escape his lady's gaze when everyone's movement is closely observed in case they show signs of the plague. But it would be wise to find this trollop, and seal her off from human contact.'

Saphira spoke up, as Falconer had expected her to.

'I could go down the lane and check the women for the signs of red plague. It would be easier for me than a man.'

Falconer was about to suggest to Bullock that Samson would be a wiser choice, but he was too late. Bullock patted Saphira's shoulder gratefully.

'I agree. And you know how to protect yourself from the dangers of the plague. I saw how you masked your face when you attended the crusader. I accept your offer with gratitude.'

Falconer gritted his teeth, thinking that a few years ago Bullock would never have put a woman in the way of any danger. But today his friend looked tired, and ready to accept any help. Not that he blamed him. The whole situation was a great burden. He just wished it was not Saphira who was the logical choice. Bullock made another suggestion about how to isolate the woman, if she were found.

'I have been thinking about where to put those who we find are infected with the plague. Brother Aldwyn, here ...' He indicated the monk, who had finished his prayers and was once again attending to the conversation. '... suggested that we use Bartlemas hospital.'

The old monk nodded his head eagerly.

'Yes, the last time I was there, there was only one inmate, who can be moved easily to make way for the infected. After all, it once served as a place for lepers, and is outside the walls. Those who remain inside the town will be pleased to see any potential source of infection being moved away from them.'

Bullock slapped a hand down on the table, causing Doukas to steady his ink pot and glare.

'Good. It is settled then. I can get someone from outside the walls to take a message to Oseney Abbey to let them know. And I shall get Thomas Burewald to accompany you, Mistress Le Veske. He will ensure that none of the brothel madams object to your work, and I can trust him not to get ... distracted. His wife is a ferocious woman.'

He smiled at his characterisation of Mistress Burewald. But he was lucky he didn't say what he did a few moments later, for Burewald himself suddenly burst in the hall. His face was aghast, his lips tight.

'Constable Bullock. The Grey Friars have put word out that they are holding a prayer meeting in their friary for anyone in the town who cares to attend. They are going to defy your curfew, and I have seen several people on their way to their church already.'

Bullock groaned and prised himself up from the comfort of his chair. He saw the dark pit opening up before him.

*

It was but a few hurried steps from the portico of the castle to the entrance of the Franciscan friary. The church, built in the very walls of the town, had a large nave that was a public preaching hall for the friars. Their own services were conducted in the greater calm and intimacy of the choir to the east. When Bullock, accompanied by Doukas and Falconer, arrived at the town entrance, the assembly had already begun. Some fifty people from the town had gathered, and were seated on benches listening to a sermon from a young Franciscan. Falconer recognised him immediately. It was Friar Fulbert, and his sermon – more of a harangue really – followed closely the tenor of the harsh words he had used when Falconer had last seen him.

'St Francis told his first followers – "I admonish and exhort the brothers in the Lord Jesus Christ to beware of all pride, vainglory, envy, avarice, worldly care and concern, criticism and complaint. And I admonish the illiterate not to worry about studying but to realize instead that above all they should wish to have the spirit of the Lord working within them."'

Bullock was about to move forward into the main part of the nave and put a stop to this, but Falconer's curiosity got the better of him. He put up a hand to restrain the constable, having in the back of his mind the thought that Fulbert might incriminate himself over the thefts and murders.

'Let us hear what he has to say first.'

Bullock grunted in irritation, but held back. Fulbert, his burning eyes suddenly staring directly at the small band of men who had just entered the church, carried on.

'He also said that a day would come when men would throw their books out of the window as useless. That time has come. This plague has been sent as a punishment on the town for those who set themselves up against God, priding themselves in knowing more and more about God's world. The constable will not tell you, but even now an avenging angel is walking the streets destroying those who imagine themselves cleverer than God.'

There was a buzz of shocked comment from the assembly of townsfolk, who never needed much provocation to launch an attack on the members of the university. So many hard-working people resented what they saw as the privileges enjoyed by the students and their mentors. Some now followed Fulbert's eyes and turned in their seats to see what he was staring at. They saw Bullock at the back of the church along with a master of the university and a swarthy foreigner, who might well be a Jew. The mood of the townsfolk was changing, and the Franciscan was relentless.

'But God has said that the deaths of a few are not enough. He has sent the red plague in order to clean out the whole town. Two killers stalk the streets of Oxford – the plague and an avenging angel. Your only salvation lies in driving the vainglorious and the foreigners out.'

Fulbert's gaze was pinned precisely on Falconer, when he said those final words. The buzz of whispered comments rose to a scandalised rumble, and Falconer could see a few of the men present were ready to rise up and riot. Someone needed to act quickly, and Bullock responded in the only way he knew how. Even though they were in church, he drew his sword from its sheath, causing a frightening hissing sound. For added emphasis he struck it on the stone slabs of the church floor. It rang ominously – a clear warning to all those assembled. Everyone's eyes were now on him, and not on Fulbert. Though Falconer knew how soul-weary his friend was, the constable's body seemed to grow in stature, and his voice rang out firmly and loudly.

'Everyone here is in breach of my curfew, and is risking not only his own life but the lives of others. I have seen the red plague, and I know how it leaps from one man to the next. Any one of you could be infected and even now be passing the pox on to the person sitting next to them.'

Falconer could see people shifting nervously on their benches, trying to edge themselves away from those either side of them. One or two men and women at the back of the church were already getting up and making for the door out into the street. Bullock called out to them as they sneaked past him.

'Will Mossop, Agnes Brown, Peter Withey, I see you.'

He turned to glare at the rest of those present, and cocked a thumb at the dark-skinned man next to him.

'Isaac Doukas, here, is a scribe and will note down all your names, and if the red plague comes to your door, we will know why.'

Doukas made a play of getting his quill and ink out of his satchel, and began to scratch out on the parchment's surface. He didn't know anyone of course, but Bullock began calling the names out one by one. Soon enough, the once agitated congregation melted away like ice on a pond when the sun strikes it. When his congregation had disappeared, Fulbert glared at the trio of Bullock, Doukas and Falconer, then descended the steps, and stormed away into the gloom of the distant choir. Relieved of scrutiny, the constable's shoulders slumped visibly, and because his hands were shaking, Falconer helped him return his sword to its sheath. Doukas returned a perfectly blank sheet of parchment to his satchel, along with the tools of his trade. He laughed harshly.

'I hope you weren't serious about taking their names, constable. I'm not that swift with my penmanship.'

Bullock looked him in the eye.

'I don't need them written down, Doukas. They are in here.' He tapped his forehead with a stubby finger. 'I shall know them all again. Now, let us return to the castle and await Mistress Le Veske's investigations in Grope Lane. Are you coming, William?'

Falconer was looking off to where Fulbert had disappeared.

'You go, Peter. I have matters to discuss with Friar Gualo.'

Bullock saluted his friend, and he and Doukas left the church. Falconer stood pondering for a while, then followed Fulbert into the friary.

115

Chapter Eighteen

Saphira stepped out of the little cubicle where Peggy Jardine lay, and unwound the linen mask from her nose and mouth.The wrinkled face of Sal Dockerel fell when she saw how solemn the Jewess looked.

'Has she got it, mistress?'

Saphira nodded slowly.

'Yes. When did Peggy start complaining of muscle pains and headaches?'

'Yesterday morning. She was sick too, but we just thought that she had fallen for a child. An occupational hazard, you understand, mistress.' Sal's sad eyes pleaded with Saphira. 'It couldn't be just that, could it? Pregnancy, I mean?'

'I'm afraid not. There are already reddish spots in her tongue and throat. In another day or two, large red spots will appear on her body, just like I saw on the carrier of the disease.'

Sal shook her head sorrowfully.

'Why has this happened to Peggy? She's a good girl.'

Saphira wasn't about to point out that the Christian church wouldn't see it that way. Peggy Jardine was a doxy and a sinner to them. But to Saphira she was just a poor girl who was fighting for her life. Now she had to ensure that Peggy had not and would not infect any others.

'I will arrange for her to be taken to Bartlemas hospital.'

Sal began to protest, but Saphira stood firm.

'She will be best cared for there.' She hesitated for a moment. 'Can you tell me if Peggy ... entertained any other men since laying with the knight?'

The brothel madam looked stricken.

'Well, of course she did. As I said she was a good girl and men liked her. But it was only a day or two after that the constable closed the town gates. Business has been non-existent since then. Can Peggy have passed on the pox to others, then?'

Saphira tried to look on the bright side.

'It is possible but unlikely, if it was only a day or two after de Wolfson lay with her. She would not be infectious until much later.'

Sal Dockerel slammed her fist down on the table.

'Damn that crusader knight. I wish now I had turned him away. But his gold was good, so why should I? I even bit it to make sure.'

Her wrinkled face suddenly fell as she recalled her transaction with de Wolfson. She looked fearfully at Saphira, thinking how she had put the coin that the crusader had handled into her mouth.

'I've been feeling a bit off colour lately. Do you think I could have ...?'

Saphira held the linen mask over her mouth, and told Sal to open hers.

*

Falconer followed Fulbert into the Franciscan friary beyond the church that was physically located outside the walls of Oxford, and accessed from the town through the church. The entire friary was an anomaly, being part of Oxford but not of it, because it was not strictly within the walls rather it was a fat boil growing out from the walls. Bullock had had to rely solely on the word of the friars that they too would observe the rule of isolation imposed on the town as a whole. Falconer wondered if someone like Fulbert felt obliged to obey that proscription. He could after all simply walk out of the southern gate of the friary, and disappear.

The cloister stood immediately beyond the church to the south, and the choir door led straight into it. When Falconer opened the door, he saw Fulbert walking in the southern range of the cloister directly opposite him with the open square between both men. Fulbert appeared oblivious to Falconer's presence, his head down and his steps hurried. Falconer knew the layout of the friary quite well. Not only was it like the normal plan of every friary in England, he had visited his friend Roger Bacon here when he had been imprisoned. He guessed that Fulbert was making his way to the dormitory, and the small number of individual cells beyond. One of which had housed Bacon when he had been out of favour with the pope. Unlike the usual cloister, which had four sides, this had only three, the fourth being the old exterior town wall. So the only way to follow Fulbert was to go the long way round, and he had to hurry. It would not be long until the whole friary would be assembling in the church to observe the liturgical office of compline, so he knew he did not have much time. And he didn't yet know what he might find wherever Fulbert was making for. Though he almost hoped it was lots of stolen books.

After leaving the cloister, Fulbert walked past the archway leading to the dormitory, and made for a row of doors. Falconer had been right – it was one of the cells the friar had been making for. He was in time to see Fulbert opening the third door in the row and entering the cell, closing the door behind him. Falconer now ran the rest of the way, knowing Fulbert was trapped in the small room beyond. Approaching the door, he placed his ear to it and heard a muffled conversation going on. Fulbert was with somebody, and Falconer was left in a quandary. Should he go in and confront Fulbert? Was this his cell, or that of another friar? What would he find inside? He might only succeed in alerting Fulbert to his suspicions, but not have enough to prove his guilt. But, hearing the sound of sandals slapping on stone close by, he finally took a decision, and pushed the door open.

*

'Then both Sal Dockerel and Peggy Jardine have the red plague?'
Saphira nodded a confirmation to Bullock's question. Doukas took

up his pen and scratched his notes on a new scrap of parchment. In a darker corner of the castle hall, Aldwyn knelt and began to pray. A mood of gloom had descended on the hall as Saphira was giving her report. It was little consolation for the constable that there had not been any reason to suspect more of the denizens of Grope Lane were infected. Bullock pulled a face, and scrubbed at his whiskery chin with his stubby fingers.

'We will move them to Bartlemas under cover of darkness.' He looked inquiringly at Saphira. 'Can both of them walk?'

'Sal will be able to, she is not as far gone. But Peggy will need a cart or something similar. She is too ill to walk unaided.'

Doukas laid his quill down.

'I suggest you move them both in a cart, constable, and cover them up too. Though it will be well for the townsfolk to know you are isolating the problem, some may react badly to seeing those who have the pox. And you should supervise the move yourself in case there is a disturbance.'

His dark eyes held Bullock's until, wearily, the constable nodded in agreement. Saphira noted the subtle change in the room as Bullock, usually so decisive and reliable, gave in to the demands of the outsider. She had never seen Peter so overwhelmed, and it worried her. She spoke up.

'I could at least accompany them as far as East Gate, Peter. They will feel less fearful, if I do, don't you think?'

Bullock took Saphira's offer in the way it was intended to act – as a way of passing control back into his hands.

'Yes. I will get a message to Bartlemas, so that you are met. I have one of my men who is lucky enough to live outside Eastgate on duty to act as a messenger with the outside world. Once the women are outside the gate, they can be isolated from causing any more contagion. The hospital is sufficiently out of the way in the countryside to be effective in ensuring that.'

His old self apparently restored, the constable went off to organise the transfer. Saphira turned to those left in the room.

'Do you know where William is?'

*

The cell in the friary did indeed house books, but only a half-dozen. The cell was clearly the domain not of Fulbert, but of Friar Gualo. The elderly friar was stretched out on a low pallet set against the far wall of the small room. With only a slit for a window, a burning candle, used to banish the darkness, was the only luxury in the cell. It afforded enough light for someone to read by. But it wasn't Gualo who was reading. Surprisingly, considering his attitude to books, it was Fulbert who had a large tome in his hands, which he must have just picked up. At Falconer's abrupt entrance both men had looked his way in shock. Fulbert was the first to speak, recovering his composure more quickly than the older man.

'What on earth do you think you are doing, disturbing our peace so late in the day?'

Falconer was not to be put off from his task, and peered at the book the young man held canted towards the candle-light. Disappointingly, it was not some heretical text, and did not figure amongst the list of books stolen by the book thief. It was in fact a well-worn copy of the *Rules of St Benedict*. Fulbert could tell what Falconer was thinking and smirked.

'Did you think, after all I said in my sermon, that I would have some secret desire for that which I condemned?'

He would have said more, but Gualo sat up and laid a hand on his companion's arm.

'Fulbert is doing me a kindness, Master Falconer. My eyes are failing me, and despite his contempt for books, Fulbert has undertaken to read to me each evening before we retire.' He waved his hand to encompass the few items there were in the cell. 'I am allowed this small comfort in my declining years.'

Seeing Falconer's eyes follow his gesture around the room, taking in the three or four books lying on the end of the pallet, Gualo elucidated.

'Just some commentaries on the Bible, including quite a rare copy of a commentary on the Pentateuch by Bede.'

Falconer could see the books were not the ones stolen by the thief. Fulbert was not about to leave the matter there, though.

'Would you like to look under the bed too, in case Gualo is your book thief, and is hoarding your precious abominations?'

He lifted the coarse blanket which was all that separated Gualo from the wooden slats he rested on. The space underneath was a void, like the rest of the austere room. Fulbert stared smugly at Falconer.

'Now, if you will excuse us, compline approaches, and we must return to church.'

He stamped his palm down on the flickering candle flame, extinguishing it and bringing the conversation abruptly to an end.

*

It had been a long day capped by the trip to Eastgate with two pox-ridden people, and Peter Bullock felt weary to the bone. But he had been thinking a lot lately. More than was his normal habit. He was a man of action still despite his years. He was almost as old as the century, and had spent most of his life fighting battles of one sort or another. He had fought in Ireland and Wales, and once in France under the leadership of Henry. That had been a humiliating excursion resulting in the French occupying Poitou, Auvergne, and Saintonge. It had been to expiate memories of that defeat that he had signed up to fight in the Crusades. It had been a harsh and brutal experience not at all alleviated by any vision of Christian piety. All he remembered about it was episode after episode of bloody massacre and looting. He had returned to England disillusioned, and found himself idle and footloose. It had been a mercy to get the post of constable of Oxford which he had held now for some twenty years. But still the lust for action stirred occasionally in his bones. The doleful transfer of the two unfortunate women from Grope Lane to Bartlemas hospital was not what he had imagined himself doing when he started out as constable.

Ignominiously stowed on a hand cart pushed by Thomas Burewald, and accompanied by Saphira Le Veske, the pox victims had been wheeled through the back lanes of Oxford. Mistress le Veske looked dishevelled, but there was a gleam in her eye, and Bullock wondered if his old friend William was responsible. Their intimacy was the worst-kept secret in Oxford, though he was sure de Bosco, the chancellor, was unaware and fortunately so. He was not so sure that Doukas hadn't picked up the signs, however, which may not be such good news for Falconer. For now, he couldn't worry about it. Reaching the East Gate without being seen, Bullock had roused Tom Inge from his slumbers, and got him to open the small wicket gate in the main door. Two hooded figures waited outside the gate, their faces masked with linen cloths. As Sal and Peggy stumbled weakly though the small gate, Bullock could not but think they were being passed over the threshold of Hell. A shiver had run down his spine, and sleep refused to come.

Chapter Nineteen

Her errand of mercy with Sal Dockerel and Peggy Jardine last night still much on her mind, Saphira returned to the brothel in Grope Lane. She wanted to be sure that the other girls were not showing signs of the plague. They were a sullen bunch without their mistress to control them, and it was some time before Saphira could get them all to gather in the hall. One by one she got them to open their mouths so she could examine them. The bolder ones stuck their tongues out in a lascivious manner, expecting to shock her. One even ran her tongue around her lips that had been rouged to emphasise their allure. Saphira was impervious to it all, and her business-like manner soon cooled their playfulness. They were probably relieved that she only asked to see the inside of their mouths and any exposed flesh on their arms and shoulders, rather than examining them beneath their skirts for another sort of pox. Still, the whole business took a long time, what with all the exaggerated play-acting at the beginning, and it was only when Saphira had finished and declared they were all free of red plague, that one of the younger girls piped up.

'Hey, what about the old boy next door? Who's going to collect the rent while Mistress Dockerel is away?'

An older girl idly scratched herself between the legs, and snorted.

'Not me. Peggy did it once or twice, and said he tried to touch her up.'

'Then who's going to do it now?'

The bunch of girls glared at each other and began to argue who would carry out this onerous task in the future. While they argued, Saphira felt a cold chill down her spine. If Peggy Jardine or Sal Dockerel had called on this lodger recently, then perhaps he had been given the pox too. She interrupted the squabble with a sharp enquiry.

'Hasn't anyone gone to see if he is well?'

The older woman pouted.

'None of our business, mistress. He has no money for our services, so there's nothing in it for us.'

'Except a small kindness.'

Saphira's comment seemed to strike home, and the young girl spoke up.

'I'll go round and see if he wants anything.'

Before Saphira could stop her, the girl darted out of the front door. She followed her as quickly as she could, worried that the old man might be a victim of the plague and liable to pass it on. When she got to the ramshackle house next to the brothel, she heard an ear-splitting scream. Across the dusty hall she saw a rear door standing open, with the young whore standing in it silhouetted by the light shining in the back room. She crossed the hall and gently moved the girl aside, expecting to see a man covered in red spots. What she saw was even more horrendous. The old man's body lay on the floor covered in flies, and his severed head lay a yard from it, a darkened mass of blood joining the two.

*

Later in the day, after Falconer had been found and had attended at the scene of Master Gerard Anwell's murder, he sought out Saphira. She had returned to her home to try and sleep. She didn't think she would be able to, but did in fact doze off in the kitchen, hunched over the long, oak table. She awoke to the sound of someone hammering on the street door. It turned out to be William and she let him in, despite feeling itchy, grubby and not at all appealing. She had slept in her clothes and they were as creased and dishevelled as she felt. Falconer appeared unconcerned by her appearance, but then he never cared much about his own appearance, wearing the same black robe day after day. But even he looked careworn to Saphira today.

She gave a short, sharp grunt of a laugh at their mutual dishevelment, and pushed a flagon of sweet water from the underground spring below her house towards him.

'We both look as though we need refreshing.'

Falconer poured the water into a goblet and drank deep, knowing the water was safe.

'I have just come from Grope Lane.'

'Was it the same killer?'

'It is likely, don't you think? I cannot say if any of Anwell's books have been taken, but the one that was left on the floor beside his body is testament to his interest. It was covered in blood that must have sprayed from his neck when his head was cut off ...'

Saphira winced at the brutal imagery, but Falconer ploughed on regardless.

'It was a text by Maimonides. Our hater of anything outside the canon of the Church would deem it demonic, I am sure. It certainly was a splendid example of illustration – beautifully gilded.' He grinned sardonically. 'It made me think of Aldwyn's last prophecy.'

'What was that?'

'"There will be gilding in the temples, but the sword's cutting edge will not cease its work."'

They looked at each other in silence for a while, neither quite sure what to believe in connection with the monk's pronouncements. Saphira thought about William's latest encounter with the Franciscans. She stared at William across the other side of the kitchen table.

'Do you still suspect Fulbert?'

Falconer shrugged wearily.

122

'I cannot be sure. I don't know what I had hoped to find in the friary. A hoard of proscribed books perhaps, or a blood-encrusted blade.' He laughed harshly at his own foolishness. 'Fulbert may have known all along that I was dogging his footsteps. He certainly tried to make it clear to me with the tender scene of his caring for Gualo, that he spends every hour with the old man. When he is not praying at the divine offices. But if compline ends his day, then he has plenty of time to slip out of the friary after dark to steal books. And kill masters of the university. But then Richard Yaxley, the feretarius at St Frideswide's also expressed the same sentiments to me the other day.'

'But your only reason for suspecting either of them is their antipathy to the gathering of scientific knowledge?'

'Which they see as pulling down the edifice of the church and challenging God, and not as I do, the seeking out of the meaning of God's wonders.'

Saphira sat up in surprise at William's words. It was not like him to acknowledge even the existence of God, let alone refer to God's wonders. She assumed he must have been confused by this bewildering case, and she resolved to set him back on track.

'Remember what you told me the first time we met?'

Falconer looked at Saphira, bringing to mind that first meeting. It had been in Bermondsey Abbey, where she had been hunting for her errant son, Menachem, who had been hiding away as an apparent Christian convert after fleeing the sad death of his father. Falconer had turned up at the abbey seeking shelter from a rainstorm. His first sight of Saphira had been most unusual, and he could picture the scene even now.

The prior of the abbey had asked him for some assistance, and he had followed him down a staircase, and out into the yard. The men had paused briefly at the archway, hesitant about diving back into the rainstorm. Falconer instinctively looked around before stepping into the darkness. Out the corner of his eye, he caught sight of something pale halfway down the junction of the wall to the guest quarters and that of the monastic dormitory. Something pale, topped by a flapping bundle of material. Realising what it was, he smiled to himself. Taking the prior's arm, he steered John de Chartres across the streaming courtyard, and away from the shapely vision of a slim woman's bare leg topped by her rumpled, dark gown which had apparently snagged on the leaden down-pipe that she was attempting to shin down. He had successfully diverted the prior's attention away from the vision.

In trying to recall his first words to her, he could only bring to mind that inspiring first sight of Saphira's bare legs. Later he had met her face to face in more normal circumstances. Her face had been pale and the features drawn by her anxiety over her son, but it was a face of great beauty with a chiselled nose, and high cheekbones. The eyes were green and almost almond in shape, suggesting some eastern origin to her. She still looked as good to him now.

'I forget. What did I say to you when we first met?'

Teasingly she chided him.

123

'Don't you recall? You said, "I myself am seduced by the logical. Too much, some people say, for my own good."'

'And what is your point?'

'That you should put all prejudices out of your head in this case, and start using logic again.'

Falconer was about to protest that his suspicions concerning Fulbert and Yaxley were not to do with prejudice. But in his heart he knew they were. Yaxley was an irascible pillar of the church establishment, fixed in beliefs that Falconer had found shifting from under him. And the young Franciscan reminded him too much of the way the order had treated his old friend Roger Bacon, whose whereabouts he was still ignorant of. Bacon had compiled a great encyclopaedia of knowledge, and it had been taken from him and hidden away.

He smiled at Saphira, conceding the point.

'I consider myself corrected. What do you suggest I do?'

'I have been thinking about the targets of the book thief. Whoever the person is who is doing this, he knew which master had books that he disapproved of. Do you agree?'

Falconer nodded, beginning to see where Saphira might be going.

'You think the thefts, and later, the murders were not random.'

'Indeed. And if so, then could the killer be someone from the university, rather than a monk or friar? A student, perhaps, who knew every master who was attacked?'

Falconer knew that, in his heart, the same idea had been brewing. But he had been too fearful of giving it room. That is why he had chased chimeras in the form of God-loving monks and friars, and semi-literate troubadours. If he was to return to logic in his pursuit of the thief and murderer, he knew where to begin.

'I need to examine the university records to see if there is a common thread that links the masters together. And I need to do it urgently as I have already wasted too much time.'

He went to rise out of his seat, but Saphira stopped him.

'William, it is too late to rouse the chancellor and his minions now. Only last night I despatched two unfortunate souls to their fate. And today I have examined the mouths of numerous prostitutes, and seen a man with his head struck from his body. Life calls me now.'

Falconer saw the lustful light in her eyes, and nodded agreement.

'True. We should do something about it.' He paused. 'Oh, and I remember what else I said to you at that first meeting.'

'What was that?'

'That, if we were solve the riddle and find your son, we needed to let a little of the mystical into our hearts.'

*

Peter Bullock was dog-tired, but he could not keep himself from wandering Oxford's streets. There was a palpable sense of fear emanating from the houses he walked past. The halls, where lived the students of the university and their masters, were shut up tight against the demon who stalked the streets in search of masters who had transgressed against God. The townsfolk had not much to fear from him, but another horror was outside their window shutters waiting to sneak in and kill. The plague was not as choosy as the book thief killer, and perhaps that made it all the more horrific. Red plague did not discriminate against the ungodly alone.

At least the twin scourges meant the streets at night were safe for the constable. Unless the book thief changed his tactics. Bullock shivered, but it was not through fear this time, but cold. He had been thinking a lot about the murderous book thief, and was not paying too much attention to where he was. So he was surprised to find himself standing in front of Falconer's home, Aristotle's Hall. He was sure it was because in his heart he feared for his friend's safety. For no reason other than a feeling of fatalism, he slipped into the doorway of Nun Inn opposite and hid in the shadows. There, his mind began to roam.

It had long ago occurred to him that, if masters of the university with unorthodox views were being targeted by this book thief and murderer, then his old friend William would surely become a victim sooner or later. Brother Aldwyn's gloomy prophecies – or more accurately his recitation of Merlin's prophecies – had contributed to Bullock's sense of impending doom. Talk of a rain of blood, whether it was by way of the pox or these numerous murders, had caused him to consider who was the most likely next victim. His inevitable conclusion had been his friend. The final horror of consigning the two women to their fate last night had convinced him that something would happen soon. Perhaps this very night. Especially with Will Plome back on the loose.

Standing in the doorway waiting for something to happen, though, shortly became tedious. He was beginning to think he had made a mistake, and besides his extremities were aching. He was cold to the bone, and was wondering if he had failed to beat Falconer at his own game after all. Having been out-thought by William so often in the past over murders, he had hoped this time for once he had found a way of getting ahead of him. But it seemed that he was doomed to failure, and nothing was going to happen. He was just about to step back out into the moonlight, when he heard the sound of boots on the cobblestones of the street.

He ducked back into his hiding place, and eased his sword a few inches out of its sheath. The apparition he saw almost took his breath away. It was a warrior dressed in an iron corselet held in place with wood, and leather straps. It passed him without being aware of his presence, and stopped outside the door of Aristotle's Hall. The strange figure pushed at the door, but found it barred in some way. Pulling out a dagger, the figure poked at the gap between the door and the frame, seemingly not caring how much noise was made in the process.

Bullock watched for a few moments, then took a step towards it and drew his sword. The swish of steel alerted the apparition, and it turned round swiftly, dagger in hand. In that instant Bullock saw who it was, and had the pleasure of knowing he had, after all, beaten Falconer to it.

'Hello. I might have guessed it would be you.'

The warrior grinned humourlessly.

'I needed to be seen whilst about my business, but not by you. And not to be caught either. Sadly, that can only mean one thing for you, constable.'

The figure lunged forward, his dagger seeking Bullock's heart. He parried the thrust with his sword, and stepped to one side. It felt more like a lumber though, and Peter knew he was out of practice for this sort of fight. Stumbling, he turned and saw that the warrior had drawn his own sword in the extra time he had given him. They circled each other, and then Bullock swung another blow, which his adversary parried easily with his dagger. A stabbing thrust with his sword followed and it almost caught Bullock unawares. He half stopped it with his own sword. They had only traded a couple of blows and Bullock was breathing hard, his heart thumping in his chest. The warrior laughed, and opened himself up mockingly to a blow from Bullock. The constable took his chance, but as he raised his sword, he felt a crushing pain inside his chest, and his sword arm failed him, feeling weak and useless. His vision darkened, and as he slumped to the ground, he saw his nemesis drawing back his sword for the final blow. His last thought was that at least he had died in battle and not in his bed like a weak-bladdered old man.

Chapter Twenty

The Feast of St Gerard, 24th September

Falconer would have liked to talk some more with Saphira about the possible murderers, but he could see the last few days had affected her. So, with her still asleep in bed, he left the house in Fish Street in the early hours of the morning. Last night she had agreed to meet him later the next day at the residence of the chancellor of the university. There, they would examine the university records for any clues to the murderer's identity. He decided to make his way first back to Aristotle's Hall. He knew he had neglected his students recently, and should check on them before pursuing the hunt for the killer.

As he turned into the narrow opening of St John's Street, he saw close to the other end of the lane that there was some disturbance. People were running to and fro from one side of the lane to another. His weak eyes were not good enough to make out exactly was going on, but he could tell from the shouts and agitated movement of those concerned that something bad had happened. As the disturbance was close by his own doorstep, he immediately feared the worst for his own students. He knew he would not forgive himself, if any one of them had been harmed while he had been with Saphira. He hurried on down the street, and saw that one of those in the small cluster of people was his former student and now newly-made regent master, Thomas Symon. He seemed to be taking charge.

'Thomas. What is going on here?'

On hearing Falconer's voice, Symon looked up, his face pale and anguished. He strode towards Falconer.

'William. You should not come closer.'

He tried to take his former mentor's arm, but Falconer would have nothing of it.

'Oh, Lord. Has one of my boys been taken ill or harmed? I must see him, if he has.'

He could tell now that the crowd was gathered around a fallen body in the doorway of the house opposite Aristotle's. He thought perhaps someone under his roof had fallen sick of the pox, and staggered out into the street only to collapse. As if to confirm his fears, he saw the faces of some of his clerks.

'Peter Mithian, who is it who has been taken ill?'

The young man he spoke to looked at his master with a face of incomprehension.

'Master? Nobody has been taken ill. It's ...'

He failed to get any more words out, and none were needed. Falconer knelt done beside the body in the doorway, and saw for himself. The sight took his breath away. He leaned back on his heels and looked up at the strained face of Thomas Symon.

'It's Peter Bullock.'

Symon nodded.

'I told you not to look.'

'Bullock dead? How?'

Falconer gently wiped the lank grey locks of hair from Bullock's face, and stared into the empty eyes. Symon squatted beside him.

'You can see there is a wound in his chest big enough to be a sword thrust. But ...'

The young man hesitated, unsure if Falconer wanted him to continue. They had both been involved together in investigations concerning murder. Symon had taught himself a deep understanding of the workings of the human body, and acted as his former teacher's advisor on matters to do with wounds and their causes. Falconer welcomed his opinions normally, but this was different. Now they were talking about a mutual friend. But Falconer grasped his arm and squeezed it hard.

'Tell me what you are thinking. If we are to find Peter's killer, then we must treat this like any other murder.'

Symon grimaced, but carried on nevertheless.

'I am not sure it can even be called murder.'

'How do you mean? You say there is a sword wound in his chest. I can see it.'

Falconer gingerly poked a finger in the rent in Bullock's tunic despite the blood that had soaked into the cloth.

'Such a thrust would have pierced the heart. How can it not be murder?'

Symon indicated the ground under and around Bullock's body with an open palm.

'Look here. At the blood.'

Falconer frowned, staring at the blood on the ground.

'I see the blood. What are you trying to tell me?'

'There was a fight undoubtedly. I heard it myself, and even saw the victim fall.'

Symon lived in the tiny Colcill Hall next door to Aristotle's.

'I saw a man leaving, and saw the constable lying in the street. Though I didn't know it was Peter Bullock at first.'

'So you saw the aftermath of the murder. What's all this about the blood though?'

'There's simply not enough of it. If the constable had been stabbed in the chest while he was alive, the blood would have squirted copiously and rapidly from his body. I have read Avicenna's *Canon of Medicine* in which he suggests the heart is the root of all faculties and gives nutrition, life, apprehension, and movement to several other members.'

He paused, unsure if he was making sense to Falconer, so he made it clearer.

'If it stops its work, blood does not come forth so readily from a wound.'

'But you say you saw him fall.'

Symon looked at the ground, trying to put his thoughts in order. When he did speak, he spoke slowly and carefully, ensuring what he said was accurate.

'Yes, but I am sure he collapsed *before* his attacker made the final blow. I think Peter was dying of a seizure of the heart already. Some survive with what is called the half-dead disease. Some simply die.'

Falconer gazed at his dead friend, and patted his head.

'Whatever the sequence of events, Thomas, Peter died as he would have wished: in battle. And whoever this man was, he was Bullock's killer. You said you saw him leave. Can you describe him?'

Symon nodded, fixing the image in his head before he spoke.

'Yes. He was a large man, maybe a little overweight. I could not see his features as he was turned away from me and he wore an iron helmet. And strange thing was he wore some sort of old-fashioned corselet on his upper body made up of metal and wood and leather straps.'

*

They took Peter Bullock's body back to the castle on a hurdle. Falconer bore one end and Thomas Symon the other. Thomas Burewald, who had been called for as Bullock's second-in-command, began the formality of the hue and cry, though the strange killer was long gone. The story of Bullock's death had already reached the castle, for John and Margaret Peper, Agnes Cheke, Robert Kemp and Simon Godrich all formed an impromptu guard of honour in the courtyard. Their search for Will Plome over the last few days had proven fruitless, as they had not been able to talk to many people. The doors of the town were firmly closed to them in fear of the plague, and they had all but given up. They had been lounging in the castle courtyard practicing their skills, when news of Bullock's death had preceded the arrival of his body. Their worst fears had been realised -- another murder had taken place with Will still on the loose. Now they stood in two ragged lines as the makeshift bier passed between them, their faces ashen.

Aldwyn had opened the derelict chapel, and he now ushered the bearers of Bullock's body into the chilly sanctuary. Falconer and Symon manoeuvred the hurdle close to the altar slab, and slipped the body on to its surface. It seemed that Peter Bullock was to have a solemn and royal lying-in-state. Everyone stood with their heads bowed as the elderly monk intoned a prayer, and then they plodded out of the chapel, their hearts heavy with the tragedy. Aldwyn was speaking to Thomas Symon, but soon came over to Falconer.

'Master Symon has told me of the apparition he saw. It is as predicted by Merlin.' He quoted by heart the passage from the Prophecies. '"*There shall come people dressed in wood and in iron corselets who will take vengeance on the White Dragon for its wickedness.*"'

Falconer felt his anger rising, but controlled it. If it had been anyone but the foolish, old monk speaking, he would have been tempted to strike out.

129

'I hope you are not suggesting that Peter was a wicked man, Aldwyn?'
The monk blushed.
'Certainly not. But the pattern of the prophecies continues, and if
Bullock was not the intended victim, then who was?'
He stared meaningfully at Falconer, who turned away stunned by
the thought that, if he had not tarried at Saphira's house, Bullock
might still be alive. He would have liked to have come face-to-face
with the murderer at last, even if it had put his own life in peril. He
knew he would have gladly exchanged his own life for that of his
friend. He looked once more at Bullock's lifeless body, only to see a
faint, derisory smile on Isaac Doukas's swarthy face.

*

Later, when he had apprised Chancellor de Bosco of the constable's
death, Falconer raised the matter of the killer possibly being a member
of the university. De Bosco, aware of the continued presence of Robert
Burnell's man in Oxford, went grey. He found himself in a dilemma.
Should he protect the reputation of the university and refuse Falconer's
request to examine the university accounts books, and risk Burnell's
later censure? Or acquiesce and risk finding a murderer amongst the
masters or students? He turned to the Northern proctor, Roger Plumpton,
who happened to be with him at the time. De Godfree, the other proctor
had not been seen since the announcement of the red plague.
'What do you think, Plumpton? Can we allow Master Falconer to
search the records for evidence of a killer?'
The proctor rubbed his flushed and jowly face, pondering the matter.
A small smile flitted across his lips before he answered. He seemed
happy to agree to Falconer's request.
'It can do no harm, chancellor. And if it leads to weeding out a
rotten fruit from the barrel, then all well and good.'
Still it was de Bosco's nature to prevaricate, but after Falconer
suggested that delay might result in another death, he had given in.
Appointing Plumpton his deputy, De Bosco deliberately left Falconer
to it, so as to avoid the distressing sight of the records being rifled. It
was fortunate that he did so, because it meant he also avoided seeing
a certain Jewess also examining the private documents. Plumpton
showed Falconer into the room where the university records were
stored, and having watched him for a while, got bored and also
departed. This gave Falconer an opportunity to sneak down to the
back door of the building called Glassen, and let Saphira in as
previously arranged. She gasped when she saw the records and the
size of their task. But it was Falconer who immediately voiced his
worries about the killer to Saphira.
'We are using up a lot of our time in searching for a murderer amongst
these records.' He waved a hand at the piles of books and scrolls in
the table before them. 'But the description of the man who attacked
Peter fits Will Plome. Are we wasting our time?'
Saphira shook her head. She had been deeply shocked when William
had broken the news of Bullock's death. But it made her all the more
determined to find his murderer.

130

'We must carry this through, or you will always regret it. Especially if Will is found to be innocent, and we lose the real killer for want of a little effort.'

Falconer sighed and waved a hand.

'Hardly a little effort.'

Indeed in front of them were receipts for fees paid by members of the university on admission, lists of 'cautions' or pledges of valuables deposited as surety, lists of graces granted by the university, and lists of candidates for degrees. The university records could be at best described as chaotic. But these records in some way or other could link the dead masters with their killer. It was, however, for one name in thousands that they were hunting, and at this stage it looked very daunting. But there was only one way to approach the task – to begin and to persevere. The candles burnt low, but still they ploughed on. Saphira was hunting for references to the names of the masters who had merely had their books stolen and survived, and Falconer for student names associated with Roger Stephens, John Bukwode, Edmund Ludlow, Gerard Anwell ... and himself.

The day grew darker, so they lit more candles and ploughed on. On one occasion, Plumpton poked his head round the door, observed the presence of Saphira and looked as though he was about to object. But seeing the hard glare in Falconer's eyes, and the woman's deep concentration, he disappeared again. Finally Falconer saw a pattern of sorts beginning to emerge. He looked across at Saphira, who had pulled the white linen snood from her head, and was running her fingers through her thick, red hair.

'Do you have anything?'

She shrugged.

'There are many names of students who attended lectures by John Catche and Robert Knyght.' These were another two of the known masters who had lost rare books before the killings began. 'How about you?'

Falconer hesitated, not wishing to jump to a false conclusion.

'I have a few names. Shall I see if they match yours?'

The room suddenly felt cold, or maybe the shiver that ran down Saphira's spine had another cause. It could be that one of them would speak the name of the killer. She nodded, and he began his recitation of names.

'William Gyllot.'

There was no response from Saphira other than a slight shake of her head, so he drew a line through the name.

'Roger Kranard.'

Again nothing, and another crossing out.

'Laurence Staynton.'

'I have him once, but only once.'

Falconer hovered with his quill over the name.

'Leave him in for the moment.'

No line was put through the name, but a question mark was placed beside it. Falconer went onwards scratching out names or leaving them in. Finally he got to the last name on his list.

'Geoffrey Westhalf.'

Saphira frowned, and looked at her list. Her lip formed into a rounded shape.

'How many matches?'

'Every master including myself taught Westhalf, except for Ludlow with whom Westhalf was a boarder.'

'So all your names are connected with Geoffrey Westhalf. Mine too.'

Falconer inked his quill and drew a circle round Geoffrey Westhalf's name.

'Then I think we should talk to the young man.'

*

As they walked the deserted streets of Oxford, Falconer began to regret allowing Saphira to come with him. Darkness was falling, and if their theory was correct, Geoffrey Westhalf could well be a violent killer with an obsession about ungodly knowledge and those who possessed it. He might not take kindly to a Jew, who knew about medicines and poisons and was a female to boot, taxing him on his activities. Falconer's problem now was that he felt he ought to corner Westhalf alone. However, Saphira Le Veske did not like being treated as a weak woman and he knew it to his cost. As they crossed the High Street, he hesitated before entering the dark alley opposite them that was the mouth of Shidyerd Street. As if reading his mind, Saphira smiled, and squeezed his arm.

'Don't worry. I will stand safely behind you. And if he lets us into the hall, I will wait outside, if you want. I trust you to protect me.'

Falconer grunted in surprise.

'What has brought this strange change of nature on? I had imagined you would be the first to enter, and confront him with his evil deeds.'

'I can be demure and ladylike, if I please. Besides, if he attacks us, I would rather he tangled with you first, and gave me chance to flee.'

Falconer growled at her teasing, and went ahead down the narrow alley. Saphira had made a joke of it, but she was actually fearful of what might happen when they confronted Westhalf. She hesitated to follow William, but it was too late to worry about that now, and she really did put her trust in him. She gathered her skirts, and followed him into the darkness. The top end of Shidyerd Street was a place where, if you spread your arms, you could almost touch the houses on either side. She felt a prickling on her neck, and imagined eyes peering from the darkened houses at their passage. Everyone in Oxford was fearful of who might be abroad after hours. Even in normal times dark brought out the rats and drunken revellers. Now, worse still, plague stalked the streets. Fortunately, the lane opened out towards its southern end, and she hurried after William catching up to his long strides. Soon there were fewer shadows, and the back of St Frideswide's Church towered above them as they approached Beke's Inn. This was where the student had lived alone since the death of Edmund Ludlow. A death that they were both now thinking to lay at the door of Geoffrey Westhalf.

Chapter Twenty-one

When they got to it, the door to Beke's Inn was ajar – something very unusual for these fear-ridden times. Saphira looked at William questioningly, and he stepped forward, pushing the door wide open with the palm of his hand. It was dark and cold within with no fire burning in the hall. Falconer called out.

'Geoffrey Westhalf. Are you there? It's Master William Falconer.'

He stood for some moments on the threshold, and fancied he heard a sound from deep inside the house. But it came only once and never again. It might just have been the timbers of the old house creaking as the chill of evening settled on it. There was no other response to Falconer's enquiry, so it seemed Westhalf was not there. But Falconer did sense some sort of presence. Something malevolent hovered just out of sight. However, he was not a man to give in to fright and lurid imagination, so he made to step inside. Then remembering their agreement, he first turned back to Saphira.

'Wait here. It may be nothing, but I think something is wrong.'

Saphira nodded and watched as William entered the darkened house. The silence seemed to envelope him, and she waited. But soon she became fearful of what he might have encountered. Moreover, the dark street behind her back gave her the shivers. So, despite their agreement, she crossed the threshold and followed him into Beke's Inn. The main hall was chilly, and she could see that the fire had not been burning for a long time. The ashes were cold and grey with not even a faint glow at their heart. There was no sign of William in the hall. Where had he gone? There was a wooden staircase leading upwards, but she could not hear him walking around on the upper floor. It was as though the earth had swallowed him up. She took a deep breath, and crossed the hall, finally seeing a door in a sort of alcove on the other side. She had not spotted it before, and had thought there was no other exit from the hall. The door swing open even as she stepped towards it. She tensed herself ready to fight or flee, and breathed a sigh of relief when she saw the familiar, tall figure of Falconer. He looked at her quizzically.

'I see you didn't observe the rules of our agreement for very long.'

She pouted.

'Not at all. I let you go first, and now I am ready to run. See – I have my skirt gathered in my hand.'

She was indeed holding the loose material of her dress up slightly so as not to impede herself if she had to take flight.

'Is Westhalf not here, then?'

Falconer pulled a face.

'Oh he's here, but not in a state to be interrogated.'

She went to go past him into the small back room that must be the student's quarters, but Falconer held his arm across the threshold.

'You shouldn't go in, or at least you should take some precautions first.'

The look on Falconer's face told Saphira all she needed to know.

'The red plague?'

'Yes.'

She turned away from William, and lifted up the skirt of her dress to reveal her linen undergarment. Having torn a strip of cloth from it, she divided it in two, and gave a piece to Falconer.

'Put this on your mouth, then we are both protected.' She looked him in the eye. 'I assume you want to go back in too?'

'Yes. Though I don't know how useful it will be to ask him questions. He is alive, but incoherent. But then his room is evidence enough of his wrong doing.'

Saphira frowned at his cryptic comment.

'What do you mean?'

'Just look around you when you go in. You will see what I mean.'

She wound the torn piece of cloth over her nose and mouth, tying it roughly at the back of her neck, and went into the back room. It was larger than she had expected, and had a window that overlooked the rear yard of the house. The shutters were closed, but as her eyes adjusted to the faint light that percolated through the cracks, she saw what William had meant. A bed was tucked against the wall on the far side of the room, and between the bed and the door were several piles of books. More books than even Saphira had seen in one place before. Her long-dead husband had been obsessed by the Kabbalah, and had owned some twenty volumes. Here, there must have been ...

'I would guess around a hundred books and parchments.'

Falconer's muffled voice spoke in her ear from behind the linen mask he wore.

'He must have been stealing them long before his activities came to light. De Bosco only knew of a few thefts before the murder of John Bukwode took place.'

He picked up a couple at random from the pile nearest him.

'Look. *De pentagono Salomonis* and *Sapientiae nigromanciae*. I wouldn't mind owning those myself.'

Saphira had become aware of a stale smell in the room, an odour of unwashed body. She cast her gaze down on to the bed for the first time, and in the tangle of sheets, saw the shape of Geoffrey Westhalf. The boy stirred a little and groaned. She crossed to the window, and pushed open the shutters. A cold and welcome breeze blew into the room, and the moonlight shone down on Westhalf's body. He was shivering, more from fever than the cold now blowing through the room. And as Saphira carefully pulled back the sheets, she saw clear evidence of what ailed him. Falconer spoke first.

'The rain of blood, they say. I can see why.'

Westhalf's whole face and body were covered in ugly, red spots,

134

as if blood had literally rained down on him. Saphira could see they were of the type that she had also seen on the crusader, Sir Hugo de Wolfson. The spots that Samson had said were the most malignant and deadly form of small pox. They were flat to the skin, not raised like the ordinary type. Westhalf's chances of survival were poor, and he was already deep into a prolonged fever. Before Falconer could say any more, Westhalf groaned and tried to prop himself up in one arm. He saw Falconer's shape but darkly, noticing merely the black robe of a regent master. He quaked as he spoke with fear in his eyes.

'Master Ludlow?'

His voice came out like the croak of a frog, and as his mouth hung open, Saphira could see the lesions on his tongue. It was astonishing he could speak at all. Falconer thought the boy must be delirious and had blanked from his mind the murder of Edmund Ludlow. Or was fearful that his former master had come back to haunt him.

'Not Master Ludlow, Westhalf. It's Master Falconer.'

Westhalf's eyes were red and bleary, as if he couldn't really take in what was being said to him. But he beckoned to Falconer, and seemed intent on saying something to him. Falconer leaned over him, putting his ear close to the boy's mouth despite Saphira's warning of the dangers of the transmission of fluids. Westhalf, a brightness shining in his eyes momentarily, murmured something that Saphira couldn't catch. She grabbed Falconer's arm and pulled him away from the dying boy.

'What did he say?'

Falconer frowned.

'He said he could die in peace, because he had looked upon the face of God.'

*

They found the key to Beke's Inn and locked the front door. Westhalf was beyond salvation now, indeed almost beyond assistance. They could arrange to move him to Bartlemas, but the chances were he would die from being moved. With the door locked, at least there was no chance anyone else would catch the pox from him. As they walked back to the castle, Falconer glanced at Saphira and spoke.

'We shall have to tell Bullock about Westhalf and ...'

He paused, realising what he had just said, and felt quite ill. Saphira stroked his arm, and he groaned.

'I forgot. I am so used to going to Peter for the mundane jobs – removing bodies, mollifying irate townsfolk and the like – I just thought ... Well, I didn't think, did I?'

'It was perfectly natural. Life without Peter will be very strange. He has been a part of your life for so long.'

They walked on in silence, each with their own thoughts until they reached the castle courtyard. Falconer saw Thomas Burewald emerging from the chapel where he must have been in communion with Bullock's body. His face was solemn. Falconer crossed the yard to him as he needed to tell Burewald what he had been going to tell

135

Bullock. It already felt odd to refer matters to this man, who was almost a stranger to him, instead of Bullock.

'Burewald, I have another case of the red plague to advise you of. It's Geoffrey Westhalf, a student at Beke's Inn. He's ...'

Falconer paused seeing tears flowing from Burewald's eyes. The watchman swallowed a sob, and with an embarrassed grimace wiped his face.

'I'm sorry, Master Falconer. I've only just heard that my brother John – he's a glover by trade, and has a stall close by Carfax – he's got the plague too. I've got men moving him to Bartlemas now.' He took a deep breath. 'I'll get them to go by Beke's Inn too.'

Falconer patted him on the shoulder.

'It's hard, isn't it? Especially with Bullock no longer here to help us.'

Burewald cast a glance back at the chapel, where the constable's body lay.

'Actually, I was just talking to him. I felt a bit of a fool, but it helped, I think.'

'Not a fool, Burewald. I always turned to Peter in a tight spot, now I shall at least ask myself what he would have done. It's only a shame that he wasn't around to witness the conclusion of the hunt for the book thief killer.'

Thomas's ears pricked up at Falconer's statement.

'The constable told me something of what had been happening with the regent masters' deaths. Are you now saying you have solved the matter?'

Falconer nodded his head.

'It would appear so. Westhalf, the student who is mortally sick at Beke's Inn, was surrounded by stolen books. And he is of a size to fit the descriptions we have of the thief. He favoured sober grey robes too, which is why he may have been taken for a Franciscan. Unfortunately, he will not survive to stand trial.'

'Some may say fortunately – for him. Though I dare say natural justice will be seen to have been done. If Bullock's murderer dies horribly, I for one will not grieve.'

Burewald squared his shoulders, and walked back towards the town and his new responsibilities. Saphira looked at him as he went under the archway in the castle walls.

'He will do well, if the guilds and aldermen have the sense to appoint him in Peter's place.'

Falconer agreed with her. Still, Oxford would be a strange place without Bullock, and someone else would have to tidy up the loose ends in his place. Falconer noticed John Peper sitting on the side of the cart that held the troubadours' properties, sifting through them disconsolately. He had a spear in his hand which must have been used as the spear of the Roman centurion when depicting the Crucifixion. Falconer called over to him.

'You've still not found Will Plome then? Only you should know there is no need for him to hide any more, as the real book thief is found.'

Peper put the spear down, and walked over to where Falconer and Saphira stood.

'No. Not a sign of him anywhere, though we looked high and low. But then, the search was made harder because most folk were reluctant to even open their door to us. The few who did open up only spoke through the smallest crack between door and doorframe. But what they told us was they had not seen Will since last year, when we were last in Oxford.'

'Did you speak to the shrine keeper at St Frideswide's? Yaxley, the feretarius?'

Peper frowned.

'But that was where he was found last time. He wouldn't have gone there again, surely.'

'Did you not even check with Yaxley? Will sees the shrine as the safest place in Oxford, and it wouldn't matter if he had been found there before. He does not think like you or I.'

Peper got angry at Falconer's scornful comment, and made a sharp retort in reply.

'No, I didn't think it worth checking. We were close by, and I suppose I may have asked, but saw Burewald just then, and heard about the constable's murder. It was put out of my mind.'

Seeing her husband getting red-faced and annoyed, Margaret Peper hurried over. She was used to John getting into unnecessary conflict due to his temper and strove to cool the situation down. But John Peper could not be calmed down, and poked a finger at Falconer.

'He said I haven't done my job properly. What does he know? Will Plome is my friend, God help me, and I wanted to find him.'

Falconer was riled now, and replied in kind.

'Then, if he was your friend, you should have taken more care and carried out your search more painstakingly. Not found, he may be a danger to himself and others.'

It took Saphira to calm the situation.

'William. Master Peper. Don't forget that Peter Bullock lies dead only yards from where we are standing. Give him a little respect. After all, if he were here, he would be banging your stupid heads together like a couple of troublesome clerks.'

Both men looked sheepishly at each other, and Peper was the first to turn away. Grumbling about returning to St Frideswide's in search of Yaxley, he walked across the yard and out the gate with his wife, Margaret, following him. Falconer watched the Pepers leave, then walked towards the chapel with Saphira following him.

Chapter Twenty-two

The sight of Peter Bullock lying on the stone altar of the chapel gave Falconer the feeling that his friend was just slumbering after a night of strenuous activity. It was as if the constable had been out in the night calming excitable and drunk clerks and angry townspeople as he so often had done. If words could not calm the situation, he would have drawn his old, rusty sword and laid the flat of the blade against a recalcitrant youth's arse. That usually achieved the desired effect. The clerks may have been studying logic as part of their course, but summary justice in the form of Peter's judicious sword trumped the application of logic every time. Falconer laughed quietly, and drew a disapproving look from Saphira. He tried to explain.

'I was just imagining him solving knotty problems with his own brand of practical good sense. You know, it used to irk him that I didn't always take his opinion about a murder seriously. I always had to hunt out what was the least obvious answer to his mind. Well, this time he beat me to it. He must have been hanging around outside Aristotle's Hall because he'd worked out who the murderer was, and that I was next in line.'

He peered short-sightedly at the pale, waxy face of his friend.

'Congratulations, Peter Bullock. You won in the end. Tell me you knew it was Westhalf all along.'

Bullock was unmoved by Falconer's admission of defeat, and his still features didn't betray what he had known. In fact to Falconer, the constable looked as though he was ignoring his revelation of the name of the killer. Almost as though he was saying, 'No, old friend, you've got it all wrong, after all. Think again.'

Falconer gripped the cold stone edge of the altar on which Bullock's body lay and frowned.

*

Yaxley didn't want to allow the Pepers access to the shrine at first. They were mere travelling players, who made their money singing bawdy songs in taverns, and he knew the woman performed lewd dances too. They were not the sort who would pay the right dues to see the saint's remains. But then, it was obvious they didn't want to see the saint. They were still looking for their travelling companion – the fat boy who had embarrassed the feretarius more than once.

'I told you I thought I saw him hanging around here again recently. That is all I know.'

John Peper was insistent though.

'But when did you see him exactly?'

Yaxley waved a dismissive hand in the man's face.

'What does that matter? I don't even know for sure it was him. I only got a fleeting glimpse in the dark. A shadowy movement, no more. But then I thought it couldn't have been him because Bullock – God rest his soul – had imprisoned him. So I don't know why you think he could be in the church once again.'

'So it was after Will had been taken and imprisoned by the constable that you saw him?'

'Thought I saw him. Yes, it was early yesterday morning, if you must know. Now be off with you.'

John Peper looked at Margaret.

'That would be after the time he escaped from the crypt.'

Yaxley yelped in annoyance.

'He escaped? Don't tell me he came back here again.'

He pulled a grim face, and waved a finger at the Pepers.

'If he is here, hiding in his usual place, I shall make sure you pay the church for the inconvenience.'

John bowed in the most servile way he could muster.

'Could you go and look, sir. Then we could take him away with us, and he won't bother you again.'

The feretarius scowled, but then gave in and crooked a finger.

'Very well, come with me. The way into the Holy Hole is close by the altar.'

They walked up the nave, their footsteps echoing in the cold and unusually empty church. Yaxley stopped by the edge of a worn slab and saw that it had been moved. He groaned.

'Here, help me with this.'

Peper and Yaxley prised up the slab and lifted it away, revealing a dark hole. They both heard a whimper. Peper dropped to his knees, and peered fearfully into the gloom below his feet.

'Will Plome, are you there? It's John. John Peper.'

He heard the whimper come again, like the sound of an animal cornered in its lair.

*

Saphira was used to William plunging into deep thought, and would have waited patiently for him to explain. But this time she was worried by the ashen look his face had taken on.

'William, tell me what is wrong.'

Falconer looked up at her.

'Peter is right.'

This strange comment made Saphira all the more concerned. Was William still imagining that the constable was alive, and speaking to him? Was he sick? Falconer saw the look in her eyes, and smiled wearily.

'I'm not mad. It's just that I was thinking about Peter's frustration with my devious mind, as he called it. He hated it when I contradicted him, but he knew in the end that I had got it right. So I just considered my conclusions again.' He took a deep breath. 'Tell me how sick

Westhalf would have been, if as is likely, he picked up the plague directly from de Wolfson on that first day.'

'By the twelfth day at the latest, he would have been incapacitated, possibly even after ten days. He would have been weak and feverish, his limbs would ache.'

Saphira suddenly understood what Falconer was thinking.

'Ah. You mean Westhalf may have attacked Roger Stephens and killed John Bukwode, but he would have been in no fit state to have murdered Bullock in his failed attempt to rob and kill you. He may even have been too feverish and weak to kill Edmund Ludlow and Gerard Anwell. Tell me, how did he seem to you when you spoke to him on the night Ludlow was discovered?'

Falconer groaned and thought back to his meeting with the student. He had been weak, feverish, and sweaty. Falconer had put it down to the events he had witnessed, but of course it had been the early stages of the plague. Desolate, he stared at Saphira.

'If only I had recognised it, he might have been treated early enough to ...'

'To later murder you. But then ...'

Falconer broke in on her train of thoughts, eager in his pursuit of the implications of this new revelation.

'I have also been thinking about something Fulbert said.'

'Are you coming back to thinking him the killer, then? And not Geoffrey Westhalf?'

'What? Oh, no. I am certain that Westhalf was the book thief, and therefore also the person who attacked Roger Stephens and killed John Bukwode. But those attacks were carried out in haste and anger, and were not planned. The other murders, and the attempt on my life that led to Bullock's death, were much more considered. No, what Fulbert said in his sermon that Bullock and I interrupted was that there were two killers stalking Oxford. Of course, he was referring to a murderer and the red plague, but it has made me consider the possibility that, if Westhalf was Bukwode's killer, but was too sick to carry on, then there *are* two killers in Oxford. And that Ludlow, Anwell and Bullock were killed by the second one.'

Saphira gave him a worried look.

'Then this new killer is still free, and you are still probably his next victim.'

'Yes. It's like being knocked back to point one on a Game of Tables.'

*

'He said that he would not come out until the Devil had gone away. He said he had seen the Devil, and that He chased him all the way to St Frideswide's, then told him to be silent.'

The Pepers had come back to the castle without Will Plome, but with the story of where he was and what had happened to him.

In the grim surroundings of St George's Tower, John Peper told his story to Falconer, Saphira Le Veske, Isaac Doukas and Aldwyn. The old monk was immediately scrabbling through the pages of his book

140

of Merlin's Prophecies. Falconer glanced his way, as the old man frowned, flicking backwards through the tome.

'What's wrong, Aldwyn? Is there no prophecy that covers the arrival of the Devil Incarnate?'

Aldwyn was unperturbed by Falconer's sarcasm.

'There is no specific statement at the section we have reached in the prophecies, but I am reminded of the beginning of the text.'

He found what he was looking for and read it in a sombre tone.

' *"The Prince shall forsake men of the church, Lords shall forsake righteousness, counsel of the aged shall not be set by; religious men and women shall be thrust out of their houses; the common people for fear shall not know which way to turn; parents shall be hated by their children, men of worship shall have no reverence of others; adultery shall abound among all; with more ill than I can tell of, from which God us defend."* If that is not warning of the arrival of the Devil, I don't know what is.'

Aldwyn slammed the book shut, and Isaac Doukas gave Falconer a look that clearly said he was on the side of the monk in this strange affair. Saphira was less impressed, and whispered in Falconer's ear.

"If we are now looking for a new killer, then we should do as you always have done, and collect the small truths to see how they point to the greater one. That method always irritated Peter, so surely you can bear to annoy him one more time by finding his killer in the same way. We need to talk to de Bosco about the masters who were killed after Bukwode. He might know of something that links you and them together.'

Falconer was glad to have good reason to leave the castle, and all the reminders it carried of Peter Bullock. Moreover, he did not want to reveal yet his thoughts concerning the murderer who was still at large. Everyone looked so glad that Geoffrey Westhalf had been exposed, and that Will was no longer a suspect. He thanked the Pepers for their efforts at extricating Will Plome, and told them that he thought Will was safe enough in the Holy Hole for the time being. What he didn't tell them was that he wanted Will locked away until he had sorted the mystery out.

'Let him stay where he feel safe for the moment. Meanwhile, I have business with the Chancellor. So you must excuse me.'

Free of the stifling atmosphere of the castle, Falconer felt he could breathe again. Hurrying along at his side and keeping in step with his loping stride, Saphira had a question for him.

'What of Will Plome? Is he once again a suspect?'

Put on the spot, Falconer had to agree that Plome could not be ruled out.

'If we are looking for another killer, he must still be considered. After all, he was at the scene of one murder, and was at liberty when Anwell and Bullock were killed. All this talk of being pursued by the Devil could be his way of excusing his actions.'

'But if it's wasn't Plome, then what about the Franciscan, Fulbert? He would be able to sneak out of the friary in the night in between prayers, wouldn't he? Or is he a milk-and-water sort of priest?'

'Indeed he would be able to be about the town when everyone else would be asleep. And as for your other question, he is robust enough to wield a sword, I would say. But if we are to attribute the initial book thefts to Westhalf, then what was Fulbert's reason for killing?'

'How do you mean?'

'We suspected ... I suspected him in the first place because of his avowed distaste for books and scientific knowledge. If he is not the book thief then he is simply a murderer. What I need to ask myself is, would Fulbert kill for his beliefs?'

Saphira nodded her head.

'I take your point. But we do not scratch him from our list of suspects. Falconer grimaced.

'No. Nor do we discard Yaxley for the same reasons.'

Their conversation had carried them to the Aula Vitrea – the House of Glass – where William de Bosco resided. They entered the hall, and persuaded a servant, who kept a respectful distance in case they brought the plague with them, to summon the Chancellor. He had a word of caution though.

'It is quite late, master, and the Chancellor is in the habit of retiring early.'

'Tell him I am William Falconer, and must speak to him concerning the urgent errand I am carrying out for him. I am sure he will see me.'

The servant cast a suspicious and rather scandalised look at Saphira, making it clear he disapproved of her presence in the house of a celibate. Falconer stared hard at him in the way he did with recalcitrant students.

'And he will be pleased to entertain Mistress Le Veske also.'

With pursed lips, the servant bowed, and disappeared through the inner door that led to de Bosco's private solar. It was quite some time before the servant returned, his face like thunder. He had obviously lost the battle with his master over allowing visitors to see him at such a late hour. His message was quite curt.

'The Chancellor will be with you shortly. May I get you some wine?'

The offer of wine was clearly made with the assumption that a courteous guest would decline. So Falconer deliberately replied in the positive.

'That is an excellent idea. And don't fob us off with the Chancellor's poor Rhenish. Mistress Le Veske is knowledgeable about the wine trade, and will know, if you do.'

The man scowled, and went on his errand. Saphira laughed gently and chided William.

'Poor man. He clearly sees it as his duty to protect the Chancellor from the likes of you, and you went and spoiled it. And as for my expertise with wine, he will now put me down as that Jewess who's in trade.'

Falconer was about to reply, but the servant returned with a jug of wine and two fine gilded goblets. He poured the wine, but retreated before Saphira could taste it and complain. Falconer was actually glad of the opportunity to drink, and took a deep gulp. Saphira sipped it more gently.

'Actually, it is a good wine. A Burgundy, I think. You must have cowed the poor man.'

Falconer laughed.

'I just hope he didn't spit in it before bringing it through.'

Saphira paled, and pushed her goblet away from her.

It was some considerable time before de Bosco himself emerged, and in the mean time Falconer had drunk deep. When the Chancellor did come into the hall, he was wearing a voluminous robe with a fur collar that covered a long white linen shirt that peeped from under the robe. He had probably been roused from his bed, but gave the appearance of being pleased to see Falconer. He even made a courteous bow towards Saphira Le Veske.

'I am glad Inkpen saw to your needs. He can be very protective, when someone arrives late. Overly so. Now tell me, do you have some news about the murders? Plumpton told me you left your researching of the records with great speed. I assumed you had found something significant in them.'

'Yes, it led us to a student – Geoffrey Westhalf. Sadly, he is dying of the plague.'

For a moment, de Bosco looked relieved that the murderer, though a student of the university, had at least had the good sense to die before his misdeeds were made known. He was already plotting ways the whole matter could be hushed up. Then he saw Falconer's solemn face.

'Does the matter not end there?'

Falconer shook his head.

'I'm afraid not. You see, he could not have been the killer of those masters who died after Bukwode, and not of the constable either.'

De Bosco pulled a face.

'Shame. Then the mystery is not solved. Oh, by the way, I was most disturbed to hear of Bullock's death. He was a fine man, and will be sorely missed.'

Though Falconer knew de Bosco was a diplomat and probably sought only to please, he was glad of the man's obsequy.

'We are near a conclusion, but we are here firstly to seek your help.'

De Bosco raised his eyebrows. It was rare for William Falconer to seek his assistance. He guessed this must be a strange case indeed.

'And how can I help you, master?'

'Of the men who died, I am most interested in any connection between John Bukwode, Edmund Ludlow, Gerard Anwell, and ...' Falconer grimaced recalling that Bullock had died instead of him. '... and myself. If you can see any.'

De Bosco frowned and paced the dark and by now chilly hall. He pulled his thick robe around him. From the look on his face, Falconer saw that something had occurred to the Chancellor, but that he was reluctant to state it openly. He urged him to speak.

'Tell me what you know, sir. My own life, if no other is at stake here.'

Having uttered those words, he wondered if the threat on his life was perhaps an incentive rather than a deterrent for de Bosco keeping quiet. Fleetingly, he thought he saw the same idea crossing the Chancellor's mind. But de Bosco was not that underhand. The chancellor raised a finger to his lips as if to express his desire for discretion.

'I can tell you of the first three and how they may be connected other than by scholarship. As for your connection to them, you must answer that yourself. I cannot see it.'

Falconer sighed. He had hoped de Bosco might have the key.

'Well, tell me anyway. How are Bukwode, Anwell and Ludlow connected?'

What de Bosco then told him suddenly hit Falconer like a hammer blow. He grunted as if actually punched, and thanked de Bosco for his confidences.

'Chancellor, you have helped enormously. Now we must go.'

De Bosco was, as ever in the presence of Falconer, bewildered.

'I have helped? I don't know how. You would do best to speak to Roger Plumpton. He knows more about this business than I do.'

Falconer bowed abruptly, and took a puzzled Saphira by the arm. He guided her out of Glassen and back into the street. There, he looked around cautiously before beginning to walk the silent lanes towards Jewry. Saphira followed until they were at Carfax, then she stopped him. They stood alone, the only two people on what was normally a bustling crossroads at the centre of Oxford.

'What is going on, William? Tell me.'

'I know who the murderer is. Well, I think I know, but I need to expose him. Make him confess, because I don't know if I can prove anything.'

'And how can I help?'

Falconer's instinct was to tell her to go home and lock her door behind her. But he knew that would not be acceptable to Saphira Le Veske. He racked his brains for something that would help.

'There are three things you can do. I need you to get John Peper out of the castle grounds, so that I can talk to him without anyone else knowing. Then you have to lure Will Plome out of his hidey-hole. Oh, and bring Yaxley with him. Can you do that?'

Saphira sighed deeply.

'I know you are not going to tell me who you suspect so I might as well do something useful. They are tasks one and two. What is the third?'

'I need Fulbert to know I am aware of the killer's identity.'

'Hmm. That is not a task for a woman – going into a friary at night. I will talk to Thomas Burewald. He could play a part and convince Fulbert you need to see him urgently.' She paused to give William chance to speak. But when he didn't, she tried to wheedle the truth from him. 'Is it Fulbert you suspect, then?'

Falconer kept a straight face.

'Wait and see.'

With an inscrutable smile, he hurried off in the direction of Aristotle's Hall, leaving Saphira to her tasks.

Chapter Twenty-three

The Feast of St Cosmas and Damian, 25ʰ September

Brother Aldwyn was roused from his slumbers by the urgent voice of William Falconer. His fuddled brain could hardly decipher the regent master's words at first.

'What was that you said, Master Falconer?'

He opened a heavy eyelid, and tried to make out the scholar's blurry features. Falconer's face was as excited as his voice. His blue eyes sparkled and a broad smile split his features.

'I said, Aldwyn, that you were right.'

'Right?'

The monk could not work out to what Falconer was referring. Since when had he ever been right about anything in the scholar's eyes? But he found he was soon to be enlightened. Falconer grasped his shoulders so tightly it made the old man wince.

'You were right all along about the prophecies coming true. It's all in the next section of your book.'

Aldwyn corrected him pedantically.

'Geoffrey of Monmouth's book. And they are Merlin's words not his.'

A peculiar look came over Falconer's face. A sort of a grimace melded with a secret smile. But it was fleeting and the monk wasn't sure if it had been there in the first place. Perhaps he had imagined it, or Falconer had had a momentary bout of indigestion. He put the thought from his mind. After all, the regent master had admitted his errors, and was ready to accept the veracity of the prophecies. Aldwyn rose from his bed with a little gentle assistance from Falconer, and hobbled over to the table where the book lay. But before he could get there, Falconer skipped ahead of him, and hefted the book in his big hands.

'I have arranged for the players to enact the relevant section. They are assembled in the courtyard. Come.'

Close by the dying embers of the central hearth in the hall of St George's Tower, another figure rose from his slumbers. The swarthy head of Isaac Doukas appeared from under a sheepskin, and his eyes blinked blearily.

'What's happening, Adwyn? What's all the noise?'

Falconer answered the questions for the old monk.

'You will see soon enough, Doukas. Come, follow me.'

He strode off through the main door, the precious book held firmly under his right arm. Doukas scratched his greasy head, and got to his feet. Following the regent master and the old monk out into the courtyard, he was presented with the strangest of sights. Dawn was breaking, and the rising sun cast a pale, watery light across the yard. At one end of the yard, a large cloth had been hung between two poles about ten feet high. The scene depicted was of green fields bordered by dark woods. A few crudely sketched-in but grand-looking buildings probably designated London. Or maybe it was Jerusalem. Who could tell? The fact that the paint was cracked and faded did not detract from the effect. The sun's beams burst through a cloud and lit up a pretty picture of a country scene. More England than Outremer, certainly. Doukas screwed up his eyes and stared at Falconer.

'What is all this?'

Falconer grinned broadly.

'Wait a moment and all will be made clear.'

Peper's little troupe of players, whose backcloth the bucolic scene was, were busying themselves around their cart. They pulled out masks and costumes, some of which they discarded. Others they distributed amongst themselves. They were so engrossed in their task that they failed to see the three people coming through the castle gate. They were halfway across the courtyard before Agnes Cheke looked up from her task of selecting a sword made of wood from the stack of make-believe weapons. Their real sword had disappeared the other night, and Agnes didn't want anyone to know in case they thought Will had it and had used it. Then, when she saw the rotund figure next to Saphira Le Veske, she threw the wooden sword on the ground.

'Will Plome! Wherever have you been?'

She rushed across the courtyard, and almost bowled the young man over. She embraced him firmly before standing back and playfully boxing his ears.

'Thought you could step out on your own, did you? Since you learned to read, you thought you were better than us.'

Will Plome blushed, and shook his head vigorously until Agnes thought it might come off. She grasped it in both hands and plonked a kiss on the boy's forehead. John Peper, who by now had crossed the courtyard with the rest of the troupe, wasn't so forgiving. He waved a finger at the runaway.

'You still have a lot to answer for, Will Plome, what with all these murders. Not to mention the money I gave you to prepare the way for us in Marcham and Abingdon.'

Plome hung his head.

'Sorry, Master Peper. But the Devil has been on my tail, and I could not help myself.'

He cast a wary glance around him for, though Saphira had convinced him that the Devil would not harm him, his emergence from the Holy Hole had caused him some trepidation. Especially when it turned out that his nemesis, Yaxley, was going to accompany the woman to wherever she was taking him. He recognised some of the other people in the courtyard. His fellow players, naturally, and Master Falconer, who always came to their pageants when they came to Oxford. And Yaxley, with his sour face. And the pretty woman with red hair who had enticed him out of his hiding place. She was Jewish, but could not be the Devil, even though the priests said Satan came in all sorts of pleasing disguises. Now, the old monk could be the Devil in disguise, as his face looked sombre enough. But surely even if the monk were the Devil, he could easily outrun such an old man, so that didn't matter. He was not so certain of the stocky, dark-skinned man dressed in a leather tunic standing next to the monk. He looked fearsome, especially when he grinned, as he was doing now. Just as he thought he had weighed up the possible incarnations of the Devil present in the courtyard, two other men hurried in from the street. One was a Franciscan monk dressed in grey robes. He strode straight over to Falconer.

'I hope taking me away from my devotions has a purpose to it, Falconer. Burewald, here...' He indicated the other man who had entered the courtyard along with him. '... said it was essential that I come.'

Thomas Burewald, acting constable, shrugged his shoulders in resignation at Falconer, showing what a hard task it had been to get Fulbert to come to the castle. Falconer remained unperturbed.

'Indeed it was, Brother Fulbert. And just as soon as another guest arrives, we can begin.'

Falconer had added to the invited audience the name of one of the proctors, Roger Plumpton. Since speaking to the chancellor, he had learned that the proctor had been very close to Robert Burnell when he had been in Oxford. Falconer suspected him of being somehow involved in events, and so had sent a message to the chancellor asking that Plumpton represent the university at an event in connection with Peter Bullock's funeral. He had silently asked forgiveness of Peter for using his name in this way. In a way there had been some truth in what he had said. Bullock would be buried on the morrow, come what may.

For a while, Falconer felt anxious that Plumpton would not come, and the rest of the assembly were beginning to get restless, then finally the proctor's plump figure appeared in the gateway of the castle. The assembly was complete, and Falconer was relieved.

'Master Plumpton, welcome. We were about to begin without you.'

Plumpton wiped some beads of sweat off his upper lip, and looked around nervously.

'Doesn't this gathering contravene the constable's proscription on assembly? I know the man is dead, but the plague is still lurking about, is it not?'

Saphira tried to settle the man's nerves.

'I can assure you, master, that the plague will soon have run its course. If there are no more cases in the next day or two, Peter Bullock's action will have been vindicated. Don't you agree, Thomas?'

She looked towards Burewald, the acting constable, and he nodded gravely.

'It would appear so, mistress. We know how Sal Dockerel and Peggy Jardine came by the plague, and we can guess that the crusader knight's passing through the market was what infected Geoffrey Westhalf, Alice Lane – who her family say was out buying fish – and ...' His voice broke slightly, but he managed to continue. '... my own brother, John Burewald. We know of nobody else.'

Fulbert's harsh voice broke in.

'Your list is not complete, Burewald. Only yesterday one of our friars showed the symptoms of red plague.' He raised a hand to stop the outburst that was to come from Burewald's lips. 'You were to be informed, and I can assure you that the brother is isolated and being cared for. He too was probably in the market on that fateful day. He replenishes our larder when we run short of our own produce.'

Saphira stepped in to emphasise what she had said.

'So you can see all the cases are of people who caught the plague from the knight. No new cases have been reported, and if none are by tomorrow, I dare say Master Burewald can lift the proscription on meetings and movement. And we can all thank Peter Bullock for our salvation.'

There was a moment's silence, then Falconer spoke in the most solemn tones he could muster.

'The prophecies of Merlin have seemed to be fulfilled in the last few days. So in order to solve the riddle of the murders that have been taking place, I examined the text closely for clues. In the process I made a startling discovery. But to make it clear, I must go back in time and show the truth of the prophecies.'

Falconer opened the heavy tome in his hands, and cradled it on his left arm. He turned the pages until he found the point in the text he wanted, and looked over at Peper's troupe of players. John Peper nodded and the actors retreated behind the backcloth. A breeze suddenly blew across the courtyard, and fluttered the cloth causing the fields painted on it to ripple slightly. To Saphira's eyes it made the vista look as though it was seen through a heat haze. Falconer began to intone the words of Merlin's prophecies.

"The island shall be called by the name of Brutus; and the name given it by foreigners shall be abolished. There shall be peace in his time; and corn shall abound by reason of the fruitfulness of the soil."

John Peper emerged from behind the cloth methodically swinging a scythe with a wooden blade, emulating the actions of a reaper. Falconer continued his recitation.

"Luxury shall overspread the whole ground; and fornication not cease to debauch mankind. All these things shall three ages see; till the buried kings shall be exposed to public view in London. Famine shall again return; mortality shall return; and the inhabitants shall grieve for the destruc-tion of their cities."

Continuing the mime mirroring Falconer's words, Margaret Peper sauntered over to her husband, swinging her hips. She pressed herself against his thigh, and he dropped his scythe. Saphira heard the indrawn breath of Brother Fulbert expressing his disapproval of such a lewd display. He might have intervened, but suddenly a figure leapt out from behind the cloth, and everyone gasped in horror. The masked man with the lanky build of Robert Kemp the juggler capered around the Pepers. His mask was in the form of a skull with a broad set of sharpened, white teeth and gaping blank eye-sockets. Two enormous ram's horns protruded from the brow of the devilish head. The Pepers fell in a heap to designate their mortality. Further emphasising the point in a reference to the current plight of the inhabitants of Oxford, Agnes Cheke staggered across the scene, red spots painted all over her face. It was a chilling reminder of the plague that still stalked the streets.

Thomas Burewald watched and was puzzled. The Le Veske woman had said it was important to get the Franciscan to come to the castle, and that Falconer was going to solve the riddle of the book thief murders. He had immediately assumed that she meant Falconer suspected Fulbert, and merely needed to lure him to the castle in order to incarcerate him. Yet here they all were indulging in some play-acting concerning a book of prophecies. Falconer looked to be unconcerned about a murderer being on the loose, let alone the persistent fear of catching the plague. But he recalled, however, that Bullock had told him how, no matter how mad the regent master's schemes seemed, they always got results. So he held back on his worries, and continued to watch in silence. He still shivered at the sight of the pox-marked woman, even though it was fakery, and moved a little further away from the other observers of Falconer's pageant.

Falconer lowered his gaze to the book, and carried on reading.

"Then shall come the lion, who shall recall the scattered flocks to the pasture they had lost. His breast shall be food to the hungry, and his tongue drink to the thirsty. Out of his mouth shall flow rivers that shall water the parched jaws of men."

Robert Kemp, the tallest of the players, had donned a white tabard with the Cross of St George emblazoned on it. He wore a crown and clearly was meant to represent him, who was once called Longshanks, and was now Edward, King of England. He strutted amongst the other players who mimed drawing refreshment from his generous gestures. But there was to be a darkness on the horizon. Simon Godrich, clad all in red, lurked at one side of the bucolic backcloth. Falconer carried on his recitation.

"A red dragon will next dwell in the death. For plague shall again return; mortality shall return; and the inhabitants shall grieve for the destruc-tion of their city."

Once more, John and Margaret Peper, and Agnes Cheke fell dead to the ground.

"But another dragon without wings will arise to replace the Red Dragon, sneaking in the city unknown."

Another mysterious figure stepped from behind the curtain, he was large and clad in a black cloak with the hood half-obscuring his face. What was visible revealed a skeleton-like mask. Saphira was as shaken as the other members of the audience to this strange pageant. All the players were on the stage, so who could this mysterious figure be?

149

The implication of William's introduction was that this was truly the murderer. Falconer smiled fleetingly at the effect he had created, and went on.

'Listen well to this section of the prophecies. *"After this shall be produced a tree upon the four square ..."* This can only be Carfax, surely. *"... which having no more than three branches, shall overshadow the surface of the city with the breadth of its leaves. Its adversary, the North wind, shall come upon it, and with its noxious blast shall snatch away the three branches."*

Here Falconer paused to ensure he had everyone's attention. Then he went on.

"The first will wither from a surfeit of learning. Then the second shall perish in its own red sap: pallor and dread will be clear to see on its leaves. The third shall die a sudden death, its very core not able to stand the terror."

All those present clearly understood the prophecies had identified the last three people killed. Edmund Ludlow, Gerard Anwell, and Peter Bullock. Falconer's reading continued inexorably though.

"He will seek out the lion, killing as he goes. He will pursue the Lion through all the narrow byways of the city, but in the end he will break his horns against the walls of Oxford."

The strange hooded figure chased Robert Kemp from the stage and disappeared behind the backcloth. There was a momentary silence, before a babble of voice broke out. Thomas Burewald's voice climbed above them all, a note of exasperation in it.

'But then who was behind the mask of death, Falconer? What is the identity of the killer?'

Saphira, herself perplexed by William's play-acting, suddenly saw a movement at the back of the crowd of onlookers. It was Will Plome, blending back into the audience, a grin on his face. She realised who had played the murderer in front of the backcloth, and marvelled that no-one had seen him slip away before his entrance. Falconer raised his hands, and the babble of questions was slowly silenced.

'The murderer's identity is still clouded in obscurity, and I shall need time to interpret the prophecies. I do believe that Peter Bullock knew, and shall keep his body company tonight. I shall pray that he makes it clear who killed him and the others. Tomorrow we shall bury him with all due solemnity.'

The disparate group of people, each wary of his companion whether from fear of plague or suspicions that he might be the murderer, began to disperse. Saphira sidled over to Falconer, and whispered in his ear.

'That was very a very sly move. I suppose you now expect the real killer to show himself to you tonight in the chapel.'

Falconer merely smiled, and tipped his head to one side in an irritating gesture. Saphira punched him lightly on the arm.

'All I can say is, for your own sake, if not for mine, take care. He still wishes to kill you.'

Chapter Twenty-four

The chapel was a cold place, and Falconer had availed himself of a homespun cloak to wrap around him. Even so the stone floor seeped cold into his legs as he was kneeling before the altar. Peter Bullock's body lay on the altar shrouded now in white linen. His face covered, his outline blurred by the shroud, Bullock had ceased to be the person Falconer had known for almost twenty years. And for that transformation, he was grateful. He could not have borne to look upon his old friend all through the night of his lonely vigil. But he did start recalling some of the more remarkable events they had been involved in.

'Remember when I made you lock Smith gate so that we could catch a murderer? We ended up causing a student riot that day which will go down in history. I think you forgave me – after a year or two. We failed to see eye to eye so many times, but it didn't interfere with our friendship, did it? Remember when the Jews attacked Edward Petysance parading his relic down Fish Street. It was a provocation the young hotheads in the community could not stand. And one of them paid for it with his life. You were glad that only one death had occurred and told me it could have been worse. I suppose my observation that it couldn't have been worse for the young Jew who died was a little intemperate. Even if it was true.'

Falconer stopped his muttered reminiscences, imagining he had heard a noise close by. He glanced nervously at the body on the altar, wondering if Bullock had moved in protest at his affirmation of being in the right after all this time. He held his breath, but when nothing else stirred, he began again, recalling more pleasant memories for a change. The two candles set at Bullock's head and feet slowly began to burn down.

He didn't know how much time had passed, or even if he had fallen asleep, but he was suddenly aware of a presence behind him. His knees ached, but he didn't move, merely contenting himself with a slight turn of his neck to the left and then to the right. Looking out the corner of his eye over his right shoulder, he could just discern a darker shape in the darkness of the recesses of the chapel. He wasn't wearing his eye-glasses, so he could not make it out clearly, but he imagined that the figure didn't intend for him to see itself properly just yet. He spoke out, and his voice echoed in the cold and oppressive space.

'Is that you come to see if the constable has spoken to me yet? Told me your name – the name of his murderer?'

151

There was no reply but he could hear the sound of someone moving closer to him. The whisper of light feet on stone slabs, and of a long cloak dragging over them. He felt an ache in the centre of his back, but schooled himself not to turn round. He would show no fear, though it shot through his veins like a stab of lightning. If the apparition would not speak to him, then he would to it.

'There are several names that Peter could have whispered in my ear. Friar Fulbert, for example, or Richard Yaxley. They both profess to despise scientific learning, or the esoteric knowledge of the ancients, but something didn't ring true for me especially about other things the killer should have known and they didn't. Still, they could be responsible. One of their names could be yours. Or are you Roger Plumpton? Did you sell your soul to Robert Burnell, Chancellor of England, in return for future favours? De Bosco told me that it was Plumpton who gave Burnell the selected names of Welsh scholars who might stir up Oxford, if the king ever invaded Wales, and who could cause trouble for Edward. Names like Bukwode, Anwell and Ludlow. I might have been on that list as my mother was Welsh too.'

Falconer heard a grunt from the ghost standing behind him. It sounded like surprise, and he smiled.

'But then you didn't know that, did you? That I had Welsh ancestry. How could you, as even I didn't know until two weeks ago. Until the town was closed up because of the red plague, in fact. Roger Plumpton certainly didn't know'

This gibe brought a response from the lurking figure, who spoke in a hoarse and clearly disguised voice.

'Don't you realise that you were my target all along, Falconer? You have attracted the displeasure of the highest in the land, who wishes to be rid of you. All the rest has just been to sow seeds of doubt and confusion.'

Falconer tried to ease his frozen legs that seemed locked in place as he answered the taunt.

'Oh yes, I became suspicious of the play-acting that you indulged in, when I saw how you seemed to actually want to be seen at the place of each murder. We will leave John Bukwode out of this, because although he is Welsh and had many esoteric texts in his possession, I think he only gave you your initial idea for confusing the constable. Geoffrey Westhalf killed Bukwode in a blind panic at being discovered stealing. Your first murder was that of Edmund Ludlow, where you ensured the fulfilment of one of Merlin's prophecies with your arrival on horseback – the Man of Bronze. You thus ensured Ludlow's neighbours would hear the horse, and remember it. It was only a curious coincidence that the original thief, Westhalf, was in the hall too. As for Anwell's murder, I guess you thought that someone whose head was chopped off would easily be found, and associated with another prophecy. Unfortunately, the find was not immediately made because of Anwell's reclusive nature. But eventually it was, and caused the sort of stir you had anticipated. So that all turned out well. But your attempt on my life was the most dramatic. Who was supposed to see the prophetic figure clad in a corselet of metal and wood? One of my students perhaps, or a neighbour such as Thomas Symon? It was the latter who did see you, by the way. Then Bullock went and spoiled it all, for he recognised you, didn't he? And for that he had to die. But by then the whole sorry mess had given you away to me. As I was sceptical of Merlin's prophecies being anything more than a fantasy weaved by poets and the deluded, I could not believe they were coming true. But what it did confirm for me was that whoever was playing out this fantasy, knew the prophecies well enough to copy them. Everything pointed at you.'

Falconer now looked over his shoulder, and saw that the figure had hidden his face in the Devil's mask from the players' cart – a hideous, sharp-toothed visage with ram's horns sticking out of the temple. The Devil growled in anger and launched himself at the kneeling Falconer, who tried to rise and avoid the attacker. But his knees, long bent before the altar where the body of Peter Bullock lay, would not respond. Falconer fell backwards, thinking he had misjudged his situation and was about to die. A dagger appeared in the devil's right hand, its blade glittering in the candlelight. Falconer fell against the altar, and held up his arm in a hopeless gesture of self-defence. Then just before his attacker was on him, a shape rose from behind the altar, and with an anguished cry interposed itself between Falconer and the Devil. It was Will Plome, and he had a spear in his hand. It was the spear of Longinus, that the players used in the tableau of the Crucifixion – a poor copy of course, but sturdy enough to kill. Either by accident or by design, the spear got jammed between the base of the altar and the onrushing man. The figure impaled itself on the spear, and with a terrible gurgle, pitched on to the floor, snapping off the thin shaft of the spear as it did so.

Falconer let out a big sigh of relief, and looked at Will, who was on his knees, sucking a splinter out of his hand. He grinned.

'I killed the devil, Master Falconer.'

Falconer laughed, and clapped Will on the back.

'You did indeed, Will. Now help me up please, my legs are numb from so much kneeling.'

Once he was up and had shaken his legs do that they functioned again, Falconer stepped over to the prostrate figure on the floor. The Devil lay on his back, with the broken shaft of the spear protruded from his chest. His mask was slightly askew on his face. That had been another clue for Falconer, the masks. Not only had Will claimed to have been pursued by the Devil, but Geoffrey Westhalf had spoken of looking on the face of God. Of course it could have been an hallucination brought on by the boy's fevered imagination, but Falconer thought it had a more prosaic origin. The players' mask used in their depiction of God in the mystery plays they performed. Sure what he would see beneath the Devil's mask, he pulled it away.

Epilogue

The Mass of the Archangels Gabriel and Michael. 29th September.
Michaelmas Day

Falconer eased himself up from the saddle of his rouncey, and stretched his legs. The gates of Oxford were once again open, and the outside world beckoned. He was waiting at Eastgate, staring out through the arch at the long road running to the village of Headington and the lands belonging to St Fridewide's priory. Beyond that the road turned south-east and ran all the way to London. But that was a long way, and Falconer was having difficulty taking the first step. Like a prisoner used to his small cell, who is afraid to emerge into the light, Falconer's freeing from the confines of Oxford was followed with unease at the broad horizons open to him. His situation was caused by more than Oxford being declared free of the pox. Regent Master William Falconer had taken the extraordinary step of relinquishing his post at the university.

There had been something stirring in his breast for months, if not years, and the nearness of being killed by Isaac Doukas and having Peter Bullock killed in his stead, had brought about its fruition. After conferring with Thomas Burewald, he had agreed that Doukas, cold-blooded killer of Peter Bullock and two regent masters, should be buried inconspicuously outside the town walls. His death would be put down to the red plague, and no more action would be taken. What more could they do? He had been the agent of very powerful men who could not be pursued by a mere town constable. And so Doukas had been dispatched at night into an unmarked grave. Peter Bullock's burial, on the other hand, had been carried out with all the solemnity that the aldermen of Oxford could muster. He had a fitting send-off for such a tireless and uncomplaining servant of the town. Immediately afterwards, Falconer had returned to Aristotle's Hall, his spirits dampened by the final confirmation the funeral had given that Peter was dead and gone. He retreated to his solar in the eaves of the hall, and examined at his life.

The room was of sufficient size to contain his experiments, but afforded little space for his own comforts. To the left of the chimney breast was a toppling stack of his most cherished books and papers, where standard church works such as the *Historia Scholastica* were lost and buried under the more used and well-thumbed texts of the Arab mathematician Al-Khowarizmi, medical works, and studies of geography such as *De Sphaera Mundi*. To the right of the fireplace stood several jars of various sizes, some of which exuded strange

154

aromas. Although Falconer no longer noticed this, they were the first thing most of his visitors commented on – always much to his surprise. In one corner stood his bed, with a small chest at the foot of it. The repository of his worldly possessions, it was depressingly lacking in items. Just a spare undershirt, and a pair of old, worn boots that he was reluctant to throw away. The centre of the room was occupied by a massive oaken table on which was piled a jumble of items, each of some significance to Falconer's erratic searching for information about the world. There were animal bones, human skulls, small jars of spices, carved wooden figures, bundles of dried herbs, stones that glittered, and lumps of rock sheared off to reveal strange shapes inside their depths. It all looked so shabby, cluttered and irrelevant with his best friend dead. The decision that had been lurking in his mind for months was suddenly made.

Thomas Symon was surprised to find Falconer on his doorstep so soon after the funeral. He had watched his mentor retreating down St John's Street, not waiting for Thomas, who boarded next door at Colcil Hall, to accompany him. Then, Falconer's shoulders had been hunched, and his eyes cast down. Now those same eyes sparkled, and his voice was firm.

'Thomas, I have an offer for you.'

When Falconer laid out his offer, Thomas was astounded and excited in equal degrees. Thomas had been a young student at Oxford only eleven years earlier, and had been rescued from fear, bewilderment, and danger by the man who now stood before him as his friend. Now he was offering him the place at the head of Aristotle's Hall with all the treasures it contained, together with the students and responsibility for their tuition.

'William, I am overwhelmed. What of all your books?'

'I have taken one. It will be all I need where I am going.'

'Where is that?'

Falconer smiled at his young companion enigmatically.

'The world, Thomas.'

Now, he sat astride his horse at the gates of Oxford, looking out on the world beyond the university. He patted his saddlebag, where his few possessions including the sole book he had retained were stowed. His patient waiting gave way to anxiety.

*

Edward's progression to Glastonbury had begun, and some hundred souls were wending their way down muddy roads that for those at the rear of the long procession were churned into a quagmire. The king and his chancellor, however were at the head, and ignorant of the struggles of the retinue of officials, guards, cooks and scribes. A few years ago, Edward would have relished riding hard towards his destination, for the sheer exhilaration of it. But now, he was king and knew he had to progress at a more stately pace. Still he chafed at the slowness of it all, and the poor companionship that Robert Burnell provided. Edward would have preferred a fellow knight and reminiscences of battles fought. Instead he was getting dull-asditchwater reports of civil matters across his realm. Just now Burnell spoke of Oxford.

'Matters did not resolve themselves as we would have wished in Oxford, my Lord. It turned out that my man was not up to the task.'

Edward turned in his saddle and looked at Burnell, who sat a horse uncomfortably.

'You mean he did not suppress any possible future rebellion by the unruly Welsh?'

Burnell tilted his head to one side, uncertain how to proceed. He looked around to make sure no other courtier was listening. The business of getting rid of the regent master needed to be kept between him and the king. The complicity could work both ways in the future, binding him more closely to the king, or exposing him to scandal. He leaned over in the saddle until he was almost slipping off the horse's back.

'Well that too, though he did make a start by scaring the Welsh masters. Some of them died in horrible circumstances.'

Edward turned his gaze to the front.

'I don't wish to know about the means, merely the results. We need to crush the Welsh, wherever they are.'

'I believe that Oxford has ceased to be a sore upon the backside of England in so far as that goes. But as for Master Falconer ...'

Burnell hated admitting defeat, and already had plans to resolve the outstanding matter for the king. So he was surprised at Edward's next comment.

'Falconer? Who is he? Another Welshman?'

Burnell gazed hard at Edward, trying to ascertain if he meant what he said. That he didn't even know who Falconer was. Or was he just playing a game with him? He distinctly recalled the conversation he had had with the king, and the agreement he had made to dispense with the embarrassment that was Falconer. Has the king actually said to get rid of him? Or had he just misconstrued Edward's wink, and imagined the verbal command? He realised Edward was now looking closely at him.

'You seem pale Robert. Is the journey too much for you?'

Burnell rushed to put his thoughts in order. Edward for once had caught him on the hop.

'No, indeed, my Lord. I was just thinking that my creature, the Greekling, clearly misunderstood my commands concerning Oxford. I should not have trusted him. But no matter, no real harm was done, and it was justice of a sort that he succumbed to the small pox.'

'Good. The matter is settled then.'

Edward turned back to gaze ahead on the road that led to Glastonbury, and a glorious future. He smiled at having run rings round Burnell, who would never know if he had understood his king or not. It didn't really matter that he had failed, because Edward knew he had resolved the awkwardness with Regent Master Falconer himself. And in a much more subtle way.

*

Falconer breathed a huge sigh of relief. He could see a familiar figure on a white rouncey coming along the High Street. Beneath her black cloak, she was wearing an emerald green dress, that Falconer knew would mirror the colour of her eyes. She had discarded her widow's white linen snood, preferring to have her red hair unencumbered by anything more than being braided in a thick know down her back. When he had told Saphira Le Veske that he intended to leave Oxford, she had looked concerned, disappointed perhaps. He didn't know how to ask her to accompany him, fearful she would say no, or would berate him for imagining she was at his back and call. He had confined himself to stating that he would be at Eastgate at midday. She had seemed quite indifferent to him when he left the house in Fish Street. It was with relief that he saw she had taken the hint, and was carrying a saddlebag of her own. Two in fact, slung over the haunches of her sleek mount. He held back from making any comment about the inability of a woman to travel light. In fact he was lost for words for once, and limited his communication to a big grin. Saphira grinned back.

'Where are we going, William?'

He slipped his hand into the open saddlebag on his rouncey, and produced the only book he was bringing with him.

'I have a guide to our travels here. It is a rare copy of a report to the pope written in 1247 by Giovanni of Plano Carpini. Two years earlier, he was commissioned to travel to far distant lands to learn about a race which was troubling the West. It's called *Historia Mongalorum quos nos Tartaros appellamus* – the 'History of the Mongols that we call Tartars'. I encountered some Mongol envoys many years ago, and I have long wished to see their homeland.'

Saphira stared at William, an amused smile on her lips.

'Then if I am to travel to the ends of the earth with you, the least you can do is clear up a few puzzles to do with Isaac Doukas.'

'What can they be? Is it not obvious why he did what he did?'

'Perhaps. But I wondered what made you settle on him and not Fulbert or Plumpton.'

'I did think it might have been Plumpton for a while. You see, when de Bosco told me that Bukwode, Anwell and Ludlow were scholars he had identified to Plumpton as likely to make the most nuisance of themselves, if the king invaded Wales, I wondered if the proctor had taken it upon himself to be rid of them. I knew de Bosco was fearful of this too, and felt a deep guilt that he had been responsible for their deaths. But then I reconsidered Plumpton's nature, and saw him not as a murderer, but as a devious man keen to further his own good.'

'Besides, Bukwode was Geoffrey Westhalf's victim.'

Falconer nodded eagerly.

'Exactly. It was his death, accidental in itself, that gave Doukas the idea of killing two birds with one stone. Murder a few Welshmen for his master, Burnell, and throw everyone off the scent when he killed me. Plumpton could not have known of my ancestry, as I had only found it out for myself recently. So he hadn't given my name to Burnell. It had already been mentioned before Burnell and Doukas arrived in Oxford. The rest of my deduction is easily explained. Who knew of the prophecies, besides Aldwyn and Doukas. The book was there at Doukas's elbow, and he tied each murder to a prophecy. Then finally, the appearance of the Devil to Will Plome, and the face of God to Westhalf, needs no mystical explanation, when you know it was easy for Doukas to borrow a couple of masks from the troubadours' cart.'

Saphira's brow was still creased in concern.

'But if Doukas was acting for Burnell, and Burnell for the king, what is to stop them trying to kill you again?'

'I don't think Edward does want me dead. Burnell may have imagined he did, and acted somewhat beyond his remit.'

'How can you be sure?'

Falconer waved the book he still held in the air.

'Because it was Edward gave me this a long time ago. He knew of my lust for travel and learning, and my boredom with teaching. It may not have been a conscious ploy, but he probably felt that such a tale of strange people and places would stir my soul. And it has had its desired effect. Soon we will be leaving England's shores, and making for distant lands far from Edward and Burnell's clutches. Are you ready?'

Saphira scented the air, as a freshening breeze blew in through Eastgate and into the stuffy streets of the town.

'As ever I shall be.'

They both dug their heels into the flanks of their horses, and Tom Inge the gatekeeper waved a goodbye as William Falconer and Saphira Le Veske left the confines of Oxford, and entered the open fields beyond.

CPSIA information can be obtained at www.ICGtesting.com
Printed in the USA
LVOW12s0922011113

359429LV00005B/32/P